RULE CHANGER

RULE CHANGER

Sienna Snow

FOREVER
YOURS

New York   Boston

Copyright © 2017 by Sienna Snow
Excerpt from *Rule Breaker* copyright © 2016 by Sienna Snow
Cover copyright © 2017 by Hachette Book Group, Inc.

Forever Yours
Hachette Book Group
1290 Avenue of the Americas
New York, NY 10104
forever-romance.com
twitter.com/foreverromance

First published as an ebook and print on demand edition: October 2017

Forever Yours is an imprint of Grand Central Publishing. The Forever Yours name and logo are trademarks of Hachette Book Group, Inc.

The publisher is not responsible for websites (or their content) that are not owned by the publisher.

The Hachette Speakers Bureau provides a wide range of authors for speaking events. To find out more, go to www.hachettespeakersbureau.com or call (866) 376-6591.

ISBN 978-1-4555-6880-2 (ebook)
ISBN 978-1-4555-6881-9 (print on demand edition)

RULE CHANGER

CHAPTER ONE

Carmen, you have to tell him."

I shifted my phone on my ear and snipped a dying flower from a rosebush in the garden of my family estate in the Water Mill area of Long Island.

For the past fifteen minutes, I'd avoided this conversation. Arya and I had talked about anything and everything inconsequential, but now it looked like she was tired of me dodging her subtle hints.

"I will. I plan to."

"When? After the boys turn ten?"

"Arya, this isn't as easy as you think. I made the right call for my babies and me at the time."

"At least you aren't across an ocean anymore. Now the next step is to return to New York, and not stay stowed away in the Hamptons."

I'd never intended to go into hiding. Well, maybe that

wasn't true. Once I couldn't conceal my pregnancy any-more, I decided to escape to Italy, regroup, and regain my footing before I had to face life in New York with two young boys.

Only a few people knew about my condition at the time; among them were my two best friends, Arya and Milla, and their husbands, one being my brother, Max.

"Thomas deserves to know. The minute you landed in New York, the reporters were on you. He's going to find out, if he hasn't already."

I'd done my best to keep a low profile since returning to the states, but somehow a few pictures had made their way to some minor tabloids.

Finding out about fatherhood through the media wasn't how I wanted to tell him. Despite what Ari believed. I wasn't going to keep my sons away from their father. I hoped that the news wouldn't go public until I had a chance to meet with him.

I closed my eyes for a second, inhaling deep. I wasn't ready for the inevitable confrontation. The pain of our breakup still hadn't fully healed, and I wasn't sure it ever would.

At least I learned a valuable lesson from my relationship with Thomas.

I'll never allow another man to put me second ever again.

"Don't ignore me."

"I'm not. I need a few more days. I left Italy less than two weeks ago. Give me a break."

"No. You've had long enough. He's their father. It doesn't

matter what happened between the two of you. You have to tell him."

"Arya." I allowed my voice to grow cool. It was that or start to cry. "Let it go."

"Don't you dare take that Domme tone with me. I'm not one of your subs. I'm your best friend and sister."

"Then let me handle this." I pushed back the tears and cocked a hand on my hip. "I have it under control."

It wasn't as if I had a choice in the matter. It was either stay calm and stand by my decisions or fall apart, as I'd done for months after my delivery.

"Liar. This is the one thing you can't control. It's only going to get worse the longer you wait."

"I know." I sighed and threw my shears in the box of garden tools, shutting the lid hard, trying to push back the anxiety Arya's words brought forth.

Get it together, Carmen. You are a Mistress who's always in control, not a weakling. What you gave Thomas will never happen again.

"Ari, can we please talk about something else."

"Sure. So, when are you coming to see your nephews and me?"

I cringed. I'd walked right into that. I hadn't seen Ari, Max, or my twin nephews since they visited me in Italy for the birth of my boys. I missed them so much. My family, who'd support me through everything.

"I promise. I'll be there soon. I have to talk to you about something anyway."

A momentary dread swept over me. Once I told her what

I'd discovered, she'd think keeping the boys from Thomas was small on the level of turmoil in my life.

"What's going on, Carm? Something changed in your voice."

"I can't talk to you about it here. I need to make sure I'm on a secure line."

"Shit, are you in trouble?"

I pulled off my gardening gloves, threw them over the shears, and paced. "I'm not sure. Ari, don't say anything to Max. I'm still trying to figure it out."

"Well, I can't say anything to him when I don't know what's going on. I need to talk to you about something I discovered, too."

My gut told me whatever Arya knew was related to the conversation I needed to have with her.

"Carmen?"

"Hold on. Nat's here." I turned toward Natalie, my assistant.

"We have word from security that your brother is requesting permission to land."

I wiped the sweat from my brow. "When did he radio?"

Natalie continued to scrutinize me and then seemed to let her concern go. "He contacted us about fifteen minutes ago. Should I approve the request?"

"Of course. He owns half this estate. Let me clean up, and I'll meet him at the helipad."

Natalie nodded and walked toward the house as she spoke into the portable communicator.

"Hey. Why didn't you tell me Max was coming?" I asked into the phone.

"I didn't know. He said he had a few meetings and had to take care of a few things before he got home."

"Well. I guess I'm part of the things to take care of. Let me call you back later on the secure line."

"Okay. Love you. Bye."

"Love you, too." I ended the call and tucked the phone into the back pocket of my jeans.

I glanced at my watch. Hopefully, Max would stay long enough to help entertain the two hellions about to wake from their naps so I could take a nice hot shower. I rushed inside, washed my hands, and headed out the front door and across the lawn.

The hum of the propellers echoed in the distance, and a giddiness coursed through me. I hadn't seen my older brother, by three minutes, in more than five months.

Whose fault is that? He couldn't stay in Italy forever.

I ignored the thought and continued toward the landing pad.

After the boys' births, I needed to keep a low profile and avoid all speculation, questions, and media scrutiny about the missing daddy, so I decided to extend my time in Europe. If not for my two best friends, I would have lost all of my sanity. They helped me survive the high-risk delivery and the intense postpartum I suffered.

I wasn't going to fool myself into thinking my life would be easier by returning. In fact, I was expecting it to become much more complicated. All I could hope for was an amicable relationship with my ex for the sake of the boys.

I approached my head of security, Richard, who met me

halfway. "Ms. Dane." He inclined his head. "Mr. Dane is approaching."

I nodded as he guided me to the waiting area. I covered my eyes from the sun's glare and stared into the sky. As the helicopter came into view, my happiness to see my brother vanished. It wasn't MCD's corporate copter, but one belonging to Regala Enterprises.

No, he wouldn't. How could Max bring him here without warning me? I clenched my fists as my stomach knotted. Oh God, what was I going to do? The last time we were near each other, he couldn't even look at me.

Get your act together. You knew this day would come.

Max was my brother; he wouldn't blindside me. I pulled my phone from the back pocket of my jeans.

"Shit," I exclaimed. I'd missed six messages saying he was on his way and it was an extreme emergency.

I should have known better than to ignore the text beeps coming in while I talked to Ari.

My only excuse was that I'd worked all morning on upcoming projects and wanted a few minutes to enjoy my garden and have a conversation with my best friend.

Now I regretted setting my phone to do not disturb.

I inhaled deep and steadied my mind.

The helicopter landed moments later, and the door opened.

My breath hitched as the man I'd mistaken for the love of my life, Thomas Regala, stepped out of the passenger side, followed by my pissed-off-looking brother.

Thomas adjusted his sunglasses and fixed his gaze on me.

He strode straight in my direction, ignoring something Max called out to him.

The last year and a half had done nothing to decrease his devil-may-care appeal. He wore his jet-black hair cut short, a remnant of his special operations days, and the tailored gray suit hugged his well-honed form, giving him an *I'm a predator, and you are my prey* aura. The only thing marring the perfection of his face was the shadow of a slight bruise on the left side of his jaw.

I squared my shoulders and waited for his approach.

Thomas stopped barely a foot from me. Without thinking, I swallowed and licked my parched lips, but thankfully, I kept my eyes directed at him. "What…what are you doing here?"

He took off his sunglasses and peered at me.

"I came for my sons."

CHAPTER TWO

W hat did you say?" My hand shook as I tucked a stray hair behind my ear.

"You heard me. I want to see my boys."

The intensity of his golden eyes peering at me reminded me of the times we'd made love and he'd seen deep into the parts of me I kept hidden from the world.

That is the past, remember? He didn't want you.

"Who told you?"

His eyes glanced at my lips for a brief moment, making my heartbeat accelerate, before his amber gaze held mine again. "No one told me. I learned this on my own."

A wave of sadness washed over me. This wasn't my lover standing before me but the father of my children and the man who'd thrown me away like so much garbage.

Max approached from the side and took my hand. "Let's go inside. This conversation should take place in private."

I snatched my hand out of his and glared toward Thomas.

"He isn't welcome in my home." I stepped backward. "Why would he want to talk to a slut whose father embezzled from his family and caused his aunt's death?"

I tried to move further, but Thomas grasped my upper arm, stopping my retreat. "I have a right to see my sons."

I jerked my arm free and tried to hold back the tears clouding my vision.

You will not cry, Carmen. Keep it together.

He wasn't here for me. No matter how much I'd wished for him to choose me, it never happened and it wouldn't today, either. I had to remember that love was no longer an option, and the boys were the priority.

I refused to let him see me fall apart. The days of trusting him were over. "What makes you think they're yours? Especially since I'm not who I pretend to be. I'm a liar like my father, right?"

He jaw clenched, but before he could respond, Max stepped between us.

"We need to go inside, Carm. Please listen to what he has to say."

"The hell I will. He"—I gestured to Thomas—"made his opinion of me clear when he accused me of using him." I turned, ready to leave, but then paused midstep. "Thomas, you have ten minutes to get off of my property, or I will have you escorted out. And my dear brother can leave, too."

I strode toward the house, keeping my shoulders from drooping and my tears at bay until I crossed the front door.

* * *

I made it inside and turned the lock before the first drops fell from my eyes. I wiped my face with the back of my hand, closed my eyes, and released a deep breath.

At least no one saw me falling apart.

I'd submitted to that man. Trusted him with the deepest part of me, a part I'd never shared before. A secret he'd made me believe wasn't a weakness, but a gift. Then he took what I'd given him and threw it away, telling me my desires didn't match his.

I will never let myself fall into that position again.

"Carmen, is everything okay? Is there anything I can do?"

I opened my eyes to find Natalie's worried face studying me. I stood up from against the door. "Give me a moment… I'm…"

She placed a gentle hand on my arm. Even if she didn't voice her opinion, one look from her spoke volumes. "Your wee ones are waking." She handed me the baby monitor, and sweet chatter sounded through the speaker. "They prefer their mama after their naps over me."

I inclined my head and went to the nursery. Natalie knew me better than most people. She had been my primary care-taker after my mother's death, and she never stopped watching out for me. She knew all of my family's sordid secrets and remained loyal.

Through her guidance, I learned all the methods and pretenses needed to navigate the ramifications of Dad's embezzlement disaster and resulting murder. She taught me the most important lesson that helped me survive the fallout from the scandal.

"Never let them see you sweat, Carmen. Stay calm, no matter what's thrown your way. That is the best way to overcome your father's careless actions. Women are judged harsher than men."

Natalie was the closest person I had to a mother.

As I walked through the boys' playroom and approached their nursery, I smiled. Their coos warmed my heart. The love I discovered for them was more than I ever imagined.

I turned the knob to their bedroom. The moment I entered, Simon and Leo stopped their chatter and pulled themselves up against the crib rails.

Two sets of almond-shaped eyes greeted me.

"Hello, my handsome men. Did you have a nice nap?"

Everything about the boys resembled their father, from the shape of their eyes and olive hue of their skin to their wicked devil-may-care smiles. Well, with one exception: They inherited my green eyes, but on them, they almost looked emerald.

"Come here, big guy." I picked up Simon, the bigger of my boys and nuzzled his neck, resulting in a squeal and laughter.

"Maaa..." cried Leo, reaching his arms up in the air.

"I didn't forget you. Come to mama." I gathered my verbose child and cuddled him, too.

Taking them both to the floor, I sat down on the soft rug in the center of the room. For the next ten minutes, we played and giggled, letting the tension from moments earlier fade.

"I will love you boys no matter what happens in life."

Tears prickled my eyes again. There was a time before the scandals and Mama's death when joy and love were the center of my family. Back then, money never came before Max or me. I didn't have to be in control all the time or project an image that deep down I knew was a lie.

Everything came crashing down the day Mama lost her life in a car accident. Dad, so lost in grief, turned to a bottle instead of his children, then to every woman willing to spread her legs, and finally to making money. Which eventually led to his downfall. I still couldn't believe he'd managed to steal over forty billion dollars in assets before anyone noticed and then manage to make it disappear.

Unlike Dad, I will sacrifice my happiness to make sure my babies never know a day without love.

I shook the melancholy thoughts from my mind as a knock rapped on the door.

Natalie entered with two bottles and immediately closed the door.

I frowned. She never closed the door.

"Someone wishes to speak to you in the other room."

"Tell Max I'll call him later when I'm not angry enough to punch him in the face."

"It isn't Max."

My skin prickled.

I'm going to kick Max's ass!

I stood up and let the boys continue their play.

"We're going to have to figure out how to tell Arya she is a widow because her husband is dead. I don't care if he is my brother."

"I think she will agree that it was just cause." Natalie winked.

I bit my lip, inhaled deep, and opened the door, connecting the nursery to the playroom.

"I thought I told you to leave."

He ignored my statement and stared at the pictures of the boys on the wall. He traced their faces with the tips of his fingers.

"They look like me." His voice filled with awe.

I closed my eyes for a moment at the ache fisting my heart.

"Were you ever going to tell me?" Thomas asked as he continued to stare at the pictures.

"Natalie arranged a meeting at your Manhattan office in a few days."

He turned with an angry glare. "You planned on handling this as a business transaction?"

"I thought it best, considering our history."

If I kept the discussion formal, then I could keep the anger and emotion of his betrayal out of his relationship with the boys. No matter what I felt, Thomas had a right to his children. Plus, anywhere else, I'd remember everything we'd been to each other and the pain left in its wake.

"This isn't about a contract, it's about our boys. When it comes to them, I don't care what you want. I won't negotiate."

I bit the inside of my cheek as my temper flared, pushing all the heartache away. "I would never use them to get anything from you. You've accused me of too many things to make me believe you'd entertain anything but business from me. I wanted to meet to discuss our sharing custody."

"You make it sound so cold."

"What did you expect from me? I'm exactly what you accused me of. A cold, heartless, calculating Dane."

"I should never have said that. You aren't cold." He took a step toward me, then stopped when I retreated.

Dammit, this was my house, and no matter how he made me feel, I had to stand my ground.

"You don't know me anymore. You never really knew me."

"I know you better than anyone else. Better than Andrew or your father or even Max."

Hearing Andrew, the name of my long-deceased fiancé, made me cringe inside. Although I'd loved him, he never understood who I was. He was happy in his role as my submissive, never knowing he couldn't meet my needs.

"Carm, you're anything but cold." He gazed at me in the way he'd done that weekend long ago, when we'd conceived our sons.

For a brief second, I believed him.

Thomas was the only person who'd ever seen past the image I projected to the vulnerable girl deep inside. To the woman who wanted someone else to hold the reins for a change.

Then the memory of him tearing out my heart resurfaces, and I resign myself to the fact that it was all an illusion I'd created. The desire of someone who'd spent her life rejected by the men she loved.

First Father, then Andrew, and ending with Thomas.

"Look. I don't want to fight." I turned away from him and stared out the window overlooking my gardens. "I can admit now that keeping my pregnancy a secret was wrong, but at the time it was the best decision for me."

"Is there any way we can work this out?"

I rubbed my arm. "I'm not going to keep them from you."

"That's not what I meant. I want this to work."

I sighed. What did he want from me? My emotions were at war with my composure, and I was too exhausted to argue with him. I refused to cry in front of him and demand to know what made him believe I was such a horrible person.

"Thomas, I don't have time for riddles. Please. Can we just talk in a few days?"

"Answer a question for me first."

What now?

"Fine. Ask."

"Why haven't you been to the club?"

I jerked and faced him. That was not the question I expected. The stark change of subject surprised me but also helped recompose my shields. He was the only man who ever shook my defenses.

"Thomas. I don't have time for this."

"I tried to find you." He stepped toward me, but I raised a hand to keep him away.

This made no sense. Why would he look for me? I wasn't his submissive, and he wasn't mine.

"As you can see, I've been too busy to visit the club."

"That isn't what I meant." He ran a hand through his hair. "You disappeared. I looked for you everywhere. After we rescued you and Milla, you all but vanished. I tried to use the tracking system Arya and I designed to trace operatives, but she changed the programming. She told me to get lost and not to bother calling Max."

I smiled. Ari would protect me even though she'd known Thomas longer. I guessed I could forgive her for marrying my shithead of a brother.

Last year, I stupidly agreed to help my other best friend Milla Duncan stop a human trafficking ring, masterminded by Vladimir Christof, an international terrorist who'd plagued Arya, Milla, and me for the past ten years.

The original plan was to find the building where the sales for the women and children took place, attach software to their server, and be home before evening. As with all great plans, ours went to hell in a handbasket. We were recognized and then held hostage. Thomas along with a group of federal agents rescued us.

"Well, what did you expect? If I'm a liar and slut, what would that make her husband?" I folded my arms and leaned against the wall. "We Danes stick together, you know," I said with as much coldness as I could muster. It was better to pretend I didn't feel anything than let him see how much he hurt me.

I hadn't seen or spoken to him since that dreadful day almost a year ago. Arya had told me about Thomas's attempts to contact me, but I was determined to move on with a life that didn't include him.

"Stop freezing me out, and listen to me for a second. I made a mistake. I…know I hurt you. Carm, I'm so sor…"

The doorknob turned, and Max entered the room. "Regala, you've had your five minutes. I think the rest can wait."

"No. I have to say this." He stared at me. "I'm sorry, Carmen. More than you can ever know. I want to try again. Not because of the boys, but for us."

I shook my head, refusing to listen. The patch I'd placed on my heart was tearing open, and I wasn't sure if I could trust him again.

"I don't believe you. I'm not foolish enough to delude myself a second time. All I can offer you is a chance to get to know the boys, but nothing more."

He released a resigned sigh. "I'm not going to give up. I want the boys, but I want you, too."

I remained quiet as he exited the playroom. My mind reeled from Thomas's last words.

A few minutes later, I heard the rumble of the helicopter taking off.

After a few more seconds, I turned, glaring. "How could you, Max?"

CHAPTER THREE

I didn't have a choice, Carm," Max said as the rumble of Thomas's helicopter grew fainter in the distance.

"Of course you did. I just needed a few more days until I returned to Manhattan and met with him."

Natalie was personal assistant to both Max and me. She was a stickler for organization and would have told Max the reason I couldn't make our normally scheduled strategy meeting.

"This would have happened whether I brought him here or not. He saw the pictures in the tabloids and knew the rumors were true. Consider yourself lucky that he only found out now." Max paced back and forth. "He's their father. He had a right to know." He ran a frustrated hand through his hair. "I couldn't imagine missing six months of my sons' lives."

My anger disappeared, and guilt replaced it. "What

choice did I have? The Regalas made it clear what they thought of me. He…made it clear." I held in a sob, but Max saw my reaction and approached me, gathering me in his arms. "He said he loved me and then threw me away."

Seeing Thomas released all the pain and emotions I'd spent the past year containing.

"Shh." Max stroked the back of my head. "I know he hurt you. I didn't betray you. I punched him when he first came to my office."

I pulled back. "Really?" That explained the bruise on Thomas's jaw.

Max smiled. "No one messes with my baby sister and gets away with it."

"Why did you tell him where I was? Couldn't you have waited a few more days until I was back in Manhattan?"

"He runs all US-based security for our company. He knew where you were the second you arrived back in the country. Besides, he was going to see you whether I wanted him to or not. Coming with him was the best way to help you keep the upper hand in the situation. He's the only man I've ever met who can rattle your unshakable control."

At that moment, laughter echoed from the other room.

I sighed and then shook my head. "When I decided to come back, I knew I'd have to face Thomas and eventually his family. His grandfather hates me, and I made a promise to myself that I wouldn't let him do to my boys what Dad did to us. I will protect my children."

"It's Thomas's job to protect Simon and Leo, too. He knows our history and won't ever put the boys through the same thing. I don't see him as the type of man who'd let anyone mistreat his children. Besides, you have bigger things to worry about. Like the fact..." Max released me, pinched the bridge of his nose, and walked toward the window.

I finished the sentence he hesitated to complete. "Things have been too quiet since the incident with Christof's brother, and Thomas has the means to protect me in case Christof decides to move against me."

Ten years ago, I helped Arya and Milla develop an intelligence software for MI6 through an MIT internship program. We never expected the agency to use our program in an actual operation, especially against Vladimir Christof. The agents used our software to freeze hundreds of millions of his assets and infiltrate his network. Which eventually led to the arrest of ten of his top men.

To this day Christof was determined to recoup the losses he incurred because of us. He'd initially focused on Arya with her skills in computer engineering and her government software. When that failed he decided Milla was a better asset because of her shipping contacts. Which led to last year's fiasco that resulted in Milla and me becoming hostages.

Now it was my turn, and if what I discovered last night during my foundation audit was any indication, I was in deep trouble. The respite I thought I had from Christof was just another illusion I'd tried to make real.

Max stared at me in surprise. "Yes, Thomas is the best

person to protect you from Christof. Arya must have said something."

"I was talking to her a few minutes before you landed. She mentioned she was worried, but she never went into any detail. Tell me what's going on."

"Arya put out feelers on the Dark Web about the three of you. She's worried he might be getting ready to move against you. Christof isn't one to wait, particularly when you're on his shit list for the stunt you pulled last year."

"I wasn't the mastermind of that adventure. Arya and Milla were the ones in charge."

God, I felt like I was a teenager trying to defend myself to my big brother. No matter how old we get, we seemed to fall into these roles. With all the chaos in my life, at least some things never change.

Overall, I knew Max had a point. Every time I thought about what could have happened to Milla and me when Christof's brother held us hostage, shivers went down my spine. Especially knowing I was carrying my sweet boys at the time.

"Carm, there was chatter about your whereabouts, your finances, and the boys."

I crossed my arms around myself. "I guess it was too much to hope that he would forget about me?"

"Carm, you're a smart woman. I never mistook you for delusional."

"Thanks," I muttered. If he only knew.

"How many years did he hold a grudge against Arya for something she did in graduate school?" Max gripped the window ledge. "And after what happened with you and Milla this past year, we knew you'd be next on his list. He was just biding his time. And on top of everything else…"

He didn't have to finish. I knew the next part since I'd thought of it myself, a few moments ago.

"I was involved in the capture of his brother and turning him into an informant against him."

The moment I'd met Christof's brother, Abram, I knew he was a submissive who would do anything to please me. I'd used his desire to redirect his interest in Milla toward me, allowing the FBI enough time to rescue us.

I never expected his need for my approval to extend beyond his loyalty to his brother. In an attempt to prove to me that he deserved me as his Mistress, he relayed as much information about Christof's organization as he was privy to.

"Christof has a long memory, and the three of you can't seem to stay off his radar."

"He's the one who won't leave us alone. First, Arya for Arcane, a software that had nothing to do with him, then Milla for her shipping empire, and now me. Let me guess, for my work with the foundation."

"That, too, but you left something out."

I frowned. "What?"

"Your access to Arcane."

"I'm not the computer nerd, plus the program is old news. We implemented the project nearly two years ago. I think you're reaching."

"Don't for one minute let your guard down. Arya and

Milla aren't such easy targets with Lex and me in the picture, but you're vulnerable."

"I can protect myself," I argued.

"You're doing a bang-up job. You're on the verge of falling apart by spending a few minute in Thomas's presence."

"Fuck you, Max!" I rubbed my temples. "The two situations have nothing to do with each other."

This was what I got for leaning on someone. They saw me as fragile.

"I know, but accepting help doesn't mean you aren't strong."

My gaze jumped to his. I opened my mouth to argue but shut it instead.

"You think allowing others to help will break the 'unshakable Carmen Dane' image you have the world believing. I know the real person underneath."

He has me there.

"I can't fall apart. I have those two boys to raise."

"Yes." He walked over to me. "But you aren't alone. Those boys have a father who runs one of the world's top security and protection firms. He won't let anything happen to any of you."

My shoulders dropped. "I guess you're right. Thomas would protect anyone he cared for with his life. Just let me figure out how to talk to him about the boys before I spring this crap on him."

"Your relationship isn't the only thing you need to figure out."

His change in tone had me turning to look at him.

"Great. More bad news. What else could be wrong?"

He pulled out his phone and handed it to me. "Read this."

I scanned the screen, and my stomach plummeted. There was page after page of transactions from our family's South African education foundation to a private account held in my name. The sum totaled over thirty million dollars.

Arya and Max had learned about the discrepancies I'd discovered before I could tell them. Hell, I only discovered them last night while I was reviewing all the foundation's accounts for tax payments scheduled to go out.

My gut screamed Christof was behind this somehow, but until I had proof, no one was going to believe that I wasn't behind the siphoning of the charity's assets.

"Max, it wasn't me. I didn't do this." My hands shook. "I don't even have an account in that bank. Oh God, Max. After what Dad did, who's going to believe me?"

"I do, and so do Arya and Milla. Arya has started tracing where the funds are going, and Mil is scouring all the books to see who's had access to any of the accounts."

"But if it becomes public, it will ruin me. Everyone will think I'm like Dad."

"No, they won't. We will stand by you."

"Max, I lived through this once, and I can't do it again. You never experienced the innuendos and gossip the way I did. No matter where I went, I was the daughter of the embezzler. If it weren't for meeting Ari and Mil, I wouldn't have had any friends at MIT. No one wanted to be associated with someone like me."

"I didn't have it much easier. I just didn't give a fuck what others said."

Etched forever in my memory was that fateful day during my last year of undergrad when the indictment came through. Agents had stormed our home searching for evidence and freezing all our accounts. They'd even searched my dorm room, essentially turning me into a leper at my over-the-top prestigious school.

I couldn't even buy a piece of gum without borrowing money from the handful of friends I had remaining. Thank God, it was proven that most of our fortune came from my mother's side of the family and had been in conservatorship until Max and I turned twenty.

Dad had hurt so many people and destroyed so many lives. I couldn't blame the woman who ended up killing him and herself. She loved him, and he'd taken every cent of her inheritance.

The craziest part of it all was that Dad's lover turned out to be Thomas's aunt.

"You don't understand. I deal with it to this day; you don't. It is one of the reasons Thomas and I aren't together anymore."

A chill crept up my body, making me shiver.

"What am I going to do? I can't leave this as a legacy for Leo and Simon."

"You are nothing like Dad. Neither of us is." Max gently gripped my shoulders and stared into my eyes. "You aren't doing this alone. You have us. Let us help you."

He was right. The only people I could rely on besides

Max were Arya and Milla. They'd fight beside me no matter what the situation. Thank God I had one man in my life who'd never let me down.

I nodded. "Okay."

Another helicopter echoed in the air.

"I don't want to leave you like this, but my ride is here." Max kissed the top of my head. "You could always come with me."

"No, my home is in New York City. The only reason I ever come back to Boston is to visit you guys."

Max stepped back and moved toward the door. "The invitation is always open." His phone beeped letting him know the crew was ready for him. "It's time for me to go home to my wife and kids."

I gave him a halfhearted smile. "Give them my love. Tell Ari I'll call her later today."

Max glanced at me as he crossed the threshold. "Think about what I said. We miss having you around, and Ari's jealous that you got to spend time with Milla."

"It wasn't like we saw each other every day. She only came to see me last month so she could leave Briana with me and go on her first vacation with Lex post-baby."

"That's just technicalities with her."

I shook my head and sighed. "Poor Ari. Such a hard life. She had to spend weeks with her husband and boys at her private estate in Kauai."

He shrugged his shoulders. "I'm just the messenger. Love you, sis."

"Love you, too."

Max left the room, and I opened the door to where the boys played.

Two sets of vivid green eyes peered at me.

These babies were my life, and I refused to pass down the same legacy I'd inherited. As of tomorrow, I'd deal with Thomas, Christof, and whatever cards life threw at me. It was time to take back my power.

CHAPTER FOUR

Carmen?"

I looked up at Natalie and set aside a prospectus I was reviewing on a new property that MCD was considering for purchase. We'd arrived in Manhattan early in the morning, and once the boys settled in at my penthouse, I'd thrown myself into work and all the projects needing my attention.

"Yes."

"It is almost four thirty, and the boys have just woken from their naps." She waited in the archway of the door. "This might be a good time to get them from the nursery."

I glanced at my watch.

Shit. Natalie was right. I'd lost track of time.

A twinge of guilt hit me as I realized I was so engrossed in work that I'd forgotten to check on the boys. From the moment of their births, I hadn't left their side, but Natalie had insisted Simon and Leo were in good hands with Stacey, the nanny she'd hired.

Before I had the boys, I only used the New York apartment as a place to sleep. I'd spend most of my days working. But now with Simon and Leo in the picture, it was time to look for a more permanent place, a home with a backyard and neighbors. Maybe even some land to raise horses, like the estate I'd grown up on, the one Max and Arya now shared.

I sighed. "You're right. Let me gather my things, and I'll finish my work later this evening when the boys go down for the night."

I also needed to remember to get a status update from Arya on any news about Christof. Ever since Max told me about what Arya discovered, I was determined to make sure nothing would taint me in the eyes of my children.

"I told Stacey to come back around eight."

I scrunched my brow but continued to collect my things. "Why?" I asked.

"You have to attend the AlySas charity gala."

There goes my chance to do any extra work.

The organization technically belonged to Arya and Milla. They'd created it in remembrance of the two daughters Arya had lost when she was younger. The foundation's goal was to help women in developing nations learn skills to sustain the lives of their families.

Annoyed, I put a hand on my hip. "Tell Arya to go. I've covered for her for the past year and a half."

Natalie raised a brow. "You need a night out. Leave after the kids fall asleep, but go out."

"The last thing I want to do is hobnob with a bunch of pretentious gala hoppers."

"They are your people. Remember?" Natalie said with a smirk.

I frowned and shook my head. "Please don't remind me."

The "New York elite," as many liked to consider themselves, were from generationally wealthy families. Most could trace their heritage back to the *Mayflower*. My great-great-great-grandparents came over on a Dutch ship a few years after. They developed a fortune far greater than all the "elite" put together.

"I've spent most of my life avoiding them, and I'd rather spend hours listening to someone recite the boring sections of the encyclopedia," I mumbled as I picked up my coffee cup and drank the last of my brew.

Natalie chuckled. "I wouldn't know since I'm the 'hired help.'" She quoted using her fingers and laughed again.

"You know all their little secrets. I fear for them if they ever crossed you."

The lightened mood relaxed me. I set my mug down and packed the last of my papers in my bag.

"Please," I begged, "tell Arya to go. I just don't have the energy to face the questions."

Natalie nodded. She understood my reservations. "You're going to have to face them sooner or later. And I double-checked: Arya is going to come down from Boston when Max is out of the country on business."

"You could have told me that from the start." I glared at her, and she returned my disgruntled gaze.

"You need a night out, Carmen. I don't like seeing you like this. There's more to life than just work and the boys."

"An evening at a gala isn't my idea of a fun night out."

God, how long had it been since I went out? The last time I remembered doing anything remotely fun was the night I helped Milla and Lex get back together after they'd separated.

"Well, if the gala isn't your cup of tea, then go to the club."

Club? Did I just hear her correctly?

Natalie knew little about my lifestyle, so I never expected her to tell me to visit the club. Well, we never discussed it before anyway.

"I…um…Nat?"

She lifted her hand to keep me from babbling in speech worse than my boys. "I raised you, Carmen. I may not understand your needs, but I've always known what you were into."

"Why didn't you say anything before?"

"Because sexuality is a private thing, and it wasn't my place to tell you how to feel. You'd had enough people turn your world upside down. I wasn't going to judge you for seeking out something that gave you a sense of control."

"Thank you, Nat." I wasn't sure what else to say. Until today, she'd never mentioned anything before, but her unconditional support meant so much to me.

I'd kept the kink part of my world private for most of my life, especially from the societal elite. Only others in the community, which included my closest friends, knew about my preferences. It wasn't until my first year of college that I discovered the kink community.

It was a few months after Dad's embezzlement had become public knowledge and my life felt out of control. The few friends I'd had, with the exception of a handful of people that included Milla, had all but disassociated themselves from me. No one wanted to be around the daughter of someone who swindled nearly forty billion in assets.

One night Milla took it upon herself to show up at my apartment on campus to drag me out of my self-imposed isolation for a night out on the town.

I expected her to take me to a dance club, but it turned out to be a fetish club.

I still remembered Milla's words as we walked into the building.

"I've wanted to bring you here for years. I think tonight you may find a piece of yourself that you never knew lived inside you."

Initially, I was shocked. I'd never known this type of thing even existed. It fascinated me, from the very first scene I observed. I'd felt the pull the submissive had toward her Dom and loved seeing the control the dominant partner possessed. It was a melding of minds, with control being the gift given between them.

I'd wanted that control and, from that day forward, spent all my free time learning from any Master or Mistress willing to teach me.

"I mean it, Carmen. You should go to Dominion after the gala. It can be your reward for enduring the company of snobs."

"How do you know the name of my club?" I couldn't hide the surprise from my voice.

She lifted a brow as if I'd asked a stupid question. "I do read the documents I handle for you and Max. My skills aren't solely utilized for filing. Who's the one who made sure six of your establishments passed inspection while you were away?"

"Sorry." I winced. "I deserved that. My only excuse is that I just assumed you didn't pay attention to that part of my and Max's businesses."

Natalie cocked a hand on her hip. "Now, back to the subject at hand."

"I'm not sure if I'm ready." I moved to the door.

Natalie stepped in front of me. "Go have fun. Stop thinking for one night. There is nothing that says you can't enjoy yourself even in the midst of chaos."

I nodded my agreement and walked toward the elevator leading to my penthouse. Natalie may have very limited knowledge about my lifestyle, but her stance on things and advice were better than a seasoned Mistress.

I slowed for a second and covered the sudden ache deep in my stomach.

What if I wasn't who I thought I was? Especially after what happened between Thomas and me.

I shook the thought from my mind. That was an experiment, which went horribly wrong, nothing more.

I will never submit to any man again.

Natalie was right.

I needed an evening out. A night where a slave honored

me with his submission would help me regain my bearings, while helping me lay to rest the submissive side of my desires only one man knew about.

I pushed the access code for the elevator and smiled to myself.

Mistress Carmen was back.

* * *

I peered out the floor-to-ceiling windows of the elegant ballroom of the Mandarin Oriental, New York, trying to ignore all the curious glances and speculations about why I was dateless and where I'd spent the last year.

For the past three hours, I'd maintained my calm exterior even though inside I was ready to punch the next person who asked me about my personal life. No one straight out said anything offensive, but the questions about motherhood and family kept coming up.

The one thing they wanted to know but were too polite to ask was who my boys' father was. I carefully navigated those conversations to foundation business.

I bet if I were a man, no one would dare ask me personal questions like those. Everything would revolve around the endeavors of the charity, nothing more.

Being around this crowd makes you bitchy, Carmen.

I shook my head and continued to gaze at the glow of the lights in Central Park. Hopefully, I'd get a few more minutes to myself before the gracious goodbyes started.

"Ari, you owe me big-time," I muttered to myself.

No matter how much I begged, Arya refused to fly down for the charity gala. She ignored every plea I'd made about her being better at getting the big donors to loosen their purse strings. The girl had the magic touch of getting even the stodgiest and most miserly wallet to open for her causes.

I couldn't blame Arya for avoiding the event. She hated these things as much as I did, and public speaking nauseated her.

I opened my clutch to check if any messages had come in while I was at dinner.

There was a message from Caitlin, one of my dear childhood friends. She was the "it" designer everyone in the fashion world was raving about.

Hey, woman. Heard through the grapevine that you're heading to Dominion tonight after the charity thing. I'll meet you there. I need a break and I also learned you're taking a sub for a scene. Don't you dare start anything until I get there and have a front-row seat.

Well, hell. No getting out of this now. Someone must have seen my name on the club roster and spread the news.

I was relieved Caitlin would be there. My first public scene in three years would be easier knowing a person I respected was cheering me on. Plus, she had an uncanny ability to help me relax and become less stiff, as she liked to call it.

But first I had to get through the formal farewells. If I were lucky, I'd get it over with in less than twenty minutes.

I slipped my phone back in my purse, turned, and then came to an abrupt stop.

"Hello, Ms. Dane. I hear you and your friend are looking

for me," a man with a heavy Russian accent said as he smiled at me.

Christof!

I stared into the ice-blue eyes of the one man I knew would think nothing of killing me in front of hundreds of people. He held the striking beauty of a fallen angel. Even though I knew he was in his midforties, he looked no older than someone in his early thirties.

His eerie resemblance to Andrew disturbed me. I'd seen a handful of surveillance images over the last few years, but the impact of him in person made an indescribable fear encompass my body. Maybe it was the bone-deep evil I sensed under the polished façade.

My hands shook as I tucked a stray hair behind my ear.

"I'm sorry. I don't believe we've met."

"Oh, come now, Ms. Dane. We may have never met in person, but you and your friends have played a heady game of chess with me for over ten years. Let's do this formally, then." He reached out and lifted my hand to his lips.

The urge to snap my hand back tugged at me, but I remained calm.

"I am Vladimir Christof. It is a pleasure to finally meet you in person."

"What…what do you want from me?"

He gave me a calculating perusal, continuing to grip my hand, making it clear I wasn't to pull away. "Oh, there are many things I want from you, but this is about what you can offer me."

"I have nothing to give you."

"I know your secrets, Ms. Dane. You'd do anything to keep the taint of your father's crimes from affecting your life. What would you do to keep your children from living with the same shame? Would you sacrifice your safety and reputation for your sons?"

At that moment, he'd all but confirmed my suspicions about the missing money from the foundation. My gut had been right. I really hoped the girls had pinpointed how to get the money back into the organization's accounts.

"Don't you dare threaten my sons. I don't care who you are." I kept the fear out of my voice, keeping it cool. "Nothing you can do to me will make me sacrifice my children."

"Ah, there's the passion I knew existed under that calm and collected veneer. I'm not threatening your boys. I'm making you aware of what's at stake."

"I fail to see the difference. I have nothing to offer you. I would cut my losses, if I were you. I'm not one of your weak flunkies who do your bidding."

I couldn't believe I'd just said that. Now if the fucker would let go of my hand.

Christof laughed. "You are a worthy adversary, Ms. Dane. I believe I was mistaken to focus my attention on your sister-in-law. You are exactly the type of woman who would keep things interesting. I look forward to seeing it during more intimate circumstances."

"In your dreams. Now if you'll excuse me." I pulled my hand free and took a step to leave, but he caught my wrist, his gaze boring into mine.

"Ms. Dane, your steel spine will only get you so far. You

have the means to make restitution for the many losses I've incurred over the past few years, including the unfortunate circumstance with my brother."

"I've done nothing to you that wasn't due to your obsession with us." I gritted out my words. This man was crazy. "You need to let me go before I have you arrested."

"You came here without your security. By the time you contact them, I'll be gone."

"You're a bastard."

"Yes. Then again, so was your father. Remember the consequences of that. Expect instructions soon."

He released my wrist and strode into the crowd.

CHAPTER FIVE

CRACK!

The sound of a fire whip echoed in one of the dark playrooms of Dominion, the private BDSM club I owned on the outskirts of Long Island.

A naked male submissive moaned as the leather singed his skin, leaving a light white-and-red line across his back.

Coming here was the perfect distraction from my unexpected encounter with Christof. After he'd left me, a numb haze had surrounded me. I couldn't believe a wanted international terrorist was walking around Manhattan without a care in the world. He had no fear of being recognized or caught.

Once the fog cleared long enough to let me walk to my car, I couldn't help but reprimand myself for my stupidity in coming to the gala alone or in not asking my security to wait outside the event.

As the car pulled out of the hotel, I'd dialed my contact

at the FBI, but then immediately hung up. If Christof knew I was without my security detail, then he'd have tabs on everyone else in my life. I'd have to wait until I could find a secure line.

My first instinct was to go home, canceling my announced scene at the club. But then if Christof was watching me, he'd know he'd hit the mark with his comments about the boys. I refused to let him have even a minor victory against my psyche.

Thank God my boys were tucked into bed, surrounded by the impenetrable safety net Arya had created around my penthouse. I thought all the security was an overkill when she'd first implemented the technology shield, but now I was so grateful.

Standing next to me outside one of the playrooms at Dominion, Lex Duncan ran a hand through his blond hair. "I can't believe you agreed to this, Carm."

I ignored his statement and monitored the fire play, making sure all safety precautions were in place. I grunted to myself and said, "You look a little out of place in your three-piece suit."

As Dominion's attorney, Lex was notorious for his attention to detail and a stickler for safety, especially when it came to edge play. He was the one who insisted all fire play was monitored by our resident physician.

"I didn't have time to change. Plus, I don't do public scenes anymore." He stared at the couple and shook his head.

Ever since Milla and Lex had their baby girl, they kept their legendary escapades behind closed doors.

"You had to make your first night back a showstopper."

I touched the edge of the glass with the tips of my scarlet-painted nails. "They've waited over a year for my consent. So I thought, why not."

"Jesus." He ran a hand through his hair. "A little warning would've been appreciated."

The Domme circled her submissive, then crouched in front of him, kissing him on the lips. She stood up when the male tried to deepen the kiss, and resumed her strikes.

"Hey. I called to let you know."

Lex took a sip of his whiskey and spoke. "Something as dangerous and controversial as fire play warrants more than ninety minutes' notice."

"Don't get your panties in a twist. You prepared the documents a year ago, and they signed them, understanding the risks."

"Yes, but we have a reputation to uphold."

I frowned at him. "There is only so long I can hold off a federal judge and her husband. Did you want to be the one to tell Judge Sanders that her desire for a public fire scene with her spouse was denied? She's the one who keeps an eye on all our clubs."

Lex sighed. "I guess you're right. The woman is a barracuda in the courtroom."

I smiled. "See, I made the best decision and saved you the embarrassment."

"Bite me, Dane."

I raised a brow. "I thought you didn't swing that way."

The scene in front of us ended, and the audience watching the show clapped and shouted their praises. The crowd dissipated, allowing the couple some privacy, and moved to the room with the next scheduled scene. The place where Samuel, a prized club submissive, waited for me.

"You are such a pain in the ass. It's a wonder Max never thought to drown you as a kid."

"I'm a fast swimmer." I smirked, then just as fast, my grin fell as I thought of all the pain that being accused of embezzlement would cause not only me but also Max.

Lex peered at me, cocking his head to the side. "What's wrong?"

Lex had known me since before my mother's death and took on the big brother routine whenever Max wasn't around.

"It's nothing." I shook my head. "No, it's something, but I can't talk about it now."

"Does it have to do with Mil's pet project?"

"Lex, not here."

"Carm, you're worrying me. Let's get out of here and talk."

"There's nothing we can do tonight. I promise, tomorrow."

Lex didn't look convinced but conceded. "Fine, but get your ass to the house first thing in the morning."

I nodded my agreement.

A dungeon attendant approached me, inclining his head. "Mistress. We are ready for you. We have prepared your slave to your exact specifications."

I noticed the surprise on Lex's face, ignored it, and then took a deep breath.

Here we go. I could do this. Three years away from scening in public didn't mean I'd lost my touch.

"Thank you, Daniel. I will be there in a few minutes."

"Are you performing tonight?" Lex asked me. "First night back and you're giving the patrons a double show. It makes sense now, why Caitlin is here. She knew about the main act before I did."

"It's time, Lex. The last time I was part of a public scene was a few months before Andrew died. Tonight isn't about my pleasure as much as it's my slave's."

Plus, it would be the best distraction from the crazy events of the gala.

"What about Thomas?"

"What about him? What we had is over. The only thing we share is parenting the boys."

Lex shook his head. "You don't believe that any more than I do, but if it helps you move forward, I will always have your back."

"Thanks. Make sure they don't set the place on fire." I gestured to the judge and her husband. "I have a beautiful man waiting for me."

"You owe me, Mistress Carmen," Lex said, giving me the formal name I used in the club.

He did this on purpose to make sure I transitioned into the correct mind-set, clearing my head of anything but the session I'd lead.

"Master Lex, you can call it even for the time I helped you win your wife back," I retorted as I nodded to the attendant and entered the private hallway leading to the playrooms. I approached the door where Samuel waited for me.

Taking a deep breath, I placed my hand on the doorknob. A moment of uneasiness churned in my stomach. The last person I'd played with at a club was Thomas.

We'd taken a private room away from prying eyes. It was the first time I'd ever given a man any form of submission. The first time I'd allowed myself to hand over control. The first time I'd felt like a man truly understood my need for domination as well as accepted my desire to submit.

Am I wrong to do this? Can I share this type of intimacy with anyone other than Thomas?

I shook the thoughts from my head and opened the door. Naked, Samuel kneeled facing the observation windows. His breath hitched, and goose bumps appeared on his skin in response to my presence. His fists clenched against the manacles holding him to the ground. His sculpted body glistened from a sheen of sweat caused by the fifteen minutes he'd waited for my arrival.

I kept my eyes closed for a second, trying to calm my own breath, then moved toward Samuel. He was beautiful, with long-honed muscles, golden skin, cropped blond hair, and a dominating height that would tower over me if he stood.

I licked my lips and smiled.

This scene was about my submissive and the pleasure I could give him. He'd asked me to use the crop on him, and I'd read through his limits and desires. He was a boxer by profession and a sought-after submissive at night. He'd been requesting a scene with me for the past two years, and tonight, I'd give him an experience he wouldn't forget.

I nodded to a scene attendant standing in the corner of the room, who brought me my prized braided leather riding crop. As soon as I took it from him, he returned to his previous position.

I smacked the instrument against my palm, and a slight smile tugged at my lips when I noticed Samuel's erection growing. I loved when the anticipation aroused as much as the scene.

I circled him four times, making sure a graze of my fingers or the tip of the crop accompanied each turn. A flush covered his body, but he kept his gaze toward the ground waiting for my next move.

"Are you with me, Samuel?"

"Yes, Mistress."

"Good. Now we begin."

I kept my eyes on Samuel, lifting his face and placing a gentle kiss on his lips. At first, he was startled, since I never kissed my submissives, but then his face and skin flushed with pleasure.

"You're a beautiful man, Samuel. If you do well, I may consider keeping you."

A smile tugged at his cheeks as he returned his sights to the floor.

For the next twenty minutes, I kept Samuel on the verge of coming, striking him, caressing him, giving him lingering kisses that never grew deep. His skin grew a gorgeous red after each strike of the crop. He was perfect, everything I loved in my submissives. Each moan of his lips and strain of his muscles was a delicious dessert to my internal Domme's cravings.

This was why I loved domination. To make a strong man bend to the limits of his pleasure. To give him what the vanilla world could never understand. To share in his euphoria.

Sam had the pain tolerance I'd experienced with only one other man. A man I shouldn't be thinking about right now. With Samuel, there was an acceptance, an honoring of the submission he gave at my feet. His complete trust in my ability to fulfill his desires was a gift to treasure.

With Thomas, it was a battle of wills that left me feeling as if I should be on the receiving end of the crop.

All of a sudden, I felt an unexplainable hum in the air. I knew without looking who stood by the observation window.

Thomas.

Why was he here? Why would he care? Why did his presence make me feel like he'd caught me cheating? Up until this point, I almost felt like the old Carmen again.

I walked over to a bench, picking up a towel and wiping the sweat that clung to my neck and face. I took a deep breath and returned to Samuel.

I refused to let Thomas's proximity mess with my concentration.

Too late.

A desperate moan escaped from Samuel's lips, and I knew he couldn't hold out any longer.

I crouched down and cupped him with my free hand, making sure to linger on his balls. Nuzzling against his ear, I whispered, "Are you ready to come?"

"Y-yess, Mistress," he panted out.

"Come, my dear." I released my last strike against his straining erection, and almost immediately, jets of semen exploded onto the floor.

I dropped my crop and held him as his release spasmed out of him. Running my fingers through his damp hair, I leaned my forehead against his. Sam panted, trying to catch his breath.

"You did well. You've pleased me more than I can ever express."

He gave me an exhausted smile. "Thank you, Mistress. May I offer you pleasure?"

Without thought, I lifted my head and glanced behind me at the observation window. My breath hitched as my eyes collided with Thomas's angry ones. What I saw staring at me was a possessive jealousy that I wasn't sure how to interpret. Then he mouthed, "Don't you dare do it."

I turned back to face Sam and closed my eyes.

If Thomas were kneeling before me, I wouldn't have to think twice, but I couldn't do it. Not because I was ordered not to, but because I needed a meaningful connection before I allowed that level of intimacy.

I wasn't going to lie to myself; Thomas's presence was wreaking havoc on my senses.

Now with the scene over, I'd have to see what Thomas's reaction meant. We weren't together—he'd made sure of that—but I couldn't deny the pull of his command. He was the only Master I'd ever submitted to, and my body, no matter how much I hated it, responded to his order.

I shook the confusion from my mind and refocused on Samuel. Thomas could wait. Right now, my priority was my submissive.

"Thank you for the offer, Samuel." I lifted his face and smoothed away the damp hair from his brow. "But this is as far as any of my sessions go."

A moment of disappointment crossed his face, but then he conceded, accepting my words. As far as anyone knew, Andrew Shepard, my long-deceased fiancé, was the only person who I'd ever had a relationship with outside of a scene.

"Samuel, let me care for you. You did well tonight and deserve a little extra attention." I slowly removed his bindings and took him into the aftercare lounge.

CHAPTER SIX

An hour later, following my care of Samuel and a small meal with him, I stepped onto the social floor of the club. As I walked past various members, they inclined their heads in respect. In the back corner of the room near the bar, Mistress Taryn, a Domme I'd trained with when I first discovered the fetish world, stood with her submissive.

She smiled at me and lifted her glass, congratulating me on my scene. I returned her smile, but my stomach was tied in knots.

As much as I enjoyed the session, the only pleasure I received was from the control I'd held. It wasn't a true arousal where I gained a sense of euphoria from my submissive's release. When Samuel came at my command, I experienced not even a small drop of the sexual stir that had brought me into the fetish world in the first place.

I growled inside. It was all Thomas's fault. It felt like I was cheating on him. One command from him, and all I wanted to do was obey.

Why did he have to be here tonight?

Caitlin sat in a plush sofa waiting for me. I inhaled deep and made my way toward her. Hopefully, a stiff drink would make this anxiety evaporate.

The moment I reached her, she placed a tumbler in my hand.

"Drink this. Do not let him know he's gotten to you."

I downed the Moscow mule in seconds and then placed the copper cup on the table as I sat on the couch opposite Caitlin.

With knowing eyes she watched me compose myself. Like me, she had an ingrained need to keep her world in complete control. However, unlike me, she craved submission at all times in her personal life.

She was with me the day I discovered I was pregnant. She never gave me advice or judged me. In fact, it was her villa that I'd spent the last year living in. She'd walked into my office one morning, handed me the key, and told me if I needed to escape, to use it.

"I shouldn't feel like this, Cait. What's wrong with me?"

Caitlin cut me off. "Stop right there. You will not let him win. He left you and had no right to pull that trick on you. He blew your concentration, and Thomas did it on purpose. Although I did learn something tonight that you've been hiding."

"And what's that?" I asked, knowing she would tell me whether I wanted her to or not.

"You're more like me than you want to admit. Thomas is the top in your relationship."

My eyes almost bugged out. Caitlin had seen my reaction. *Fuck.*

How many people had caught that?

"Calm down. I was standing next to him, and the only one who noticed your interaction."

"That's a relief," I whispered. I still felt like a fraud.

"Stop looking at me like that. It was a riveting scene. All the touching and kissing left the audience hot and bothered. If people didn't know your history, they'd assume you were a committed pair. But…" She paused.

Here it comes. Caitlin noticed everything and never kept her feelings to herself.

An attendant delivered me another drink, and I took a sip.

"It felt like he did more for the audience than he did for you. You were perfect together. Why wasn't your heart into the scene?"

"I was wondering the same thing," said a deep voice that had haunted my dreams.

My gaze snapped to Caitlin, who looked like a deer caught in headlights, confirming what I already knew. Thomas was behind me.

I expected him to seek me out but hoped I'd at least get to relax before I added another notch to my over-eventful evening.

Thomas's words echoed in my mind. *"I'm here for my sons."*

"Master Thomas, I wish I could say it's a pleasure to see

you." Caitlin took a sip of her drink. "We were in the middle of a private conversation."

Holy shit. Caitlin didn't seem to care that she'd spoken with contempt to a house Dominant.

Thomas chuckled, not taking offense to her greeting. "Caitlin, would you excuse us for a moment?"

She glared at him. "Unless Mistress Carmen requests I leave, I will remain where I am."

I loved this woman. She knew how shaken up I was and would break club rules to protect me. But she had to remember, a submissive was to speak with respect to every Dom in Dominion. If she kept up the hostility, I'd have to say something, and that could mean suspending her.

Thomas sighed. "Carm…um, Mistress Carmen, could we speak alone for a few minutes?"

Was that a stutter? My confidence jumped a notch. Squaring my shoulders, I turned to face him. There was no getting out of this, so I might as well deal with him.

My heart immediately accelerated the second our eyes locked, and the ache in my chest intensified.

Thomas wore his signature dark leather pants and tight black T-shirt, which accentuated his muscular arms and chest.

He'd approached me the exact same way the first night we'd met.

I licked my lips and then spoke. "If this is about the conversation we had at the estate, I think it can wait until tomorrow."

He scanned me from head to toe, and a slight grin tugged at his lips.

I glanced down and wanted to kick myself. I was wearing the very outfit he'd bought for me. The buttery leather bodysuit was what I'd planned to wear the first time Thomas and I openly played at the club.

"This discussion pertains to the question Caitlin asked you."

My eyes narrowed.

What did he want me to say? That playing with someone other than him made me feel as if I was betraying what we'd shared?

"Master Thomas, you aren't entitled to an answer. You lost your right a year and a half ago."

"Tell him, Carm."

Thomas ignored Caitlin and pleaded with his eyes. "Please, Carm. I want to…I need to speak with you."

I released a sigh. I could do this.

Put on the Carmen Dane ice, listen to what he has to say, and then get away from him as fast as possible.

"Fine. Let's go to my office."

"Thank you. I apologize for taking Mistress Carmen from you." He glanced at Caitlin and then behind her. "I'm sure Master Ian will be happy to entertain you for the remainder of the evening. He's just arrived from England and could use the company of a submissive who knows every one of his preferences."

She shot daggers at Thomas with her eyes and then stood, turning so fast that she slammed into said Master. Ian steadied Caitlin and stared at her for a brief moment before she pushed past him and left the room without a backward glance.

"That was wrong on so many levels," I said to Thomas as I stood from my spot on the sofa.

Ian and Caitlin had been a couple during their youth, but mistakes on both their parts ended their relationship. To this day, their feelings remained unchanged.

Thomas's hand grazed my lower back, making goose bumps prickle my skin and electricity shoot up my spine. The mere presence of this man affected me like no one else.

"She needed to remember her friendship with you has limits once she enters the club. Whatever she thinks of me is secondary to club rules. Besides, you don't need anyone to fight your battles."

"That may be true, but doing that to either of them was uncalled for." I guided us toward the hallway leading to my office. "I haven't given you permission to touch me."

"As you wish." Thomas lowered his hand but followed me at a close distance, keeping my anxiety peaked.

"You pull off the cold, elitist Domme very well, but it's only me now. You can tone it down a few notches."

"What makes you think I'm acting?"

A group of submissives passed us, inclining their heads in respect. I grazed my hand down the shoulder of one the women who was recovering from the end of a bad relationship.

She stopped as her lips trembled and she looked toward her feet. I tipped her face up. "You are stronger without him. He wasn't worthy of you. No more hiding in corners. You've done it too long." I gestured to the social area of the club. "Go out there and enjoy yourself."

"Yes, Mistress," she whispered.

I stared her in the eyes and saw the same pain I felt. The only difference being that she'd lost her bright-eyed innocence as an adult and I'd lost mine as a child. "It was an order."

A slight smile touched her lips. "Yes, Mistress."

I continued toward my office without thought to whether Thomas followed me.

Jane, the submissive, had fallen victim to Jacob Brady, the man who helped Christof kidnap Arya and Milla. Jacob had manipulated and preyed upon Jane's trusting nature, using her naïveté to gain access to Arcane, a software Arya had built for the government. As a computer wizard and a super-shy tech geek, she'd never experienced the type of attention Jacob gave her, which made her easy prey.

Now as chief technology officer of my family's company, she had a new purpose, but she stayed away from relationships. Her being here tonight meant one of her friends was forcing her to reenter the kink community.

"Jane," Thomas called behind me.

I turned to look at them.

"Yes, Master Thomas."

"Master Nathan is in need of a slave for the night. Go to him and tell him I sent you."

Jane hesitated and glanced my way, but then nodded her head. "Yes, Sir."

Thomas allowed her to pass and entered my office.

"Thank you for doing that. What made you pick Nathan?"

"Nathan knows her history and will treat her with care.

The only other Master I'd recommend is Ian, and he isn't an option."

"You're right. Ian belongs to Cait."

I shut the door of my office and folded my arms across my chest. "Now that we're alone, what do you want?"

He quirked a brow that made me think of things best left forgotten.

"What do you think I want to discuss besides the fact you scened with another man? The fact that you caressed him, kissed him, and made him come at your feet."

I leaned against the desk, which housed a wall of security monitors. "Who I scene with and what I do is not your concern."

"The hell it isn't."

I jumped at his outburst but remained quiet.

"Tell me that you were aroused performing with that boy. Did you enjoy caressing him, kissing him, making him come? You may have everyone else watching fooled, but I know you. I know when you're turned on, and you weren't even remotely stirred. You enjoyed the high of control, nothing more."

I clenched my jaw, trying to rein in the turmoil rolling around inside me. "What does it matter how my body reacted? You aren't part of my life. You made sure of that. Besides…" I paused and closed my eyes for a second.

"Besides?" he probed, and stepped in front of me.

I stared him directly in the eyes. "Besides, I stated where I stood with you during your visit to my estate."

He remained quiet, holding my gaze.

I stood up, forcing him to step back, cocked a hand on my hip, and tilted my chin slightly, giving him my stern Domme stance. "Let me ask you this one more time, and I expect an answer. Why are you in my club?"

His pupils dilated, and his golden-halo-rimmed hazel eyes clouded to a dark green.

I inhaled deep.

Please don't look at me like that. My heart can't take it.

"I came for the mother of my children and…"

I swallowed.

"My Mistress. My submissive."

I froze at his words. God, I was such an idiot. He was toying with me.

"Don't you dare play with my emotions." I pushed him, but he barely budged. "No matter what we shared, you are no submissive." I moved around him and walked to the far end of the room, hoping some space would calm me down enough to think with a level head.

He smiled. "I want you."

"No, you don't," I countered. "You're just jealous because I'm moving on."

He scowled at my words and then strolled toward me as if he owned the room.

He tilted my chin up, his gaze flashing to my lips for a moment. "This has nothing to do with that boy. I've always wanted you. To my regret, I allowed my family to influence how I treated you. I've never wanted anyone as much as I want you."

"Don't." I stepped back. I couldn't hear what he was saying. He'd broken my heart.

"Please, *mi amor*, let me finish."

I wouldn't agree, but I remained quiet. The days of me being his love were gone. There were too many things I'd believed about us, only to find out I'd made a terrible mistake.

"I used my family as an excuse because I was frightened by what we shared." He cupped the side of my face, and it took all of my will not to nuzzle into his hold. "Being with another Dominant wasn't something I ever thought I'd enjoy. But then again, that isn't the truth of it, is it?"

I shook my head and stepped out of his caress, but he grasped my hand.

"I'm not saying I don't enjoy being in control. That would be a lie, especially with you. Your submission is one of the most beautiful things I've experienced. What I meant is that"— Thomas stepped into me again—"with the right woman, I'm willing to give up my power for her pleasure."

I bit my lip, refusing to look at him. After all this time, how could I be sure he told the truth?

I couldn't. This was a lie, and I refused to fall for it again. Rage from the past year resurfaced.

"I don't believe you." I tried to pace away from him, but he held me tight. "Why did you wait so long? What happens the next time your grandfather accuses me of something I had nothing to do with?" I jerked my hand free. "I won't let his hatred pour onto my boys." I pressed the sides of my temple, trying to will away the migraine pulsing to life in my head.

"Our boys."

"What?"

Thomas's eyes bored into mine. "I said our boys. They belong to me, too."

I nodded and my voice quivered. "Our boys."

"And I will protect them as much as you will."

I turned away, inhaled deep, and wiped the tears from my cheeks.

Fucking hell. This man has made me cry more than any other person in my whole life.

"Carm," he whispered.

I ignored him and focused on the club's security monitors.

What would the other Doms think if they saw cold, always-in-control Mistress Carmen crying, especially over another Dominant?

I'd fooled myself into believing I'd found the right man in Thomas. A man who accepted my desire for domination as well as my need for submission. What an idiot I turned out to be. The type of relationship I craved didn't exist. All I could hope for now was a little fun at the club and nothing more.

"Mistress. Give me a chance."

I ignored him.

"Mistress," Thomas repeated.

"Don't," I whispered and glanced over my shoulder.

Thomas stood a few feet from me. His eyes swam with emotions I refused to acknowledge or trust.

"It won't work." I exhaled and wiped at the tears dampening my cheeks.

"Yes, it will. I was wrong. Give us a chance," he pleaded.

I shook my head. I wasn't strong enough to have my heart broken again. "Twice I accepted a relationship where I was second. First with Andrew and then with you. I won't do it again. I'll never regret what we shared, because…because of it, I have our sons. But we won't have anything more than that."

He opened his mouth to respond, but I cut him off. "There isn't anything left to say. It's time you left my office and my club."

He must have seen the determination on my face and nodded. "This isn't over. It won't ever be over."

He turned without another word and left.

My hands shook, and I sunk to the floor as the door closed. *What just happened?*

I hiccupped as a sob threatened to escape my mouth. When I came back from Italy, I'd prepared myself for a legal battle. I never expected Thomas to want more from me than shared custody of the boys.

Now nothing made sense.

I knew deep down from the beginning that what we'd had wasn't sustainable. Nevertheless, I'd allowed myself to believe a man would choose me first, would love and accept the woman underneath the controlled exterior.

I'd been wrong, yet again.

Andrew had never been open to the real me, making me feel like it was a flaw in my domination of him. But it was Thomas who'd ripped a hole in my heart deeper than Andrew ever could. I'd believed he'd chosen me in spite of our pasts, that I was safe to expose my deepest secrets to him.

That for the first time in my life, everything came second to me.

He wanted to go back to where we were, and I just couldn't risk it again.

I laughed as a hiccup escaped. What would the world think if anyone discovered the always-poised Carmen Dane was a fraud? That a man could destroy her self-confidence.

I pushed myself to standing, wiping the lingering tears from my face.

This wasn't about confidence, but about power. I'd given it up without a fight, not just sexually but emotionally. It had started with Dad's rejection of me and ended with Thomas.

No more. I knew the road would have setbacks by the pain of the past, but my boys deserved a confident mother.

It was time for Carmen Dane to take back her power.

CHAPTER SEVEN

Let me take him, Ms. Dane."

I stepped out of my helicopter the following morning and handed Simon to Taylor, Milla's nanny.

The short, uneventful thirty-minute flight to Milla and Lex's estate along the Broad Sound was a welcome respite. I'd spent the majority of the night after returning home from the club handling two cranky children and making calls to my security contacts at the FBI and MI6 between tantrums.

I had to let the girls know what was going on before any of the agents contacted them. With any luck, I'd get in a breakfast cocktail before Arya and Milla reamed my ass.

I'd made a promise to myself that I'd never second-guess my security again. Too much was at risk and I couldn't afford to take anything for granted. I knew what it was like to grow up without a mother, and if I could at all help it, my boys would never know a life like that.

"Give me the other precious boy," Natalie said, pulling Leo from my other arm.

I frowned. "When did you get here? Today was your day off, and the drive from New York to Boston is at least four hours."

"Lex sent his plane to get me earlier this morning. He had to join Max in London and thought I'd help keep you girls in line while he was out of town." She ignored my glare and smiled at my now-cooing boy. "How are you, little one? Come here. Your mommy needs some time with her sisters. Let's go turn Zia Milla's house upside down with your cousins."

The moment I crossed the threshold of the mansion, I saw Milla and Arya coming toward me.

"*Mera behna*, what happened?" Arya hugged me and ran a thumb over the bags under my eyes. "Caitlin called about my dress for the stupid gala that Max is making me go to and then told me that you ran into Thomas at the club."

Good news travels fast, I guess.

"It's okay. I've got a handle on it."

She pursed her lips together. "You're such a liar. Do you want me to hack his security and make it oink every time he gets an alert?"

A genuine laugh escaped my lips. My computer genius best friend would use her skills to avenge me without a thought to the consequences. No one crossed her, something Max learned firsthand when he bossed her around after the delivery of their twins. She'd locked him in her computer lab, scrambled his phone, and refused to let him out until he apologized for being an ass.

"I don't think hacking one of your business partners would bode well for future endeavors."

She released me and crossed her arms. "You spoil all the fun. Just remember: sisters before stupid boys."

"I don't think that's the phrase, but we'll go with it," Milla interjected and stepped forward, hugging me. "Come on, let's get you settled. Taylor and Natalie have got the brood covered. Watch, those five kids will be nothing but angels for them and save all their tantrums for when we have them back."

I smirked. "It's the four boys that are terrors. Your princess is sweet as can be. I should know, I spent a week spoiling her rotten."

A few days after I returned from Italy, Lex arranged for me to watch Briana so he and Milla could have their first getaway post-delivery. To my eyes, Bri was the ideal baby. She rarely fussed and spent most of her time smiling.

"The only reason she's nice to you is because you're Zia Carmen and she feels sorry you're surrounded by boys all the time."

I shook my head and let her guide me into the foyer.

As we entered the sunroom of Milla's palatial house, I headed straight for the bar in the back.

Arya handed me a glass from the counter, her signature cocktail and my new go-to, a B&B, a *kick you on your butt* concoction of Benedictine and Brandy.

I downed the drink in one gulp, letting the potent liquid

heat my insides and calm my nerves. I glanced at Arya, who lifted a brow at my enjoyment of the drink and then set a second in front of me.

"Girls, I need to tell you what happened last night." I picked up the replacement drink from the bar and walked into the sitting area of the room. I set my glass on the side table next to the oversized sofas that Milla insisted made the grand glass and gold room look less stuffy.

Milla and Arya followed, plopping down beside me.

"This has to be more than whatever happened with Thomas," Milla observed, taking a sip of her coffee, which I knew she'd spiked with a little something. "It has to be a doozy if you're drinking at nine in the morning."

I ran a hand over my face and released a breath. "Thomas only added the cherry to my fucked-up night."

Milla touched my arm, giving it a little squeeze. "Start from the beginning and then we'll go from there."

I stayed quiet for a few seconds, trying to decide where the beginning was.

"Carm, we can't help you if you don't tell us." Arya tucked her feet under her.

Okay, here goes.

"Last night when I went to the benefit for AlySas, I had an encounter with Christof."

"What!" both Arya and Milla shouted.

"When I tracked him, he was last seen in Australia. When the fuck did he get into the states?" Arya pulled out her phone and started typing ferociously. "Motherfucker ghosted me."

"Motherhood has done nothing to curb your sailor's mouth." I shook my head.

"Stop stalling and spill it," Milla demanded as she pinched the bridge of her nose.

"He strolled in like he was supposed to be there and cornered me when I was taking a few moments to myself. He knew I was alone, which meant he's been monitoring me."

"What the fuck, Carm." Milla jumped up. "Where was your security? Didn't you learn anything from my stupidity? You're never to go anywhere without them." She started pacing. "He could have forced you to go with him. No matter how pretty he appears on the outside, he is the devil."

Milla's hands shook and her face had lost all color. I was positive she was reliving the terror Christof had put her through last year.

I'd seen the images firsthand, and it turned my stomach to think about it.

"Keep talking or I'm calling Thomas, and his men will be on you like glue."

"Calm down, Mil. It won't happen again. It was stupid. I admit."

"Stupid is an understatement. Have you learned nothing from the past three years? God." Milla clenched her fist and then crouched in front of me, resting her hands on my knees. "He could have hurt you."

"I know. You can't say anything that I haven't already considered. But after going over my conversation with him, I realized I'm more useful free than as a hostage." I tried to push down the fear starting to bubble up inside me. "He's the one setting me up to look like I'm embezzling."

"There's no evidence of his involvement. Milla and I have scoured the finances of the foundation, inside and out. The transactions I found link to an account in Switzerland in your name only. I need you to tell me word for word what he said."

I nodded and gave them every detail of my interaction with Christof.

"So he didn't come right out and say it, but he implied what you would have to do to keep the boys from experiencing what you went through," Arya said as she wrote down the facts.

"Ari, I don't have your superhuman brain, but I know Christof wants it to look like I'm doing exactly what I've spent my entire life hating my father for doing."

"But unlike your father, you have more integrity than he ever possessed." Milla scooted next to me, slid a hand around my back, and pulled my head onto her shoulder. "Now to get the proper people involved."

"I already contacted them. They said they will start monitoring Christof's movements."

"But?" Arya probed.

I looked at Arya. "I didn't tell them about the money. No one's going to believe me. All the evidence about the foundation funds points to me. No one else heard the conversation between Christof and me, so as of now, it is just circumstantial. I have to figure out a way to fix this before it gets out."

"You know better than to have such little faith in us. As soon as I discovered the discrepancies in the financial statements, I had supernerd over here." Milla pointed to Arya. "Place trackers on all foundation accounts and the banks involved. I'll know something as soon as the next transfer is scheduled."

"Um, Ari, isn't that illegal?" I asked her.

I loved her for wanting to come to my rescue, but I wasn't going to get her name dragged down along with mine.

"Well, you see…" Arya fidgeted.

Milla answered for her. "It isn't exactly legal, but because of our ties to security, we sold the program as a way to prevent international account fraud. And since they've been plagued by those types of crimes recently, they agreed."

"In other words, you used all your technical talk and big words to make them think it was in their best interests."

Arya shrugged. "Hey, it worked."

"Thank you." My lips trembled for a second, but then I bit them.

Arya and Milla believed in me without question. I knew what Max said, but hearing for myself filled part of the loneliness I felt.

"I love you girls. You know that?"

"Of course we do." Milla squeezed me close. "You like making everyone think you don't feel, but you're the most sensitive of all of us. Your heart breaks the easiest."

I didn't agree or disagree. Admitting my insecurities would release a flood of emotions that I wasn't ready to unleash.

"Now that we've had our hallmark moment," Arya joked and then grew serious, "are you ready to talk to a few more people about this? A few INTERPOL agents owe me some favors. They'll add an extra layer of protection, but soon—meaning in the next few days—you'll need to get Thomas involved."

"It's already on the agenda. I scheduled a meeting with him for Monday to discuss custody. After last night's events, he's the best person to provide protection for the boys."

"And you," Milla added. She stood and reached out her hand. "Let's go make our calls, then you can tell us what happened with him while getting rip-roaring drunk."

I lifted a brow as I grasped her fingers to pull me up. "And what about all our kids?"

"Nat's got them," Arya chimed in. "If she has her way, we won't see those kids until it's time to go home tomorrow."

"Come on. The sooner we contact the big bad international agents, the sooner you can tell us all about the super-hot boxer you took as your slave last night."

I shook my head at Milla and followed her out of the sunroom.

* * *

"It's time to spill it." Arya walked into Milla's crazy-big library overlooking the water of the sound. She nudged my feet off the coffee table, snatched the book I was reading out of my hand, and then all but sat on me to make space for herself on the chaise I was lying on.

"Hey, I was relaxing."

"No, you were hiding." Milla walked in and took the seat

opposite us. "Ari, there are other places to sit besides on top of Carmen."

Arya shot Milla the bird. "Whatever, she's in my favorite seat."

"Carm, you can't ignore the topic forever. Remember we're very persistent when we want information. All through lunch, you've been lost in thought. And don't tell me it has to do with talking to Ari's contacts at INTERPOL."

There is no getting out of this; might as well give it to them.

"Fine. I went to the club, picked a gorgeous submissive, and cropped him to orgasm. End of story."

"If it were that simple, you wouldn't have said to wait to call Thomas until after we spoke to the agents."

"Look, I can't handle being second best anymore. First my father, then Andrew, and now Thomas. I'm done with men who view me as lacking and disposable. I won't keep putting myself in the same situation."

"But from what Caitlin said, it looked like Thomas was about to blow his top when he saw you in that room with your submissive. That isn't the reaction of a man who thinks you're disposable."

"Cait talks too much." I glared at Ari. "Thomas made his choice when he picked his grandfather over me. I have my pride after all…" My voice trailed off as I held back the emotions resurfacing again.

Shit.

I bit the inside of my cheek to keep the tears at bay.

Arya placed her hand over mine. "What do you mean Andrew? From what Max said he suspected you two were having problems before his death, but he didn't know the details. He knows you were holding back the truth about what was going on because of your pregnancy."

That is an understatement. "There are things he never knew about; no one did." I released a deep exhale. "Andrew was cheating on me, and he'd found another woman who satisfied him."

"What?" Milla exclaimed. "From what I remember, you two were the perfect couple in the lifestyle."

"I believed the same thing. That is until I found pictures on his phone of him with another woman the week before his death."

"Who was she?"

"I don't know. Her face was covered with a mask, but the look in her eyes told me it wasn't the first time they'd been together, and there was…" I closed my eyes as the pain of betrayal I thought I'd buried began to reemerge. "Was love."

"Did you confront Andrew?" Milla asked.

"I did. He tried to make me believe it was my fault. That I wasn't the Domme he needed. He told me I wasn't strong enough to tame his dominant side."

"You didn't believe him, did you? You're the best Domme I've ever met."

Of course I did.

"No. I didn't. I knew everything he enjoyed inside and out. Plus he was more than happy to vocalize his needs. He may have been dominant in the public world, but he was a true submissive in private."

"You're such a liar. What he said tore you apart. If it

hadn't, you wouldn't have kept other men from coming into your life. Well, until Thomas."

I snorted. "And look how great that turned out. He left me the first time things got complicated."

"Stop it!" Arya shouted.

I jumped.

"Stop it. What is wrong with you? Stop letting these men affect you like this. Where did the freeze-them-out, take-no-one's-shit Carmen go? Not so long ago you had Christof's brother on his knees, peeing on himself for fear of disappointing you. That Carmen was no weakling."

I remained quiet. I had no answer.

I never expected to play Domme to anyone when the CIA asked us to help them after Christof's men had hijacked one of Milla's cargo ships. What I'd done last year was to protect Milla and me.

Our plan was to find the building Christof used as his Boston headquarters, attach a tracer to it, and then be on our merry way. But as with anything that had to do with Christof, things hadn't gone the way we wanted.

Why did Thomas have to be with the team who'd rescued us? I cringed inside remembering the look of devastation on his face when he'd found Abram, head bowed and kneeling at my feet with his hands tied behind his back. If Milla hadn't passed out, I'm not sure what he'd have done to Abram.

I tried not to analyze Thomas's reaction too much because it would leave me confused. He was the one who had left me.

"Ari," Milla called, snapping me out of my thoughts. She touched Arya's feet and spoke again. "Ari, calm down."

"No." Arya pushed her hand away. "She needs to hear this. I won't watch another of my sisters hide from the world or herself. We all had shitty hands dealt to us by our pasts. Falling apart isn't an option."

"Hey," Milla admonished.

"Shut up. This isn't about you. At least you got your fucking act together."

"Well, thanks for that," Milla muttered.

"Bite me, Duncan."

Milla stuck her tongue out and then turned to me. "Carm, you're the best Domme I've seen, trained by a legend. It's time you acted like it. Stop letting the past dictate your life."

I nodded. There was no denying anything she'd said. But I wasn't ready for a relationship. I might never be. I was never going to let another man trample on my heart.

Giving Thomas a second chance would only open me up for a second heartbreak.

"I'm done with men," I announced.

"Are you switching sides, then?" Arya responded.

"Shut it, Dane," I growled. "What I meant was that I'll play with the male subs at the club, get my pleasure, and then return to my life with my boys."

However, if last night was any indication, I wouldn't be getting any pleasure from scenes for a long time.

"That wasn't what Arya was trying to accomplish with this conversation," Milla said.

I inhaled, closing my eyes for a moment. "I'm tired of not being enough. At the club, as a Domme, I'm the best and in control. This is the only way to prevent more headaches in my life. Besides, I have Leo and Simon, and there's no room for any extra testosterone in my life."

If only I believed the crap I just said.

"Something tells me that their father will beg to differ."

"I know," I whispered. "I want us to get along for the boys and will do my best to give them a great relationship with Thomas. But what we had is history, and I'm not repeating it."

Arya snorted and mumbled *bullshit* under her breath.

We had to move away from this subject. I didn't want this weekend to end up going in circles, centered on the same conversation.

There was too much happening in my life to focus solely on the dynamics of my personal life.

"I love you girls, and I know you mean well, but I promise I'm not going to fall apart. Thomas and I'll figure it out, one way or the other."

Arya and Milla glanced at each other, nodded their heads, and then Milla answered. "Okay. We'll drop this subject. Promise no more serious talk for the remainder of the weekend. The husbands are away, the kids are taken care of, and we have some catching up to accomplish."

CHAPTER EIGHT

Time to get cracking before my meeting with Thomas," I muttered to myself as I scanned the custody agreement my attorney had drafted. Due to Thomas's business obligations, our original meeting to discuss the boys had been rescheduled three times, giving me a short reprieve.

Two weeks had passed since my weekend with the girls, and I still couldn't believe Arya coaxed me into admitting something I never wanted to admit even to myself.

"Just tell us the truth, and we promise to leave you alone."

"Fine, I admit it. I still love the asshole and wish I didn't want him so much, because I know only hurt will follow."

"Are you sure there's no hope?" Arya asked.

"There's always hope," Milla added. "Lex and I are the perfect examples of that. Our love was stronger than everything thrown our way."

"What if I'm wrong again? There is only so much rejection a girl can take."

I shook the conversation from my mind and refocused on the documents. At that moment, my computer beeped telling me I received an e-mail.

I opened the message, and a shiver immediately ran down my spine. It was a letter and pictures of Leo and Simon playing with me in Central Park two days ago.

Ms. Dane,

It was a great pleasure speaking with you at the gala. My plan was to contact you at a later date, but as always, your friends continue to snoop in my affairs. It would be in your best interest to advise them to stop. What happens between you and me has nothing to do with them.

As I told you the other night, my politeness only goes so far. I can only imagine the worry and pain you would feel if anything happened to your loved ones. I am sure your family comes first, as does mine. We will soon discuss how you can make amends for the incident with my brother.

Then you'll need to decide what you value more, your family or your reputation.

VC
PS I'll be in touch.

My stomach turned in somersaults as a headache formed behind my eyes.

How Christof obtained my e-mail after everything Arya had done to keep our personal accounts secure scared me.

I had to call her now.

Picking up the phone, I dialed Arya's personal line.

"Hey there, *mera behna*."

"Ari, I need your help," I said as I rubbed my forehead.

"What's going on?"

I stared at my screen for a moment longer and then spoke. "Can you access my e-mail account? There's something you need to see."

"Shit. Christof contacted you, didn't he? Scaring the shit out of you at the gala wasn't enough. Big bad international psychopath had to drive it home with an e-mail. Okay, hold on. I'm going to remote access your computer. When the request pops up, click yes."

She typed in the background, and within seconds, a dialog box appeared on my computer. I approved access, and Arya immediately started working on my PC.

"Fuck, this is bad." She continued to open screens. "Son of a bitch."

"Ari, I need you to stop cussing and tell me what the hell you see. I don't understand a single thing you're doing. All I see is about a million windows open on my monitor."

"When you opened his e-mail, he bugged your laptop. Motherfucker."

This was bad, really bad. Thank God our security protocols required us to use a token that generated a new password to access the company network every few minutes. But my personal files on the computer were another story. Dread crept in.

"Give it to me in English, Ari. How much shit am I in? How many of my private files did he breach?"

"Fortunately it's not as bad as I initially thought. Whomever Christof has working for him is good. When I say good, I mean supergood. But you know what?"

My headache intensified. "What?"

"I'm better. And I didn't tell you this, but after what happened with Milla last year and before you two decided to play CIA operatives, I installed extra security protocols on all MCD and ArMil equipment."

"But my laptop was with me in Italy and never got upgraded."

"I created an integration program for any employee working remotely. When you did the company software update, it installed in the background."

"Arya, I have no idea what all of this means. Did he access my private files or not?"

"Keep your panties on. He accessed the files in the folder labeled 'Twins' but nothing else. I'm blocking any outgoing traffic from your computer. Oh hell, someone is trying to open the files for the foundation. I'm going to block them. In a few seconds, I'm going to corrupt your computer."

"What! No, don't do that," I shouted. I needed those files for my projects.

"Calm down."

"Calm down, my ass. Have you lost your mind? Please tell

me you backed up my computer while you were tinkering, or I think I might fly my ass up to Boston and kill you."

"Duh."

Relief washed over me. I didn't need this kind of stress right before I met with Thomas.

I glanced at my watch. "Ari, I need you to hurry up. Thomas is going to be here any minute."

At that moment, my computer screen went blue and then shut down.

"Happy? You now have an officially dead computer."

I leaned my elbows on the desk and covered my face with my hands. "All my work. What am I going to do? I have a presentation to work on. Fuck. The documents for Thomas were on the stupid machine."

"It'll be okay, Carmen. At least the crazy terrorist doesn't have access to anything other than Leo and Simon's growth charts and your pregnancy records."

The thought of anyone having my private information left a burning sensation in the pit my stomach. What if Christof found a way to use the information against the boys or me? I'd die before I let anything happen to my babies.

"Stop worrying. You can't do anything about it now."

"Arya, a crazy Russian mobster who hates us just hacked my computer. How am I supposed to stay calm?"

"Because your best friend reverse bugged their computers," Arya said with giddy glee.

I shook my head. "I should have expected you to do something like that."

"I'm also having one of my techs at the ArMil New York

offices bring over a new laptop for you. Once you get it, give me a call and I'll copy your files onto it for you."

God. I loved this girl. Give her a computer and she could solve all my tech woes.

"Thank you, my ever faithful and wise tech-nerd sister." I sighed. "Wish me luck with my meeting with Thomas."

"Um…about that. I think it's time to get him involved in this. I thought you were going to tell him about the incident with Christof."

"He's been on assignment and rescheduled our meeting, and I was hoping the agencies would have found something."

"Until a few minutes ago, all was quiet on that front. Now it's time to get your big-girl panties on and bring Thomas in."

"I know this."

"For the record, I'm not saying you bump uglies with him. It's about getting his security company involved in protecting you and your children. It's the program he designed that I used to reverse Christof's hack. He's going to know sooner or later that I'm using his software."

I cringed. Thomas knew everything that went on with his company, especially anyone using his intellectual property.

"I'll talk to him. Meanwhile, you do your cyberspace mumbo jumbo for now."

At that moment, a knock sounded on the door, and I knew it was Thomas.

"I have to go, Ari. I'll call you later."

Hanging up the phone, I took a deep breath, put on my game face, and opened my office door.

God, he was beautiful. No, that was too pretty a word for someone so rugged and masculine. His tailored black suit accentuated his large muscular frame. His short hair and five-o'clock shadow gave him a slightly unkempt appearance. However, his hands, rough and calloused from working his family's ranch, said he was as comfortable working outdoors as in the boardroom.

"Come in, Thomas. We should get started."

Thomas stared at me as if he could see into my soul and slay all my demons. I couldn't handle his scrutiny, so I stepped back and gestured for him to enter.

He remained still and continued to examine me.

"Are you coming in?"

He tucked a stray strand of my hair behind my ear. "*Mi cielito*, what's wrong?" *My heaven.*

My breath hitched, and I wanted desperately to lean into his touch, to seek a moment of comfort. Until Thomas, no one had seen past the cold, always-in-control Carmen Dane. I'd never felt as safe or protected as during the short time we were together. In the end, I realized it had all been an illusion.

"We'll talk about it in a moment." I stepped away from him and moved behind my desk. "And please don't call me that."

Thomas frowned. I expected him to say something, but instead, he followed me and took the chair across from mine.

"It's a term of endearment. Something anyone would say to a person they cared for."

I glared at him, knowing it wasn't true. "You once told me

that your mother said to use that term only with the woman you planned to marry. Since I'm not her, you shouldn't refer to me that way."

He stood, putting his hands on my desk, and leaned forward. His gaze bored into mine, making me lick my lips.

"You are her."

What did he want from me? I couldn't let him make me believe again.

I closed my eyes for a brief moment, remembering the freedom and pleasure I felt in his domination of my body, of my heart.

Pushing down my desires, I spoke. "No, I'm not. You want a submissive. I'm a Domme. I won't ever submit to anyone ever again."

He sat down with a slight smile touching his lips as if he viewed my statement as a challenge.

"What if I say I'll willingly submit to you?"

"Then you're crazy. There isn't a submissive bone in your body."

"I'm serious, Carm." His eyes continued boring into mine. "I want you. I never stopped."

He'd lost his mind; that was the only explanation. Submission was one thing he couldn't do. He enjoyed some release of control, but there had never been a time where he relinquished all of it. I ended up feeling as if he'd topped me from the bottom. He wasn't a submissive; he wasn't even a true switch.

I rose from my chair and folded my arms across my chest. I walked around my desk and leaned a hip against it as I glared down at Thomas. "So if I said I wanted to tie you up, to flog you, to whip you, you'd accept?"

He stood, trying to remind me that he'd always be taller than me. I shook my head inside. That was not the response of a submissive.

"We've done that, remember?"

Yes, then you'd flip me onto my back and fuck me until I couldn't see straight.

"What about fingering your ass or fucking you with a strap-on? You'd submit to that?"

He swallowed but nodded. "Yes."

"Really?" I couldn't hide the surprise in my voice.

"Yes." He continued to hold my gaze. "Are you willing to be my Domme?"

No matter how much I wanted to say yes, I couldn't. Thomas was too much of a Dom to be anything else.

"I don't believe you. You couldn't do it." I broke the standoff and moved back to my chair. "I don't know why we're discussing this. It's not going to happen, so it's a moot point."

"You won't know unless you agree."

I ignored his response and moved to the reason for the meeting. "Do you have any questions about the custody agreement?"

My stomach knotted. Would he let me raise the boys here in New York?

"No. Joint custody is the best thing for our sons. And I agree the boys should be with you full-time. No child should grow up without their mother."

I heard the slight pain underlining his statement. His grandfather had raised him after his parents' deaths, and from what he'd told me, his grandfather loved him but was far from affectionate.

"What about the terms of visitation?"

"I see no problem with them."

"Is there anything you don't agree with?"

He frowned. "Carm, breathe. We don't have to decide everything today. We'll figure out how to raise our sons without hurting them." He reached across the desk and covered my fisted hands, ones I hadn't realized I was clenching.

Tears clouded my eyes. He was saying everything I'd wanted him to.

"I'm not going to lie to you. Ideally, I'd like for them to grow up with you and me as a couple."

I tried to pull my hands out from under his, but he held them tight.

"Thomas, you've got to let it go," I said.

"Not where my family is concerned. Don't look at me like that. Whether you want to admit it or not, we are family. Our sons will connect us for the rest of our lives."

"I know, Thomas." I inhaled deep. "But I can't give you the relationship you want."

"When you're ready, I'll be waiting."

I shook my head. He never gave up.

"Would you like to come over and meet them? I know you're going back to California tonight, but we can arrange it for when you get back."

Surprise crossed his face, and then a full-on smile that

had my heart stopping. "I'll be back on Friday. Would Saturday morning work?"

"Sure. Simon and Leo wake up from their naps around eleven."

"I'll be there."

We both stood, and I walked him to the door. He leaned in, and I lifted my face toward him in response before we both pulled back.

My face flushed.

"It's going to happen," he crooned. "You feel it as much as I do."

"Goodbye, Thomas."

"Goodbye, *cielito*. I'll see you next Saturday."

I closed the door as Thomas left; and I knew, deep down, I was in trouble.

CHAPTER NINE

T his is as good as it will ever get," I announced to no one in particular as I checked my reflection in my compact.

After my meeting with Thomas, I couldn't concentrate on my work anymore. There was too much turmoil bubbling inside me. My issues with Thomas were major, but all I could think about was the e-mail from Christof and the fact I'd never gotten around to telling Thomas about it.

I'd let his statement about me being the woman he wanted to marry throw me. He wasn't one to say those words easily. Even if what he said was true, I couldn't be positive he'd put our relationship before his family, and I didn't want to be the one who separated him from the only father he knew.

With one last glance at my vanity mirror, I grabbed my clutch and left the penthouse for my waiting car.

"Hi, James. Thanks for driving me tonight." I slid into the vehicle.

The stoic Russian bodyguard inclined his head. "It is my job, Ms. Dane."

I raised a brow, which resulted in a glare and him shutting the door. This was anything but a job. He was Arya's surrogate father, and since she was my sister by marriage and friendship, I was his daughter by default.

Arya had informed him of the threats from Christof, and he would protect me.

A shiver ran down my spine as an image of Christof popped into my mind. I needed to call Arya and see if she'd discovered any leads on the reverse virus she'd attached to the files on my computer. Then I would call Thomas. It was better to talk to him with all the information on hand.

I glanced at my building a second before James pulled into the street, and I held in the urge to go back, cancel my plans for the evening, and spend the night cuddling Leo and Simon.

I pushed that thought down; tonight's event was as much about business as enjoyment. Many of the power players in the world of finance and real estate would be at the party, and I was responsible for three new property development project that were currently in escrow and hadn't closed yet.

The partition of the limousine lowered. "We'll arrive in a few moments."

"Thanks, James."

As we pulled up, I lowered the passenger window and handed my invitation to the waiting attendant. He inspected my credentials and then waved us through the gates.

The party tonight was an annual event held by a well-known Dom in the area. His private estate was one of the few remaining giant properties owned by a single family in New York. Attending the event hadn't been on my agenda for the evening, but after receiving a personal phone invitation from the host, I couldn't refuse.

James stopped the car at the entrance to the mansion, and the door immediately opened.

"Mistress Carmen, welcome." The butler smiled at me. "Master Travis is very pleased you are here tonight."

"Thank you." I stepped out of the car and adjusted the legs of my white leather bodysuit.

"Master Travis requested you join him in the parlor."

"But isn't the party in the gardens?"

The butler squirmed as I stared at him, and he looked down. "Yes. I am only relaying his message."

Aha, a submissive.

"No worries." I stepped toward the house. "Please attend to the other guests. I will show myself in."

He kept his head down but peeked up. "As you wish, Mistress."

I glanced over my shoulder and gave him a last smile. He reddened and turned to the arriving cars.

I surveyed the beautiful mansion. It held the original details of its Victorian history with large chandeliers and staircases, but had clean lines and muted colors, in style with the modern owner.

I approached the hallway near the parlor.

I opened the door and found at least ten Doms and Dommes with a handful of submissives socializing.

As I approached the Doms, who were in a heavy discussion, a beautiful Latina submissive stepped toward me.

She was dressed in a form-fitting corset dress that accentuated her generous curves. She had a scowl on her face, and I braced myself for whatever she had to say. I'd never met her before, but she knew who I was. Just a few steps before she reached me, a Dom called her name, and she turned in his direction. As she reached her Dom, she glanced over her shoulder, giving me a pointed stare.

Whatever I'd done to this woman must be a doozy. For a split second, I thought it might be Andrew's mistress; the woman in the picture was a blonde and a Domme.

I walked up to Master Travis, shaking off the unusual encounter with the submissive.

"Mistress Carmen, I apologize for Sophia's behavior. I've never seen her hostile with anyone. Let alone a Domme. Maybe she's jealous."

I frowned. "Why would she be jealous?"

She wasn't Andrew's lover.

"Because of Master Thomas, of course."

I held my breath and hoped my eyes didn't bug out.

How did he know about Thomas and me? That meant others must know as well.

"I'm not sure I catch your meaning. Thomas and I have a business relationship."

Most people in the lifestyle knew about Thomas's partnership with me in his first endeavor into fetish clubs. He was well known for his high-end nightclubs around the world, catering to the twenty-five to forty crowd.

"I think you're mistaken, Master Travis," another Dom interjected. "Only a fool would assume Mistress Carmen would submit to any man."

The corner of Travis's mouth went up in amusement. "My mistake. Can you imagine two Dominants together? They'd kill each other." His words didn't match the expression on his face, and I had the distinct feeling he knew more about me than I wanted. Then I remembered Travis and Thomas were close friends, and it hit me. This was a setup.

The hairs on the back of my neck prickled as I watched Travis gaze behind me.

"Speak of the devil. Here he is," Travis announced and then leaned down and whispered in my ear, "No more avoiding the inevitable. You've settled your custody issues. Now you need to settle the personal."

"This isn't the time or place," I whispered back.

I glanced behind me, and Thomas's eyes caught mine. My breath hitched as he headed straight for me. He strode past Sophia when she tried to get his attention, and ignored any other submissive who greeted him.

Thomas came up behind me and slid his hand over my stomach. Instead of pushing it away, I gripped it, unsure of what to do.

"Gentlemen, if you will excuse us, I need to speak with the mother of my children."

Before I could respond to his declaration or gauge the response of the other Doms, Thomas had me walking toward the exit with his hand moving to my lower back.

When I realized what I was doing, I stopped and turned around.

His eyes darkened with desire as he stared me down, and my pulse jumped. I licked my now-dry lips.

Dammit. I had no discipline when he looked at me like that. The reason I ended up pregnant was that I'd lost all willpower to remember protection the last time we were together. That was the very night my heart had decided he was the man with whom I'd spend my life.

Believing that was one of the biggest mistakes of my life.

I opened my mouth to tell him to fuck off, but before I could utter a word, he placed a finger on my lips and squeezed the hand now on my waist. "Keep moving, Carm. I'm not above making a scene, and we both have reputations to protect. I left your office today because I knew you weren't ready to listen or accept what I offered. I'm finished waiting. Now move."

My cheeks flushed and I swallowed as arousal shot through me. How did Thomas always find a way to catch me off guard?

There was no point in fighting right now. He was right. The more we lingered, the more others would notice us, and this discussion needed to happen in private.

Thomas guided me to a private lounge at the far end of the house. We passed many couples and individuals who were too engrossed in the dancers preforming around the mansion to avert their gaze from the show.

Once we were alone, I planned to give him a piece of my mind. He had to get it through his thick skull that we'd never be a couple again. I couldn't trust him with that part of me.

The moment we entered the room, Thomas grabbed me and pushed me against the door.

"Thom—" I cried out as he sealed my mouth with his and my clutch hit the floor.

He lifted my legs around him as he deepened our kiss, one filled with anger and desire while pushing his denim-covered cock against my sensitive flesh. I shoved against his chest, knowing it wasn't a good idea to let it go further, but he tasted so good, the flavor of cognac mixed with his natural sweet essence.

I'd dreamed of his touch for a year and a half. I'd missed him so much.

I arched against him and moaned, pulling my face free. "We shouldn't do this. It will only make things more complicated."

Thomas fisted my hair and drew me back to him. "Oh, we definitely should do this."

Wetness flooded my pussy, and I knew I was lost. I needed him. I had to get him out of my system.

Maybe one more time will end this yearning, this desire the scene at the club did nothing to rectify.

Thomas released his grip on my thighs, allowing my feet to slide to the ground. He turned us and then walked me backward toward the sofa.

"I'm going to show you that you cannot live without your Master." He cupped my breasts through my bodysuit, causing them to pebble painfully against the fabric.

Master. The hell?

He was not getting away with that statement. I wouldn't ever submit again.

I laughed and reversed our positions so when we reached the sofa, the back of Thomas's legs hit the edge. "I don't think so." I tumbled him down onto the cushion and climbed on top of him, grabbing his hands and placing them above his head. "I am a Mistress, and I will not yield. You're the one who wanted to submit, remember?"

A slight grin touched his lips. "Let me have it, Mistress."

I threaded my fingers into his hair and sealed our mouths again. Our tongues dueled, and I rubbed my throbbing core against his straining erection. I kissed down his neck and worked the buttons of his shirt open. As I revealed his chest and abdomen, I nearly moaned. Hours of combat training, working on the ranch, and his natural athletic build created a body worthy of any woman's fantasies.

My hands and nails trailed down his pecs, over his six-pack abs, and then grazed his denim-covered cock. A shudder shook him as my fingers traced the tip. I glanced up to see his eyes squeezed shut and his arms twitching to move. I tapped his biceps. "Don't even think about it. I'm in charge."

"Yes, Mistress," he purred, and his voice triggered goose bumps all over my body.

I licked my lips and leaned my face into his stomach. His scent tickled my senses, reminding me of how much I enjoyed tasting him and how long it had been.

I grasped his belt, pulling the leather through the loop, and then unbuttoned his pants. I nuzzled his groin, and he arched his pelvis in response.

His lids flickered.

"Keep your eyes closed, or you won't enjoy the pleasure of my mouth."

His fists clenched tight. "Yes, Mistress."

Opening his snug pants, I pulled out his beautiful, pulsing cock. I grasped the base and squeezed up to the tip and back down. A drop of precum beaded at the end, and I licked the pearl.

His earthy musk exploded in my mouth, and a moan escaped my lips.

"I love how you taste," I announced, and then traced the throbbing vein running the length of his cock with my tongue. I teased him like that for a few moments, tracing, circling, and licking.

"Please, Mistress," Thomas begged with his head tilted backward into the sofa cushion. "It's been too long. I won't last."

I smiled, knowing he was on the verge of losing control. A thrill shot through me, soaking my thong completely. He was a Dom who was giving me his submission. If he desired, his strength could overpower me at any second; hopefully, he wouldn't.

I decided to end his torture and engulfed him in my salivating mouth. I slid down and then slowly up, savoring his incredible length and flavor and rubbing my tongue against the thick vein underneath. I sucked and licked, following my lips with my hands.

His hands slid down from where I had positioned them, into my hair. I could have pushed them away, but I liked the feel of them cupping my head. I continued my ministrations, taking him deeper as my own arousal intensified.

I hadn't had any form of release since the last time we were together, and the need to slip my fingers between my legs tugged at my control. This wasn't about me. A Mistress gives pleasure before she receives hers, even if her submissive desires to give her release.

What would it be like to allow Thomas control over me again?

The thoughts evaporated as his grip tightened and his breath grew harsher. "Mistress, stop. Or I'm going to come."

My lips curved as I slid down his cock again. I wanted him, the taste of him, his essence inside me.

All of a sudden he pulled out and flipped me onto my back and hovered over me.

The look in his eye told me the tables had just turned. No matter what he said, he could never submit completely. I should be upset he went back on his word, but this, whatever it was, felt right.

"I want your pleasure first. You won't deny me." He sealed our lips, and our tongues dueled once again.

I tried to push him back, but he grabbed my wrists in one hand and positioned them above my head. My heartbeat hammered into my chest.

Thomas grasped the zipper of my jumpsuit and slid it down from the base of my throat to just above my pussy. His lips followed the path of the opening, pausing at the juncture between my breasts. His jaw nudged the fabric to the side, revealing my nipples.

"I love how you're always naked underneath these body-suits."

He took one bud into his mouth, sucking and biting.

I arched up. "Harder," I called as I tugged my arms against the grip of Thomas's hand.

He obliged, allowing his sharp teeth to pinch the bundle of nerves into a tortured peak. He tightened his hold on me and then moved to the other puckered tip. His hand trailed down my body and then into the opening of my suit at the top rise of my pussy. He slid between my lower lips and circled my clit.

"T-Thomas," I cried as white-hot need fired to life inside me.

"That's it. You aren't going to hold out on me. It's never been that way between us and I won't allow it now."

I thrashed my head as he pushed his fingers into my core and curled upward. His touch melted all my defenses, making me weak to anything but the pleasure spiraling through my body.

"Let go, baby. I've got you," Thomas crooned as he covered my lips again.

My pussy quickened, and another flood of dampness poured between my legs. I rode his hand as tears blurred my vision.

"Come now, Carmen."

I detonated, causing every nerve in my body to scream with pleasure. My pussy contracted around his fingers, and I bowed off the couch.

Before I could come down from my orgasm, Thomas had

my suit off my body and pooled at my knees, where my boots held it on. He lifted me and positioned me with my stomach against the back of the sofa.

His cock traced the seam of my ass and then between my folds.

"God, you're so wet," he said and pushed in deep.

We both groaned.

It had been so long. Nothing felt like him, hard and pulsing inside me.

"Oh God," he moaned. "This is like coming home."

My heart clenched.

That's exactly how I feel.

He kissed my shoulder and nuzzled my neck. I wasn't a small woman, and he made me feel tiny and delicate. His body covered mine as his hands came to grip the edge of the couch on either side of me. The zipper of his jeans scraped the back of my thigh as he withdrew and slammed back in, reminding me he held the controls. I jarred forward, and my hands covered his to keep my balance. He rode me hard, giving me everything I knew he'd held back for so long.

My pussy rippled and contracted with each thrust. The urge to beg for release pushed at me ever more. I shook my head, but his hand came up in front of me grabbing my jaw, tilting it up.

His desire-glazed eyes bored into mine. "Ask me."

A refusal touched my lips, but my words ignored my mind. "Please. Let me come."

He smiled, holding my gaze as he continued riding me

and his other hand moved to my clit and rubbed. "Come for me, Mistress."

I held my breath as my core contracted around his cock and my mind clouded. My skin prickled and then my whole body spasmed, forcing me to exhale.

"That's it, baby."

A bead of sweat trickled down his face, and I realized I wasn't the one holding back. But I knew he was doing it for my pleasure, to give me what my body needed.

My orgasm continued to roll inside me as I cupped his face and stared into his passion-hazed eyes. He brought me over the peak one more time before clenching his eyes and allowing his release to wash over him.

CHAPTER TEN

My heart had barely calmed when Thomas shifted us on the sofa, lying with my back against his stomach. His softening cock still throbbed inside me. Neither of us was ready for the end of the connection.

This was how it had always been between us. It didn't matter if our sex was vanilla like now or with all the aspects of kink. The confusing dynamics of our relationship worked.

No matter what I told myself, what Thomas and I shared was what I needed, even if it made no sense.

The boys deserved a chance with their father. Family meant everything to Thomas, and with the uncertainty of what the future held with Christof, Leo and Simon would be safe with him.

I shook the thought of Christof from my mind. This wasn't the time to think of that asshole. Right now, I had to figure out the next steps with Thomas.

His fingers drew circles over my stomach and the fading stretch marks left by my pregnancy.

"We have to make this work, Carm. If not for us, then for our sons."

I closed my eyes at his words and responded. "Yes, we have to figure this out."

No matter how much I hated acknowledging it, this all-consuming and confusing attraction between us wasn't going anywhere.

One of his hands flattened against my abdomen, and the other played with the hair on my forehead. "I'm sorry, Carmen, for everything. I want you as much as I want the boys."

I lifted up my shoulders to sit, but my bodysuit restricted my movement. Thomas pulled me back against him, but his cock slipped out of me, followed by a stream of wetness from his cum.

All of a sudden, I stiffened. We hadn't used a condom.

"Thomas. We didn't use protection." I couldn't keep the panic from my voice.

Thomas held me tighter, forcing me to say where I was. "Calm down. If it happens again, it only means our sons needed more siblings."

I elbowed him in the stomach, and he released me. "Are you out of your mind? We aren't together, and we forgot to use a condom. Once wasn't stupid enough, but twice?" I climbed off him and covered my face with my hands.

What was I going to do now? I sighed. Whatever happened, I'd handle it. People joked that only a fertile Myrtle got pregnant on the first time; well, that girl was me.

Arya couldn't get pregnant no matter how hard she tried, and I got pregnant by sharing a glass of water with a guy.

Thomas stood, jarring me out of my self-pity. He tugged on and buttoned his jeans, then crouched in front of me.

He took my hands in his. "Carm. We'll figure it out. For us, our boys, and any other children we have. Whether you want to admit it or not, you agreed that we're together again."

"The hell I did." I stood, pushing him back.

I shrugged my bodysuit on, zipping it, and then paced. "I will allow you into the boys' lives, but don't hope for anything more from us. I won't repeat what you put me through last year. This won't happen again."

He raised a brow in response, and we both knew what I said was a lie. The attraction between us was beyond my comprehension. He was a Dom who said he wanted to submit to me, and I was a Domme who couldn't help but submit to him.

No. I can't do it. I won't ever submit again.

"You aren't a submissive, Thomas, and that's what I need," I whispered, and turned my back to him and stared at the mahogany fireplace in the large room. No matter how much I wanted or needed him, I had two boys to protect, and the only way to do that was to set parameters from the beginning.

"What we share can't be defined. It doesn't make sense, but it fits us." He approached me from behind and gently grasped my shoulders.

"I won't let you accuse me of forcing you to be something

you're not." The memory of the confrontation we'd had when we broke up flashed in my mind.

One week we were planning our future together, and then the next, after a visit to his family's ranch, I was disposable. God, he'd accused me of so many things, including pushing my will on him.

"I was wrong. I shouldn't have said any of the things I did. Carmen." He shifted to face me. "I was an idiot. Growing up, I was told a man is a man and never allows a woman to tell him what to do, and then here I was, willing to let a beautiful, tall Domme dominate me. I got scared and said things to cover my pride. I used the secrets you told me and the hurt from our families' pasts against you. I promise to spend the rest of our lives making it up to you."

I stared into his pleading eyes, wanting to believe him, but I wasn't ready. The hurt from the last year was too fresh.

"I can't do it, Thomas. Maybe one day, but not now."

"I'll do my best to wait until you're ready."

I guessed that was the best I was getting out of him. He was offering me what my heart wanted more than anything else. If only I could trust him to stand by me and not run when things got complicated, or in our case, family interfered.

"Carm, there is one thing I want to ask you to do for me while we wait to see where we're headed."

"What?"

"I'd like for you and the boys to come to my home. To my family's ranch. I want my sons to see the other half of their family."

"We can't." I stepped back.

A crease formed between his eyes. "Just like that? Why not? They have a right to get to know their family."

I folded my arms around myself and rubbed my shoulders. *How do I refuse without letting Thomas know what happened with his grandfather?*

"I can't leave right now. I just got back, and I have a business to run."

"Bullshit!" he exclaimed and ran a frustrated hand through his hair.

"Believe what you want." I tried to move past him, but he grabbed my wrist.

"Tell me why you don't want to come to my home or meet my family."

I hadn't told anyone but Arya and Milla what Thomas's grandfather had said to me a year and a half ago. Thomas's words back then had broken my heart, but his grandfather's had sealed the decision of keeping the pregnancy to myself.

"Why would I want to subject myself or my boys to the man who called me a thief and a whore like my father?"

"When the hell did that happen?" Thomas demanded.

I jerked my arm free. "After you rescued Milla and me from Christof. Seeing Diego at my office door made no sense. You and I weren't on speaking terms."

Thomas visibly cringed, then shook his head as he sat on the sofa. "I shouldn't have called you a *puta*. I'm sorry." He closed his eyes for a second. "I was angry that you allowed another man to submit to you. I didn't think that the only reason you'd do that was to save Milla and yourself."

"I get it, Thomas, but it doesn't change that it was said or that we can't be together. Just like it doesn't change the fact your grandfather came to see me."

He ran a frustrated hand through his hair as his gaze bored into mine. "I don't believe you. He doesn't leave the ranch unless it's for an auction. He would never fly across the country to New York without one of us."

My lip trembled, and then I squared my shoulders.

I will not cry in front of him. A Domme remains in control even when her world falls apart.

"You proved my point. This is why you and I will never work. I will never be first; hell, I'll never be fourth."

"I want to know every word that was said."

"Why bother? I gave you a brief synopsis. You didn't believe me. End of story."

"Carmen…"

His Dom voice washed over me, and a tingle shot up my spine, but I stood my ground and smirked at him.

"Do you really think talking to me in that tone is going to make me shake in my pants?"

No need for him to know how he affected me.

"Just tell me what the hell he said."

"Fine. Diego said I was like my father and he will die before another member of his family succumbs to a Dane. He brought up everything Dad had done to destroy his family. Then he went into great detail about how I was manipulating you and filling your head with lies so that I'd gain access to your fortune. He ended by telling me I was trash and spitting on my face."

Thomas stood, his face reddening with anger. "He wouldn't do that. My aunt's death hurt him, but he would never treat any woman that way."

He was never going to choose me before anyone else.

I held my breath, holding in the pain piercing my heart, and then shrugged my shoulders and paced away from him. "Like I said, you wouldn't believe me. You've placed him on such a high pedestal, and nothing will allow you to see what he did. The best I can now offer you is a chance to be in Leo and Simon's lives, but whatever we had is over. I won't ever be last on anyone's list again."

I held my head high and walked toward the door. I hoped that I wouldn't break down before I made it to the car. No matter how hard I tried to pretend I could handle Thomas, it was a lie. He still held my heart and continued to crush it.

Thomas grabbed me and held me against him. A tear slipped past my eyes and dripped onto his bare chest.

"I'm sorry, Carmen. Please forgive me. I just reacted to the news. I never expected anything like this from him."

Does he believe me, or is he saying that to keep me here with him?

I remained quiet. There was no point in saying another word. Nothing would change.

He pulled back, cupped my face in his hands, and thumbed my stray tear. "We have to move on from the past. Please give me a chance. Let me prove to you that I want you and will put you and our boys first."

I closed my eyes. There wasn't any moving past the things

Diego said to me. And I couldn't trust Thomas wouldn't flip on me again.

"I can't give you more than a friendly relationship." I stepped out of his hold, and he released me. "I won't lie. I loved you more than I ever loved Andrew. But then again, you hurt me more than he ever did, even with his cheating. Our boys deserve you in their lives. I know you'll be a good father."

"I'll be a good husband to you, too."

I shook my head. "No, Thomas you won't. I can't give you what you need, and you can't do the same for me. I won't pretend even for the boys' sake. Eventually we'll both find people more suited of us."

With those words, I walked to the door and opened it.

"Carmen," he said behind me, a tinge of anger in his voice.

I paused and braced myself for his words.

"Remember, it's my cum coating your pussy. No other man will ever give you what you need. You belong to me as much as I belong to you."

CHAPTER ELEVEN

Get up, lazy bones. I've come all the way from Boston to Carmen-nap you." Arya's cheery voice called out from the threshold of my home office.

"Sorry, beautiful. I have work obligations," I responded as I reviewed a proposal from a company that had been courting MCD for the past five months.

"You could at least look up when rejecting me." Arya pouted and walked in, pulling the prospectus from my hands.

"Hey," I yelled, scowling at her. "I don't have time for this. I have to get all my work in before Thomas comes over to meet the boys tomorrow."

My heart skipped a beat. It had only been two days since I left Thomas at the party. We'd communicated about the boys but nothing else. It was as if he didn't want to touch the subject of us with a ten-foot pole, and I was grateful for it.

I hadn't told the girls about what happened, but with the way the rumor mill worked, I was sure it had taken less than thirty minutes to reach their ears. The fact that they hadn't pumped me for information surprised me.

My hormones were a mess, and sleeping with Thomas hadn't helped. Every time my pants rubbed against my pussy, I remembered the feel of him pounding into me. I was so desperate at times that I pulled out my long-forgotten battery-operated boyfriend. But I couldn't reach the release I craved. Damn Thomas and his magic cock.

"Ms. Hermit, we have to get you out of here."

"Whatever," I mumbled.

She frowned at me. "Don't try to blow me off. Let's get moving."

"Look, I'm freaking out about everything going on with Christof, so I refuse to leave the building until the security around the boys and me is locked down tight."

Over the past few days, my anxiety about the unknown from Christof left a burning in the pit of my stomach. I kept going over the conversation we'd had for any clues to how he'd expect me to "repay his losses," and the only clue I could think of was that it was related to Dad's embezzlement.

I had to remember to get Max to pull any case files we had on the trial that had been set to start three days after our father's death.

"It's not like you don't have security around you."

Arya's comment snapped me out of my thoughts.

"It's different than if Thomas was leading the effort. Do you remember what happened after Christof threatened Milla? He had security for the security. I should have listened to you and talked to him about this whole mess."

Arya rolled her eyes and then gave me the "I told you so" smirk. "Well talking to him will have to wait for later."

"That still doesn't solve my worry."

"Carm, there are two guards, hand selected by Thomas, shadowing you all the time. On top of that, we'll have Milla's and my detail added to the mix."

"Ari, I already went out on Wednesday. I've met my quota for the week. You're more than welcome to veg with me at home."

"Get your ass up, or I'm going to sic Milla on you, and you know how she gets about our girls' nights."

I exhaled and pushed back from my desk. "Look, even if I wanted to go out, I gave the nanny the next few days off, and I won't leave Leo and Simon with anyone I don't trust."

"We've got it covered," Milla announced as she strolled in and plopped down on the sofa at the far end of the room. "Lex and Max are going to watch all the kids."

I hesitated. "Are you sure they can handle four mobile boys and a three-month-old princess?"

"Who cares? We had them the other weekend when both guys were out of town, and we managed. Plus it isn't like they won't call Natalie to take charge if anything goes wrong."

I nodded. "That does make a difference." Natalie could handle anything.

"Come on. You need this."

I glared at her. "How would you know?"

Arya and Milla shared a look.

Ahh. Oh, something happened.

"Well, you see. We had a meeting with Thomas and…um."

"Arya, seriously. It takes you like five years to tell a story," Milla admonished. "Thomas came to see us about the dance club we're opening, and while we were talking, you came up. He told us you two are making arrangements for the boys."

I raised a brow while crossing my arms. "And?"

Milla smiled, trying her most innocent face. "He said you guys have to finish the business you started last week."

"Did he go into details about what business it was?"

If Thomas said anything, I was going to gut him, private security, military, crazy man or not. Hell, the girls would gut me for not telling them, especially when we'd conferenced yesterday to discuss the details of financing another project.

"No he didn't go into detail, but I can assume it has to do with the announcement Thomas made at Travis's party and the just-fucked, disheveled look you had while leaving his house on Wednesday." Milla's face grew stern. "Holding out on us, were you?"

My eyes nearly bugged out of my head. "Were you there? Why didn't you tell me you were going?"

"Don't try to change the subject." Arya cocked her head to the side and pointed to the chair across from her.

I shrugged my hands in retreat and joined the girls in the seating area.

"Spill it, Dane," Milla ordered.

"There isn't anything to spill. Travis tricked me into being there, and then Thomas showed up and made his announcement about being the boys' father…and…" I rubbed my temples.

"And?" Milla asked in her best impersonation of a Domme tone.

Sighing, I answered. "We ended up fucking each other's brains out, then arguing before I left."

"At least you finally scratched the itch," Arya interjected. "What was the argument about?"

"What else? His family, the boys, our relationship." I pulled my knees onto the seat and buried my face against them. "There's no hope for us, Ari. No matter how much my heart wants to trust him, he won't ever put me first. The second I told him what Diego said, he told me he didn't believe me. It's better this way."

"Are you saying that to make yourself feel better, or do you believe it?" Milla said as she crouched in front of me and took my hands.

I looked at her. "I have to believe it, Mil. I don't have it in me to deal with disappointment again."

"Carm, I know you don't want to hear this, but Thomas is hurting, too." Arya sat down next to Milla. "I've known him longer than all of you, and he clings to his grandfather because everyone else rejected him as a child."

"I know his history, Arya."

Thomas's mother was a New England debutante who fell in love with Thomas's father while on vacation in California. His mother's family disowned her when they found out she was pregnant and married to a lowly Mexican farmer. They never knew or wanted to know that the farmer was a horse rancher who owned most of two counties in Northern California, or that he had three vineyards that produced award-winning wines. By the time Thomas's mother's family wanted to reconcile, both of Thomas's parents were killed in a plane crash, leaving Thomas to be raised by his grandfather and aunts.

"Then you understand his attachment to Diego. When we were alone, he asked me if I knew what Diego said."

"What did you tell him?" I fidgeted in my seat.

"I told him exactly what he said to you, including the part you left out about you being a high-class whore."

My cheeks reddened. "Yep, that's what I am. With all the submissives I've played with at the clubs, who would believe I've only been with two men in my life?" I shrugged my shoulders. "But hey, I'm the daughter of a thief. Like father like daughter. My dad seduces Thomas's aunt and ruins her life, and I seduce Thomas and ruin his life."

"Goddammit, Carmen, lay off the dramatics."

I jumped at Arya's reprimand.

"He's hurting. The man he loves with all his heart betrayed him and kept him from being part of his boys' lives. Give Thomas a break."

"I thought you were on my side."

Arya sighed and shook her head. "I am on your side. You're my sister, and I won't have you talking about yourself like that. You're better than that. Where's the take-no-shit Carmen gone? You need to find her stat."

Oh God. Arya was right. I couldn't do this anymore. Wallowing in my pain wasn't going to help Thomas or me navigate the future.

"I'm sorry, Ari."

"I know you don't mean it. What both Thomas and Diego did to you is shitty, but it's time to think about your boys' futures. And that involves Diego and the California ranch."

"Do you think I should go to California?" I asked the girls. "Here I feel safe, and there I won't have anyone."

"Yes, you will," Arya countered. "Aunt El is only forty minutes from the ranch. Call her, and she'll be by your side within an hour."

Leo and Simon had a right to know all of their family. If it meant taking a few hits while I was there, I'd have to do it.

A tear slipped down my cheek, and I wrapped one arm around each of the girls. "Did I tell you that I love you both?"

"Not today. Now get up and put on the fire-engine-red dress I snagged from Caitlin's new collection. It will compliment that killer supermodel body of yours. Plus, I'm in the mood to dance on a few tables."

"Um, Mil. I thought those days were over," I said as I stood and walked toward the door.

She gave me a devious grin. "What Lex doesn't know, won't hurt him."

* * *

We arrived at Columella, on Manhattan's Lower East Side at exactly eleven that night. I tried to pretend I didn't know that Thomas owned the dance club, but the cat was out of the bag, so to speak, when Milla mentioned having her family architect look at the blueprints so they got the Italian vibe correct. Arya and Milla were partners with Thomas in over twenty different clubs around the world, each with a unique flair. Columella's being Italian villa meets French Riviera.

The one good thing was that I knew I wouldn't run into Thomas tonight. He was in California. When we briefly spoke earlier in the day about meeting the boys, he mentioned he had to finish some ranch work before catching a late-night flight to New York. With the way we'd left things at the party, the last thing I needed was to run into him while dancing the night away.

"Stop brooding," Arya ordered as we approached the bouncer and he lifted the rope to let us pass. "We're going to have fun tonight, whether you want to or not."

I shook my head. "Well, if you're that determined for me to have a good time, who am I to argue?"

"That's the spirit." Milla threaded one arm through mine and the other through Arya's.

We walked into the club, and I was struck by how beautiful the interior was. Three levels of dance space surrounded us. The main floor where we stood housed a famous DJ and dancers. The other two held lounge areas and different themed music, something to appeal to all tastes.

"Wow. This place is insane," I said as we continued toward the bar.

"I know, right? When Thomas brought the idea to us, I was hesitant at first, but now that it's finished I'm so glad we took the jump." Arya cringed and put a hand on me. "Sorry, Carm. I promised myself I wouldn't bring up his name again, and here I go."

"Don't worry about it. Thomas is part of my life, whether I want him in it or not. Now let's get some drinks."

We approached the bar, and right before I opened my mouth to order, Milla pulled me into a back room that had a private bar and seating area.

"This is where we get our liquid sustenance. I called ahead to have our cocktails ready when we arrived." Milla inclined her head to the bartender, who approached us with a tray.

I raised my glass. "Here's to friends who own clubs and have private VIP areas."

"Here's to friends who own fetish clubs and give us naughty girls an outlet for our kinky desires," Milla countered with a smirk.

We all laughed and downed our drinks. After a few more concoctions from the mixologist, I was relaxed and in the mood to dance.

"Come on, girls. I'm going out into the main area to let off some steam. Who's joining me?"

"Let's finish our drinks, and then we'll meet you in a few minutes," Arya said, but the sleepy look on her face told me she'd be in the same spot when I returned.

"Girl, you need to learn to hold your liquor better." Milla nudged Arya's arm

Arya responded by flipping her off.

I laughed and worked my way onto the main dance floor. I stopped to observe the sexy DJ mixing the track and couldn't help but smile at all the girls trying to get his attention. Too bad the ladies didn't know his girlfriend was a Domme who enjoyed watching her man squirm under all the female attention. I glanced to the second level toward his Dominant. We inclined our heads in respect to each other, and I looked back to the dance floor.

"Mistress, may I have the privilege of a dance?"

I turned to the voice. Before me, stood a gorgeous, six-foot-five, well-built Latin man whom I remembered from the club. He was exactly what most Dommes liked in submissives: the look of a Dominant but with a natural desire to submit.

"Hello, Elonso."

He waited and glanced down. "Would you please do me the honor?"

Maybe he'll be the perfect distraction to my man issues.

"It would be my pleasure."

I allowed him to guide me onto the floor and we started dancing. He had amazing moves and made me thankful that Milla insisted I take dance lessons during graduate school. Her words were, *"Bella, you're too stiff. How are you going to attract those Latin men you like so much if you can't move?"*

"May I ask you a question, Mistress?" Elonso spoke as he twirled me.

"Of course."

"Why didn't you take any of us for a scene until the other day?"

I answered on a dip, "I have too many things going on in my life right now, and I'm not into casual scenes. The night with Sam was a first in over five years."

"I'm very happy you're performing again." Elonso grinned

at me. "Keep me on the list for when you decide to enter the dungeon again. Sam can't be the only one who gets the privilege."

I couldn't help but return his smile. He was charming and easy to be around.

He lifted me to standing, and I gripped his muscled arms.

"I'll make sure you're the first one I contact if I decide to play again." I lifted my hair off my back and allowed the air-conditioned air to cool my neck.

We danced for a few more minutes, laughing and talking, then moved to the high-top tables to rest. I ordered a water from the server, when all of a sudden, I knew we weren't alone.

Thomas.

CHAPTER TWELVE

Cousin, it's good to see you." Elonso turned me to the side and hugged him. "Mistress, let me introduce you to one of my favorite family members. He owns the club."

Thomas stared at me, and a smile tugged his lips. "We know each other well. So well that we have two sons together."

There he went again with his one-line zingers.

"Excuse me. Say that again."

The shock on Elonso's face told me he hadn't heard of Thomas's big reveal at Travis's party. He looked back and forth between Thomas and me as if he was trying to figure something out.

"But, Mistress, I thought…you're both Dominants… how…Do you belong to Thomas? Is that why you haven't taken a submissive?"

Before I could answer, Thomas did. "You have it wrong,

Eli." He tucked a strand of my hair behind my ear. "I'm the one who belongs to her."

Goose bumps prickled my skin, and my heartbeat accelerated.

Oh God, why would he say he was my submissive when it wasn't true? Why was he doing this?

"But, Thomas, that doesn't make sense. Both of you are known for your skills as Dominants. I've never heard of a Dom and a Domme together." A chuckle escaped Elonso's mouth. "I can't wait to see how this turns out."

"There's nothing to see. I am who I am. I will always be a Dom, but with her, it's negotiable."

Elonso tilted his head and gave us a skeptical frown, then nodded. "I hope you both know what you're doing."

"We do," Thomas countered.

Elonso ignored him and took my hand. "Mistress, I'm sorry if I overstepped tonight."

I leaned in and kissed him on the cheek. "No, you gave me exactly what I needed. A fun night of dancing and laughter. Be good. I'll see you at the club."

Thomas growled but remained quiet, and Elonso's eyes flashed at him. For a submissive, he was all testosterone right now. As I watched the standoff between the cousins, I noticed their family resemblance.

No wonder you're drawn to him.

After a few moments, Elonso smiled at me, then turned and moved into the crowd on the dance floor.

"That must have been some dance. He was practically drooling at your feet."

I noticed the underlying tone of jealousy in his voice, and it both scared and excited me. I never knew I held that kind of power over him.

He walked forward until he had me trapped against the table with a hand on either side of my waist.

My throat dried up, and I licked my lips as a slow, steady throb ignited inside my core. The Dom in him wanted my submission, but the Domme in me wouldn't yield.

I jutted my chin toward him and stared into his eyes. "Why did you give him the idea we're together? You aren't my submissive. You don't have it in you to be one."

I still hadn't figured out what we called what happened between us. Thomas was the only man I had ever allowed to take over, but I also knew I was the only woman ever allowed to top him.

No, that was a lie. I never truly topped him.

"I want you to trust me, to see that what others think doesn't matter to me. The only thing that is important is what you believe." He grazed the side of my neck with his five-o'clock shadow.

I tilted my head without thought and bit my tongue to keep from moaning. I gripped the table behind me to keep my balance and not jump him in the middle of the club.

He leaned in again and lightly nuzzled the juncture of my pulse. "I wanted him to know that what we have together doesn't shame me or affect my manhood."

I want to believe you, but how do I know you're telling me the truth?

I placed my hand on his. "What happens when your

grandfather finds out? Don't you think it'll get back to him? He isn't going to take it well, knowing his prized eldest grandson enjoys the domination of a woman."

Thomas pulled me toward him, wrapping his arm around my waist, and then slid his hand up my back. "I spent the last few days thinking about nothing but us. I'm going to prove to you that I won't let anyone come between us." He grazed my lips with his. "Not my family." Kiss. "Or our society." Kiss. "And definitely not our pasts." He sealed our mouths, deepening the embrace.

His taste exploded on my senses, and I clutched his shoulders. This man turned all coherent thoughts to mush. We explored each other, not caring who was around us. By the time we pulled apart, I was barely able to stand and his erection pushed against my pelvis.

He leaned his head against mine and steadied his breath.

"Thomas, I can't think when you overwhelm me like this. You caught me off guard. I have to think."

He tightened his hold on me. "I'm beginning to realize that it's better if you don't think."

"I don't understand what's happening between us."

"It looks obvious to me." He pushed his straining cock more against me. "I want you, Carmen. I wanted you a year and a half ago. I never stopped."

I closed my eyes, trying to comprehend what he was saying. "Thomas, what we share frightens me. Why would you let me take control? It doesn't come naturally to you."

"Because with you, all I can think about is your pleasure.

And if that means giving you the submission you need, then I will."

"I won't submit to you. I gave you all of me, and then you told me I wasn't good enough. That I wasn't the kind of woman you could see spending your life with. So if you're expecting anything else, then this can't go any further."

A sadness flashed in his gaze, making my breath hitch. "I'll take you any way I can." He cupped my face. "There's something you should know about yourself that I think you won't readily admit, especially after what happened between us."

I waited for him to elaborate.

"You want to submit. I've seen it every time I've taken over. You craved it. You enjoyed every minute of it. My stupidity in how I handled things with you ruined the trust we'd built. I'm so sorry."

I wanted to argue with him, but how could I argue against something I'd been telling myself?

I looked away, hoping to hide the truth from him, but he tugged my face back to him.

"Carm, you'll always be a Domme. That's part of who you are, and what happened between us doesn't make it any less so. As it doesn't make me less of a Dom."

"What if I can't?"

"It won't change the way I feel for you." He kissed the tip of my nose.

I wanted to believe him, everything in me said believe him, but the uneasiness remained. Until we figured out what happening between us, I wouldn't have my answers.

He stepped back and extended his hand.

I hesitated, knowing that I was about to change the path I'd set for my relationship with him. Maybe Arya was right. I had to give him a chance.

I slid my palm over his. "Take me home, Thomas."

"Yes, Mistress."

* * *

Thomas and I walked toward the exit of the club, and from the side of my eye, I saw Arya and Milla leaning against the railing of the second-level dance floor. The kiss that Arya blew me and the fist pump Milla sent my way told me they'd seen more than I wanted.

Well, Carmen. Who told you to make out in the middle of a nightclub?

"I have my car here." Thomas inclined his head to the attendant, and within seconds, his Maserati arrived.

"I guess it's good to be the boss," I observed.

"It has its perks."

Thomas opened the door, and I slid in. He went around the driver's side. Once situated in the seat, he turned to me. "Ready?"

I nodded but then shook my head. "Thomas, are you sure? This will change our relationship, and like I said, I may never completely submit to you in exchange."

He grazed his thumb over my bottom lip. "I know what I'm doing, Carm. You're what I want."

"Okay then, let's go." A smile touched my lips. Time to see if he could handle my Domme side.

We rolled out of the parking lot and stopped at a traffic light.

"Lower your pants and pull out your cock."

He jerked the brakes and glanced at me. "Are you serious?"

I raised a brow in response, and a crease formed between his.

Without any more words, he did as I said. The moment his hardening cock sprang free, I grasped it, squeezing up and down.

"Drive," I ordered.

He looked at the light and realized it was green.

I worked his cock with my hand, making sure to thumb the angry, weeping head. I licked my lips as my mouth watered to taste him.

"Do you see something you want to work into your mouth?"

My eyes jerked up to Thomas's face. He was studying my expression.

"For that, I'm not going to let you come." I squeezed harder. A rough groan escaped him, and his grip on the steering wheel tightened. I continued my ministrations, bringing him to the point of orgasm but stopping moments before the eruption happened.

"Carmen…," Thomas growled.

I stopped his torture, and I slid closer to him without releasing my hold on him. Shimmying from side to side, I lifted my skirt to reveal the red thong that matched my dress.

"Do you like?"

Thomas swallowed and tried not to look too long without losing his attention on the road.

"Yes, Mistress," he answered through a raspy voice.

"Your job is to get us home before I make myself come." I pumped his cock a few more times. "If you do that, I will allow you to pleasure me."

"I will," he stated and sped up.

"Give me your hand."

He complied, and I brought it to my underwear. "Pull it aside, but you aren't allowed to touch me no matter what I do to you or myself."

He held my thong with his pinkie and gripped my leg. I could have reprimanded him for taking liberties, but the feel of his large hand against my thigh sent a gush of wetness to my pussy, something I'd never experienced with any other man.

I resumed my strokes on his hard erection and began rubbing my clit. The first contact of my fingers sent a spasm deep inside my core. A moan escaped my lips, and I threw my head back against the seat.

It was Thomas who did this to me. My body never reacted the minute I touched it. I slid two fingers into my throbbing pussy and continued rubbing.

"Oh yes, I've needed this. I hope you get to my building soon," I called out as my squeezed my eyes shut.

Precum dripped from the tip of his cock. Thomas growled, and his grip tightened on my leg.

"Almost there," he gritted out as he lifted his hips to

match the rhythm of my hand. "Fuck. I'm going to come." He thrashed against the seat as he drove.

I released my grip on him, but I continued riding my fingers. "Don't you dare. I haven't given you permission."

"I won't Mistress, but don't stop. I have to see you come," he begged or ordered, I couldn't tell, as he pulled into my private entrance.

"Oh God," I called, squeezing my eyes tight. At this point, it didn't matter if I wanted to stop. The orgasm was almost on me.

The car screeched to a stop and all of a sudden my seat was pushed back, with Thomas dislodging my fingers from my pussy and replacing them with his mouth. He licked and sucked, causing my body to bow, then without warning, I exploded.

"Thomas," I cried out, and let wave after wave of bliss washed over me.

"My Mistress," he murmured as he continued laving attention on my clit, and I rode out my release. "My woman. Mine."

CHAPTER THIRTEEN

M y breath calmed, and I opened my eyes. Looking down my body, I saw Thomas with his head against my thigh, breathing just as hard as I was. His erection throbbed hard in his lap, and for a split second, I wanted to give him the release he needed, but he hadn't earned it, and his release came once I finished with him.

I turned my head away from Thomas and looked out the window. All of a sudden, I noticed the security camera pointed directly at the car.

Fuck. I hope the guards didn't see anything.

I lifted up and pushed Thomas back into his seat. "We have to fix ourselves. There are cameras on us."

He glanced at me and grinned. "The windows are too dark for them to see anything. Besides, does it matter?"

His words triggered the memory of a conversation I had with Arya, where she told me Thomas loved to show off his submissives, especially the orgasms he gave them.

I sighed. I wasn't a sub.

"Perhaps not, but I don't want to give the guards anything to wonder about."

We straightened our clothes and took the elevator to my penthouse in silence. I wanted to touch him, to enjoy a level of intimacy we once shared, but I wasn't ready, and I wouldn't know if it was real. Right now, I needed to remain focused, in tune with what brings Thomas pleasure. This was about Thomas and his needs; my desires came second.

A few seconds before we arrived at my floor, I gave him my orders. "When you enter my apartment, I want you to strip and go to the third door on the right. It is my bedroom. You will kneel at the foot of my bed and wait for me."

"What about the nanny and the boys?"

"They're spending the night with Max. He'll bring them over in the morning so they can meet you."

Thomas stared at me with hooded eyes, and his hand lifted for a second. I held my breath, knowing he needed the affection as much as I did, but then he dropped it. A twinge of disappointment hit my heart.

Before our breakup, we never had to worry about what every touch meant. Now we were both working through new territory neither of us knew how to navigate.

"I will follow your directive, Mistress," he said as he opened the door and we stepped inside the foyer to my penthouse.

Thomas took his jacket and shirt off, laying both on the back of the sofa, and then went straight to my bedroom, without a backward glance. I inhaled, letting my heartbeat calm, and walked to my kitchen. I filled a glass of water and drank deep. The cool liquid refreshed my insides as I leaned against the counter and tried to steady my emotions.

Why did it feel like I had no idea what I was doing with him?

Because you don't. He isn't a submissive, and you're playing a game without rules.

Rules. I needed them. I was taught to stay in charge by setting the rules. I maintained control without pushing my will on my submissive to more than they could take.

I closed my eyes for a moment, imagining that it had been Thomas in that dungeon instead of Samuel. His head bowed, his body glistening with the oil the attendants prepped him with, and his cock growing for my attention.

A low moan escaped my lips as my clit throbbed with the fantasy. If it had been Thomas, I would have allowed him to pleasure me. Hell, I'd have allowed him to fuck me.

"Mistress," Thomas called, snapping me out of my thoughts.

I straightened, grabbing a hair tie from the bowl on my counter, and gathered my hair on top of my head. Slowly, I made my way to the bedroom.

My breath caught as Thomas came into view. The mere sight of him aroused me like no other man. He kneeled naked in front of the chaise, positioned at the foot of my bed.

I walked back and forth behind him, running my fingers along his sculpted bare shoulders. Goose bumps prickled his skin as he stared straight at the bed. The moment I came into view, he lowered his head, surprising me. In all our past scenes, he never looked down. He always kept his gaze at eye level. At the time, his defiance never fazed me. I knew the Dom in him would rebel, and the enjoyment we both desired would disappear. Now his voluntarily looking down told me he was committed to submitting, committed to what he had agreed to.

What turned me on most with Thomas was that he was the strongest man I'd ever played with. He was confident in who he was. It didn't matter if he was kneeling, as he was now, or if he had me tied to the bed and towered over me. It was a heady mix of well-controlled raw power.

That's what drew me to him that first night so long ago. It was the push and pull between his strength and mine.

"What are your limits?" I asked.

He snorted. "What limits. You're the Domme. You know how far to go."

I fisted his hair, jerking his head back. He stared me in the eyes, without flinching. "Not tonight, Thomas, ple…" I stopped midsentence. What was I doing? Then I noticed the gleam in his eye and realized he was fighting me for his submission as he'd always done.

"Very clever." I ran a thumb over his lips as a smile tugged at mine. "No fighting what I want to do to you," I ordered. "You agreed, after all. The minute you stepped into my room, you became my slave."

He continued staring at me, not saying anything.

I gripped his hair tighter, hard enough to keep him on the edge of uncomfortable without hurting him. "Are we in agreement?"

His face flushed and his eyes dilated, telling me he enjoyed the sensation caused by my fingers. "Mistress, I have always been your slave. Do as you will."

I released his hair, walking away from him. I shook my head with amusement. This man had no sense of self-preservation. If he thought I wouldn't push him further than I'd ever pushed him before, then he was about to be sadly disappointed.

I licked my lips. My hot lover was submitting to my every desire.

What a delicious idea.

He said he was my slave. *Let's see how far he'll let me go without losing control.*

I wasn't stupid enough to believe Thomas would readily hand over power without attempting to reclaim it.

"One last chance. What are your limits?" I asked over my shoulder.

"A la carte, Mistress."

I closed my eyes, savoring his words.

Steadying my breath, I went into my closet and pulled out a box that I hadn't opened in nearly two years. Lifting the lid, I selected a bottle of lube, manacles, and a riding crop. The scent of the leather tingled my senses, and I licked my lips as a calm I was familiar with entered my body.

He was my slave. He was here to serve me. And for his service, I'd reward him.

I stood, returning to the bedroom, and my heartbeat quickened at the sight of him. He remained in the same position I'd left him, kneeling with his hands clasped behind his back and his gaze trained on the closet door. His erection stood long and hard pointing up toward his belly button.

My skin prickled. Thomas was gorgeous and *mine.*

He watched me approach with a blaze in his eyes that said he could see the depth of secrets I wasn't aware of myself.

I shook the thought from my head and retrieved a condom from the side table before I moved in front of him.

This time, I wasn't going to forget. When I'd visited the doctor yesterday, she'd told me not to worry since I wasn't in the ovulation phase of my cycle. She'd told me my best option was the Depo-Provera shot, which was active in a matter of days. I wasn't stupid enough to believe the incident at Travis's house was a onetime deal. Now all I had to do was wait another day until it was fully active.

"Give me your hands."

He offered them to me, and I clasped the cuffs against his wrists.

"Stand."

He followed my command, and as he reached his full six-foot-five height, our size difference hit me. My five-foot-ten frame barely came to his shoulder, and with my heels, I was only a little bit taller.

My fingers itched to draw him to me. He must have read my thoughts since he licked his lips. For a brief second, he leaned toward me but immediately pulled back.

"If you want my kiss, you'll have to earn it."

I walked us over to the side of the bed and clicked a controller that opened the ceiling, revealing a grid of metal bars.

I climbed onto the bed and reached for a braided pulley attached to the steel.

I took each of Thomas's wrists and clipped them to the rope, then tugged another cord, causing his arms to lift tight above his head. His body angled toward the center of the bed, but he remained standing.

His muscles bulged, and his beautiful ass flexed as he adjusted his stance to accommodate the restraints. It should be illegal to look that sexy. My pussy contracted, and a new wave of wetness dampened my crotch.

I hadn't felt a twinge of this type of arousal during my scene with Samuel.

That's because he wasn't Thomas.

"God. You're exquisite," I announced. "Stay like that."

I picked up the crop, rubbed it up from the back of his knee to the dip of his lower back, and then back down the other leg. His skin prickled with goose bumps, and a slight flush tinged his beautiful tanned skin. His sculpted body was mine to do with as I pleased. A blank canvas to mark as mine.

"Turn."

He complied, and his eyes collided with mine as his breath quickened. I rubbed the end of the crop over his nipples, first circling one, then the other. A shudder rocked his body. I continued lower until I reached the angry purple head of his cock pointing past his belly button. I flicked the crop against the bulbous, weeping tip.

Thomas hissed but remained still.

"Did you like that?"

"Yes, Mistress."

I did it again.

This time he kept silent.

I moved away from his beautiful cock and snapped the crop against his thighs, much firmer than I'd hit his beautiful cock. I flicked and cracked the crop all over his honed, muscular front side. Sweat glistened on his skin, and his arms bulged as he jerked against his restraints. Every strike was harder and closer to the straining evidence of his arousal.

The power of his body inflamed my insides. I pushed a button, allowing for some slack on the leather manacles, which sent Thomas onto his back on the bed.

I climbed over him, straddling his body. I positioned his cock against the soaked fabric of my thong, sliding his length between my folds and against my swollen clit.

"Oh, so good," I moaned.

He lifted his hips, but I clamped them with my thighs. "Stay still."

A crease formed between his eyes but he relaxed back down. I continued to rub my pussy against him as I unzipped my red dress and lifted it above my head.

"You're gorgeous, my every dream," he said, and his words squeezed my heart.

I held back my response as I unclasped my bra, allowing my breasts to spill out. I leaned down, rubbing my puckering nipples against his, and closed my eyes. The sprinkling of hair on his chest tortured my tightening buds.

Yes, this was what I needed. Thomas's skin felt so good. My core spasmed and I pulled back as I realized my train of thought. This was not about me. It was about giving Thomas pleasure. I shimmied my pussy away from his cock.

"Close your eyes." I kissed the center of his chest and peeked up to see if he obeyed. His gaze bored into mine. I bit the skin below his nipple and raised a brow. He sighed and shut his lids.

Trailing lower, I licked and kissed until I reached his throbbing cock. Grasping the base with my left hand, I squeezed, pumping it up and down. I felt his heat, the iron pulsing hardness of him.

With the tip of my tongue, I licked the blood-filled, sensitive vein running along the base of his cock.

"Carm," Thomas moaned. "Mistress."

His cry was like an aphrodisiac to my senses. The trail of my tongue continued until it slid into the dripping slit on the tip. His salty essence increased the saliva pooling in my mouth. Gliding lower, I nuzzled his bulging balls, then sucked them one at a time.

I continued to pump him while I teased until a guttural rumble echoed from Thomas's throat. He jerked his arms against the pulley, bringing them down, but they caught about halfway.

He pushed his pelvis up into my fist and growled as I ignored his unsaid command.

"Is there something you want?"

"Yes."

I squeezed tight at the back of his cock, causing a hiss from his mouth. "Yes, what?"

"Yes, Mistress. I need your fucking mouth on my cock."

The hairs on the back of my neck prickled. Peering up at Thomas, I realized he watched me with almost black eyes.

"Naughty, naughty. That's not how you ask," I murmured against his balls, gently pinching the skin on one side with my teeth.

He lay back down and apologized. "Sorry, Mistress. Will you please suck my cock?"

I smiled inside at the defiance he reined in, and for a split second, I thought about making him wait, but my mouth watered for a taste of him.

Opening my lips, I engulfed the head of his cock, taking him in as deep as I could bear. I swallowed, releasing the back of my throat, and he slipped in a little further.

"Oh God," Thomas cried out and pushed up until he hit the back of my throat.

I caressed his thighs as I worked his beautiful cock. I peeked up and saw his lids squeezed tight and his hands clenched against the manacles. The ache in my pussy intensified and I pressed my legs together, rocking back and forth in hopes of relieving the pressure building inside me.

I circled and sucked, bobbing up and down, enjoying the soft and hard feel of him in my wet mouth. I loved the taste of him.

I lifted my mouth for a second and said, "Bend your knees. I want to get comfortable."

He complied, and I settled between them and engulfed him again. I used one of my hands to work him with the rhythm of my mouth and moved the other behind me to the lube. Popping the top, I poured some into my palm.

I rubbed the lube between my fingers, and then brought them underneath Thomas's balls, rubbing the resistive skin.

"Carm," he growled and warned even as he pushed his hips up, giving me access to my end goal.

My hand curled around his firm, muscular ass and toward his puckered entrance. He instinctively clutched them tight, but one of my lubricated fingers slipped in as I increased the pressure of my mouth on the head of his cock.

"Fuck. I'm going to come if you do this." There was a tinge of panic in his words, which I knew was from his loss of control. Tonight he was mine, and I wanted to taste him, the way he denied me at Travis's mansion. Anal play was new territory for us, and I was positive no one had ever done this to him.

God, I hope he can handle it.

I slid another finger inside and pushed deeper, pressing my fingers to the sensitive bundle of nerves deep inside.

"Goddammit, I…," he gurgled as he pumped his hips and discharged jets of cum deep into my mouth.

I swallowed and licked, savoring his essence. A thrill shot through me, knowing I'd snapped his ability to hold back.

This was my show. Mistress Carmen still existed, even with the uncertainty of our relationship.

As the last of his thrusts calmed, he relaxed down, breathing hard, not saying anything. His eyes remained closed as I slid his cock from my mouth and my fingers from his ass.

"Let me clean up."

He didn't respond.

A lump formed in the pit of my stomach. Had I pushed

him too far? Was this a hard limit? He'd said there were none.

God, Carmen. Get it together. Don't doubt yourself now.

I cleaned up, and within minutes, I returned to Thomas, who still hadn't opened his eyes.

I pulled the lever, releasing the chain holding the cuffs, and Thomas's arms fell to his sides. I climbed on the bed and rubbed his shoulders, making sure he regained any feeling he'd lost as he'd pulled on his bonds.

"Thomas?" I inhaled and sighed. "Thomas…"

He moved so fast, I couldn't finish my statement. He sat up and gripped my upper arms, bringing me on top of him and at eye level.

My heart thundered as he stared at me with anger and lust. "I'm going to fuck your ass one day. You'll lose all of your control, and when that happens, you'll remember this moment. I gave you something no other person has had, and I expect the same."

I swallowed. "No, Thomas. You can't expect that from me. I may never be ready."

He opened his mouth to argue, so I did the only thing I could think of to soothe him. I leaned in and covered his angry lips with mine. I nipped and licked until he opened, then his kisses became all consuming. His hands moved from my arms, one going into my hair and the other to my lower back, pulling me close to him.

I slid my fingers to the back of his neck, enjoying the play of his tongue against mine.

"Carmen," he murmured and continued to devour my mouth. His grip on me eased as I held him close.

The unquenched heat inside me fired to life again, and my clit pulsed. My body wasn't the only one waking. Thomas's cock grew, pressing between us. I rubbed my dripping pelvis against him, hoping to relieve some of my need.

"That's some fast recovery," I mumbled against his lips.

His lips curved in a smile. "My Mistress does that to me."

"I need you inside me. Please."

Dammit, I'm not the one who's supposed to beg.

Thomas lifted me, breaking the contact of our mouths to slide me down onto his hard length.

"Yes," I called.

I rode him hard and fast, desperate for the release I craved. I arched my back while digging my nails into his. Each rise of my hips sent spasms into my aching core. My rhythm faltered as my orgasm loomed closer. Thomas thrust up, keeping up the pace I needed to go over.

"Come for me, *cielito*. Let me see you fly."

He leaned in, biting the skin at my pulse, and almost immediately I detonated, ecstasy flooding my bloodstream. My body bowed, and I cried out Thomas's name. I squeezed his cock with my pussy as he continued pummeling into me. A few moments after me, he followed with his own release.

* * *

I woke with a start, expecting to hear Leo and Simon calling for their breakfast. Then I remembered that they were at Max's estate and would be back later in the morning. I relaxed back into the bed, moaning as I shifted my legs. My body ached from the long night of glorious sex.

I glanced to my left as Thomas slept on his stomach. His face turned away from me with the sheets barely covering his beautiful, chiseled ass. One arm rested under his head as the other held me close. The same way he'd held me during a nightmare I hadn't expected would surface.

I'd returned from a day in the office and no one was around. I called out but no answer. As I searched for Stacey and the boys, I came across Stacey's dead body and a note pinned to her chest that read, *Since you can't decide between reputation and family, we'll make it for you. Once the money clears, the boys will come home.*

I must have screamed because Thomas had gently shaken me until I freed myself from my terror, and then held me as he told me he was there for me.

I knew I should have told him what was happening with Christof, but I wasn't thinking straight. And all I wanted to do was forget.

When I'd asked Thomas to make love to me, he never hesitated. He slid his body over mine, pleasuring me in a way that left me believing what we shared could be real and trusted.

My heart clenched. The walls I'd erected after our breakup weren't going to last much longer.

I gently touched the show of whiskers on his face. He was gorgeous, awake or asleep. He'd given me so much yesterday, even before the bad dream. He'd let me control the events of the evening even when I knew he wanted to take over. He understood the battle inside me and allowed me the freedom to hold the reins for the night.

I closed my eyes and held back a sigh. I wasn't sure if I'd actually held the control or not. Why did I feel this way every time we were together?

He was the father of my children and once again my lover. Could I hope for more? It would be so easy to fall back in love with him.

Stop lying to yourself, Carm. You never stopped loving him.

My phone buzzed, and I reached out to grab it from the nightstand. It was a text from Max, letting me know he was pulling into the garage with the boys. With one last look at Thomas, I lifted his arm, slid from the bed, and then slipped on my robe as I rushed to the bathroom.

Less than ten minutes later, I was in the kitchen, starting my coffee, and preparing a snack for the boys.

The elevator dinged, signaling Max's arrival. I met him as the doors opened, and smiled at my disheveled brother and my handsome sons, one sleeping on Max's shoulder and the other staring happily at me with green eyes that looked like mine.

"Rough night?" I asked with a smirk.

He handed me Leo, who reached out and squeezed me tight once he was in my arms.

"It was God's sick joke to give both of us twin boys. The four of them had Lex and me ready to binge drink. At least Briana decided to give her dad a break and crashed a few minutes after her last bottle."

"I thought Natalie was coming over to help."

"She stayed to help clean up and make sure Bri was

tucked in, and then told us that we needed to see what it was like to handle four active toddlers. She gave us her sweet smile, kissed all of us on the cheek, and took the nannies with her." He shook his head. "That woman raised me and left me to fend for myself."

"You had Lex," I retorted. "Want a cup of coffee? It's Milla's special brew."

I walked to the coffee machine, but before I poured two cups, I gave Leo an apple slice to gnaw on.

"Yes. Um. Carm, what the hell is this?" Max stood by the pile of clothes on the back of the sofa and frowned. "Who the fuck is in that room?" He pointed to my bedroom. "Arya never mentioned anything about you hooking up with anyone last night. Please tell me you didn't pick up some random guy."

Cocking a hand on my hip, I scowled back at him. "Language! You're only older than me by a few minutes. Don't give me that big brother shit. I can have a sex life without your approval. I've been in a drought for the past eighteen months."

"You're one to talk." He raised a brow and then waited for my response.

I picked up another apple slice and walked toward Max. "I don't sleep around. You know this. Who do you think is in that room?"

"Shit." He ran a hand through his hair and adjusted Simon as he started to wake. "So the rumors about Thomas's announcement and the disheveled way you left Travis's party are true?"

"Here you go, sweet boy." Simon smiled at me with a two-toothed grin and took his snack. "Did you miss Mommy?"

"Carmen, you can play with him and answer my question." I sighed. "Yes, it's true. We're working on it."

"How? I wouldn't worry so much if you weren't still in lo…" Max stopped midsentence and looked behind me.

I turned and saw Thomas standing with a towel wrapped around his waist at the threshold of the living room.

CHAPTER FOURTEEN

Thomas stared at the boys with a pained longing. He kept his eyes on them without saying anything as he approached us.

The second Thomas was within reach, Leo lunged out of my arms and into Thomas's.

"Da…Da…Da," Leo called, and laying his head on Thomas's bare shoulder.

Thomas held Leo close, breathing in his scent, and then looked toward Simon, who was ready to follow his brother's lead and leap out of Max's arms.

Max handed Simon over. Both boys grabbed each other's hands and gazed up at Thomas.

After a few moments of studying the boys, Thomas swallowed and whispered, "They look like me."

The emotions in his voice completely shattered the shell around my heart. "Yes," was all I said, trying to keep the hoarseness out of my response.

"They know me," he stated in awe.

"I show them your picture every morning and tell them who you are."

He glanced at me with clouded eyes. "I have so much to make up for. I've missed so much of their lives."

I reached up and cupped his cheek. "We'll figure it out."

The sound of the elevator reminded me that Max was still there.

Lowering my hand, I turned to see Max entering the elevator.

"Max, where are you going?"

He smiled. "I need to get home to my wife and kids. Plus, it's time that you worked on your own family."

The doors closed and Thomas spoke. "Are we a family, Carm?"

He seemed so confident when he announced we were one in my office, but now with the boys in his arms, his uncertainty showed through.

I released a deep breath and then nodded, not trusting myself to speak without crying. Thomas leaned down, kissing the top of my head. At that moment, the boys decided to start fighting and fussing. They began hitting each other and smashing mushed-up apple pieces into the other's face.

Thomas and I started laughing, and he set them down on the floor, which resulted in complete meltdowns.

Thomas cringed and then tried to distract the boys with any available toy in the vicinity, making the boys cry louder. I couldn't help but laugh at the panic etched across his face.

"This is normal and part of parenting. Here." I grabbed a

few napkins and handed them to him. "Clean them off while I get their bottles and a cup of coffee."

"Will you get me one, too, preferably spiked with brandy?" he said as he adjusted his towel and attended to our hellions.

I smiled, bringing our drinks over. Leo and Simon grabbed their bottles, fell back onto the floor, and sucked down their milk.

"How did you do this on your own?" Thomas asked. "Seeing the state Max was in, something tells me these guys are a handful."

"I had help from Natalie and now from the nanny." I was quiet for a few seconds. "I didn't have a choice, Thomas. I was alone, and whether I kept them or not wasn't even a question."

Sadness flashed over his face. "I'm so sorry."

"You're in their lives now; that's all that matters." I gently grabbed Leo's foot as he kicked me.

"I want them to have my name." He stated.

"They already do," I said as I continued to play with Leo's feet. I couldn't look up at him to see his reaction.

"Why'd you do that? After what happened between us, I never expected you to give them anything that reminded you of me."

During my pregnancy, my emotions went up and down about giving them Thomas's last name, let alone naming one of my boys after Thomas's father. But I knew what it was like to lose a parent. So I decided to name Leo after Thomas's father, Leonardo, and Simon after my mother, Simone.

"Because no matter how I felt, they belonged to you as much as me."

"Thank you."

"You're welcome." I took a sip of my coffee.

"That's not all." He paused, making me glance up, then spoke again. "I want you to have my name, too."

My heart jumped, and I swallowed, staring up at him. "Say that again."

His fingers twitched, but he didn't make a move to touch me. "I know you're going to resist, but hear me out. I made mistakes with you that I will regret for the rest of my life. The way I feel about you never changed. I want you to marry me."

"Um, slow down a moment. I don't even understand what's going on between us. I can't marry you. Besides…" The urge to run pulled at me, but I remained seated.

"Besides what?"

"How do I know you aren't going to change your mind? You rejected me once. It could happen again. Let's just keep our relationship going the way it is and then see where we end up." I held my breath, failing to keep the panic out of my response.

His voice grew cold. "And what way are we going?"

I squared my shoulders. "Being parents to Leo and Simon and occasional lovers."

"Fuck that." He stood up and paced. "You aren't going to turn what we have into something casual. Who held you last night? Who loved you last night? It was special, even if you don't want to admit it. Yes, I fucked up. I'll regret everything I did to hurt you." He ran a frustrated hand through his hair. "If what happened wasn't important, you wouldn't be putting up this wall."

Of course it was important. Nevertheless, I'm scared.

"Thomas, the boys have to get used to you before we get any deeper into this."

"You're just using them as an excuse."

I growled and got up, stalking toward him. "You want to know the truth?" I poked him in the chest, and he grabbed my wrist.

"Yes. Tell me the truth," he gritted out.

"I don't trust you."

Hurt flashed across Thomas's face but changed to anger within seconds. "I see. And what is going to get you to trust me?" His grip on my hand intensified, and then he released me and walked toward the mantel.

"I don't know. This is all going so fast." I pressed my finger to my temple, trying to calm the headache brewing to life. "We need to slow down. Take it a day at a time."

"No. I won't accept that. Those boys need both of us in their lives."

We looked at Leo and Simon playing, unaware of the turmoil between their parents.

"I never denied that."

"Bullshit. You kept their existence a secret from me. I had to find out through a tabloid article. Do you have any idea what it was like to find out that the woman I love gave birth to my children and didn't bother to let me know?"

He loves me?

I couldn't believe it. Too many times, I'd made the mistake of trusting words of love, only to learn I was wrong. First Andrew, then Thomas. I couldn't keep making the same mistakes.

My tempter flared. "Do you think I wanted to do this alone? Don't you think I wanted you there? You shredded my belief in what we had. Do you remember telling me that my father's crime would always follow me and you couldn't see a future for us? Especially if it meant hurting your family? What Dad did to your aunt wasn't my fault."

"I know what I said. I was wrong."

"Wrong. Are you kidding me right now?" I shouted at him. "One weekend you're telling me you wanted to build a home with me, and the next, after a visit to your family, you tell me I'm disposable. If what we shared freaked you out so much, then why did you pursue me? We could have left it as a fling and moved on."

I ran a hand across my face and pinched the bridge of my nose.

"If I recall, you handled it pretty well. You didn't even show an ounce of emotion. I couldn't believe how cold your response was."

"What did you expect me to do? Fall apart? Would it have made you feel better if I'd cried?" I clenched my jaw. "You tore my heart out that day."

I was disposable, just like I was to Andrew, to Dad, to Thomas.

"You still kept my boys from me."

"There was no proof that you'd stick around if I'd told you about my pregnancy."

"What do you want me to do to get you to see I'm here for good?"

"Nothing. I've seen too much to believe it's true," I whispered as the hurt from the past year washed away any fight I had left in me. "I'm used to being alone. It's better that way."

I turned away and walked toward the bedroom. If I expected anything from him, I'd open myself up to hurt again. Why had I let last night happen? I knew better.

God, my emotions are so fucked up. Carmen, you have to get it together.

"Where are you going?" Thomas asked from behind me.

I glanced over my shoulder and tried to speak without any affliction in my voice. "To shower. I'd appreciate if you'd watch them until Stacey arrives. Then you can leave. I think we've said all we need to say."

Thomas stepped toward me but stopped when he saw me raise my hand.

"Don't do this, Carm. Not with me. Don't freeze me out when it gets hard. I'm not giving up on us."

I ignored him and walked into my bedroom.

Shutting the door, I stripped off my clothes in a numb haze and walked into my shower. Turning the dial to the hottest setting I could handle, I stepped under the spray. I closed my eyes as the water beat down on my face, and the heat seeped into my body.

What was happening to me? I thought those feeling were long buried.

A Domme isn't supposed to fall apart at the slightest trouble.

She has to maintain control no matter what life throws her way.

I hiccupped as a sob erupted, and slid to the floor, letting my pain and heartache consume me.

* * *

Twenty minutes later, after I finally had my emotions back under control, I stepped out of the shower. Thomas wasn't at fault for my choice of keeping the boys from him. He was right. It was easier to freeze him out than to let him know his words or actions affected me.

Maybe it was all the lessons Natalie gave about controlling my reactions when people talked about Dad after Mama died.

Even before the embezzlement scandal, people referred to me as the snobby Dane. Max was the golden boy of the family. He was athletic, supersmart, and could charm anyone around him. On the other hand, I was a supershy and socially awkward twelve-year-old, and became even more so after Mama's death.

At that time, Natalie was my family's estate manager, and she ran every aspect of the house. When Dad abandoned us, she took it upon herself to raise us. One of the first lessons she taught me was that I couldn't control the opinions of others, but I could control my reaction to them.

Over the next years, her lessons helped me deal with the gossip and recriminations of the various scandals Dad put us through, from affairs with the wives of his colleagues and clients to ultimately the scandal that nearly cost Max and me everything.

Those lessons became an ingrained part of who I was, and now I used them as a way to maintain control in all things.

No, that wasn't true. For the six months Thomas and I were together, I'd given him command over so many aspects of our relationship, something I'd never felt comfortable doing with anyone else.

I walked toward my closet.

I had to figure out what was going to happen between us. Becoming lovers again was probably a big mistake, but I wasn't naïve enough to think it was going to end. No matter how hard I tried, Thomas pulled at a side of me no other man had ever reached. The part of me that would allow another person to take over. Maybe it was the Dom in him that called to the...*submissive in me.*

I sighed and closed my eyes for a second.

Was I wrong about who I was?

I pushed those thoughts back and quickly dressed. I couldn't go there right now.

I walked into an empty living room five minutes later. All evidence of Thomas was gone except his tie on the side table. My heart clenched. I shouldn't have walked away like that. I shouldn't have dismissed him.

I picked up the silk and held it to my chest.

After my conference call, I'll call him and apologize.

At that moment, the boys' bedroom door clicked.

"Stacey, were they difficult to get down?" I asked without looking toward the hallway.

"No," Thomas answered. "They were half-asleep by the time she arrived."

I whirled around as my breath hitched. "What are you still doing here?"

"We haven't finished our discussion." He moved in front of me, stepping forward as I retreated.

"There's something you should know about me." He advanced until my back hit the wall. "No matter how much you try, you can't dismiss me."

He caged me with his arms, trapping my body. I tried to push him away, but he grabbed my wrists and pinned them above my head. My heartbeat accelerated, and a tingle shot to my core.

"Thomas," I gasped. "Stacey is here. Let me go."

He grazed his stubble against the side of my face. "She told me the boys would sleep for the next three hours, so I sent her home."

"Are you sure you can handle them?"

"I'm not worried. Does my presence make you uncomfortable?" he purred.

I shifted my head to the side as my pulse rang into my ears, and stared him in the eyes. "You don't frighten me, Thomas. Don't think for a second you intimidate me."

"Oh, but I know I do. Your breath is shallow, and your cheeks are flushed." His eyes dilated, and his lips turned up on the corners. "I'm not going to let you hide from me or push me away. The trick may have worked with everyone else, but I know, deep inside, what you want. What you need."

I lifted my chin. "And what is that?"

"You need someone who'll stick with you, no matter what happens. Someone who'll love you through anything. Someone who'll believe in you and fight for you."

I clenched my jaw. "I've never had that. I still don't."

I wanted to shove him out of the way, but my body betrayed me and wouldn't move.

Cupping the side of my face, he rested his forehead against mine. "Yes, you do. I won't make the same mistake again. I know what you need. I won't let you down."

I closed my eyes, letting his words sink in. I had to give him a chance to show me I wasn't second to his family, or I'd never be able to trust him.

As if sensing my thoughts, he rubbed a finger against my lips and spoke. "Let go of the past, Carm. Let me show you all we can have."

"I won't let you do this to me again." I tugged my hand out of his and shoved past him, moving to the balcony window. "Once, I was stupid enough to have hoped for…" I shook my head, stopping the words I was about to say. "Not anymore, Thomas. I won't risk it again."

"What we have will never be just sex, no matter what you say. The second I touch you"—his fingers grazed my arms, causing me to gasp—"your body knows its Master."

"Stop. I have no Master." I tried to push his hands away, but he grasped mine.

His grip tightened. "Do you think admitting I have a hold over you makes you weak?"

I am weak. You crushed my heart once before.

"Don't you get it? Depending on you means you can hurt me again." I scrunched my eyes tight.

Fuck, I shouldn't have admitted that.

"What about me? I'm just as vulnerable as you." His lips trailed down the side of my neck, and without thought, I tilted it to the side, giving him better access.

One of his hands slid up my shoulder and cupped my throat with a small squeeze, which caused a moan to escape my lips.

My phone beeped, breaking the spell he had over me and letting me know my conference was going to start.

"Thomas, let me go. I have a conference call."

He sighed, released his hold on me, and turned me toward him. "Go. I'll be here when you're done. This conversation is far from over."

I opened my mouth to tell him to get lost and leave, but he sealed it with his. He kissed me with such need that my mind lost all thought except giving him every warring emotion in my body. My fingers slipped into his hair, and he dug into the curves of my ass, drawing me against his erection. We nipped, tasted, and savored each other until Thomas slowly pulled back.

"You have a meeting."

I refocused on him through desire-glazed eyes and tried to steady my ragged breaths. We both stared at each other for a few moments before I turned and rushed to my office.

CHAPTER FIFTEEN

I entered my office in a haze, slipping into the seat at my desk. How did we go from anger and emotional turmoil to sucking face? I cupped the sides of my temples and squeezed my head.

This man had me turned upside down. My computer pinged, alerting me to the start of the video conference.

I logged onto the video chat, slid into my seat, and spoke. "Hello. This is Carmen Dane. We'll get started in a few minutes."

"Hey, Carm." Arya came into view from the office of her company headquarters. "It's only Mil and me here. We canceled the meeting. And before you lose your shit about messing up your plans, let Boss Lady give you an update."

Milla appeared on the screen, and the expression on her face told me I wasn't going to like what she was about to say.

"Give it to me, Mil. I'm a big girl."

"So after Arya told me about your happy e-mail from the

asshole and his not-so-subtle references to the past, I did a little more digging. I found something that I don't think the feds even realized." She paused. "I don't know how to say this. *Merda*. This sucks."

"Milla, just tell her," Arya reprimanded.

"You aren't going to believe this, but I think Christof is after the money that disappeared right before your father's death. I think linking you to the same type of embezzlement was just his way of getting your attention and making you more willing to do as he says."

"What? That doesn't make sense. Every financial wizard and tech geek searched every bank in the world for that money. Are you trying to say that there is an account out there with my name on it that has forty billion in embezzled funds?"

"That's exactly what I'm saying. There are over two hundred accounts with money allocated for you and Max. Well, not you two directly but some of the smaller MCD subsidiaries left to you when your father died." The tone of Milla's voice said she was dead serious. At the same moment, a document popped up on my laptop screen.

I opened the spreadsheet, and a list of accounts appeared with the ghost companies managing them. From what I could see, there was nothing in the names or the structure of the accounts that had any link to Dad, Max, or me. Maybe I was missing something.

"I didn't want to believe it," Arya added. "But it was always there, sitting in plain sight, just no one knew how to find it. Whoever helped your dad hide the money spent an exorbitant amount of time and money manipulating banking software. Eric Dane was smart, but only a group of people could pull off this type of heist without setting off alarm bells sooner than they did."

"How does someone or a group have the ability to manipulate the programming of every major bank in the world? If you can answer that, Ari, then maybe I'll accept this as a possibility."

"Well, Arcane can coordinate, manipulate, and copycat data so government agents in the field can appear to be in one place when they are actually in another. It's pretty easy to change any similar software's parameters for financial purposes, like cloning accounts to look like they have little or no money when they're filled with millions."

"Arya, only someone like you could manipulate software to do this. When the embezzlement went down, computer technology wasn't anywhere near the caliber it is now. Moreover, even today, there are…what, maybe a handful of people in the world who have this capability? Most of us idiots out there can barely manage to turn on our computer and open a few programs."

"Yes, you're a big dummy with an MIT education and three master's degrees, one being in computer science. Anyway." Milla grew serious. "Can you admit, at least, that there's a possibility your father wasn't the sole embezzler?"

There was no way I could deny the merits of what they said. I'd always wondered how Dad had pulled the whole thing off, but I never focused on the possibilities too long, fearing what I'd learn.

All of a sudden, a lump formed in my stomach as the thought crossed my mind. "Girls, what if Christof kidnapped the both of you for Arcane? What if his ultimate goal was to use the program for the exact purpose Arya said? What if he was part of the embezzlement from the beginning?"

"That's a lot of what-ifs," Milla interjected while ignoring my frown.

"My God. You could be right. I remember Christof telling me how useful I'd be to him." Arya ran a hand over her face. "He even said he could offer me more than I could imagine if I came over to his side and help him with a software project he had his eye on. At the time, I thought all he wanted was to use Arcane to sell government secrets."

Pinching the bridge of her nose, Milla lost the humor in her voice from a few moments ago and spoke. "My gut says Christof or whoever wasn't expecting your father's murder. He left too many things up in the air, especially where the money was concerned."

"There is something else we need to consider." I tucked a piece of my hair behind my ear.

"What?"

"Unless this magic software reappears, Christof is still after Arcane. You said it yourself, Ari. The software can be manipulated for financial purposes. He can't access the original program, so he was looking for an alternative. Forty billion is a lot of motivation."

"That's true, but I feel like there is more to this. Why is Christof so fixated on you? I'm the one with access to the software. We need to keep digging. There has to be something we're missing." Arya typed away at her computer.

When she got into her research mode, she'd tune out anyone and everyone around her. I glanced back at the list Milla compiled.

Oh shit. One of the accounts matched the name of one of the biggest donors to my foundation. This was bad.

"Ari, hold on a minute before you disappear into your world of zeros and ones." I accessed a series of files and directed them to the girls. "Take a look at what I just sent to you."

Both girls scanned the documents and then looked up.

"This is bad." Milla echoed my thoughts. "The biggest donations came to the foundation from three of the accounts on my list."

She wrote down a sequence of numbers, then flipped her pad to the camera on her computer.

I swallowed, trying to push down the bile rising in my throat. "According to the list, I've been operating the foundation with embezzled funds for over ten years. I've used over five hundred million dollars for endowment projects all over the world. If anyone gets word of this, it could ruin all of our reputations."

My lips trembled.

Arya shook her head, and all the color drained from her face. "How am I going to break this to Max?"

"If this gets out, no one's going to believe Max or I didn't have any knowledge of what Dad was up to. They'll think we were in on it from the beginning."

We'd been on the cusp of adulthood when the investigation and indictment took place. By our ages, most corporate families had been grooming their children for years in preparation to take over their organizations.

It wasn't the same in our case. From the beginning, Max and I wanted to take different paths. My dream was to work in architecture and structural design, and Max's was to practice law.

Our father's actions left us no choice but to take over MCD. We put our plans and dreams aside in an effort to save a company that spanned four continents and employed over a hundred thousand people. Through hard work and serious on-the-job training, we managed to fix the mess Dad left the company in.

"That's where you're wrong. I pulled the IRS and FBI documents on the case. All the data they collected on every organization you, Max, or your father was involved in. They only stopped monitoring you this past year. And that was because they couldn't justify the expense when they'd found nothing to link either of you to the embezzlement."

I shook my head. "I'm not sure I want to know how you got your hands on the files, but thanks."

"You're welcome." Arya blew me a kiss.

"Girls, as soon as we're done, I'm going to talk to Thomas. I should never have waited so long. He'll make sure our security is as fail-safe as possible. If the current embezzlement is somehow linked to what Dad was involved in, then this is bigger than the three of us, and our contacts, can handle." A tremor of terror coursed down my spine as I remembered my nightmare from last night.

"The minute I confirmed the accounts existed, I sent in a request to our liaison at Regala Enterprises for a complete overhaul of the protection surrounding all of our families."

This was getting worse by the second.

"I can't believe you did this without telling me. The man who owns the company is sitting in the other room. Don't you think he's going to hear about it? Dammit, Mil. How do you think Thomas is going to react when he finds out his head of security knows more about what's happening in my life than he does?"

I stood up as a throbbing started in my head, and paced.

"I'm sorry, Carm."

"No, it's not your fault. I should have told Thomas after my encounter with Christof at the gala. I'm scared and feel like a fool. I've spent so many years being angry at Dad and now I'm part of the same shit."

Arya sighed. "For the record: You didn't orchestrate this and you are nothing like your father."

I moved to the fridge in my office and pulling out a water bottle. I opened the bottle and gulped it down, hoping my headache would lessen.

Returning to my desk, I stared at the worried faces of my best friends.

"Carm, *mera behna*. We'll figure this out." Arya's eyes clouded with unshed tears.

My own slipped down my cheeks. "We have to, Ari. Our children can't live with this legacy. Oh God." I covered my face. "What's Thomas going to think?"

Until that moment, I focused on security; now all I could think about was how our relationship was going to survive another embezzlement scandal.

"He won't turn his back on you."

"How do you know? He said he'd stand by me, but this isn't something distant like an aunt who Dad swindled. It's the woman he's sleeping with, the woman he said…he said he wanted to marry."

Arya and Milla glanced at each other, not hiding the surprise of my words.

"Because, I know," Arya countered. "He loves you. He told me that himself."

"There's a difference between love and wanting to be together."

"Of course he wants to be with you," Milla chimed in. "What man submits to his woman because it's what she needs, over what he needs, and then turns his back on her when she needs him most?"

"Carm, stop preparing for the worst. Trust in him. He won't ever let you down again."

I glared at them, trying to ignore their insight into my relationship as well as the hope it brought.

I squared my shoulders, inhaled deep, pushing my emotions back, and decided to stop speculating. "It's worthless to discuss this at this point. Thomas doesn't know what's going on."

Milla frowned but kept her mouth shut.

"Now to the important matter at hand. We need to get Thomas, Max, and Lex in the loop on what's happening. Anything that involves us affects them. Then once we each get our asses handed to us, we regroup here at my penthouse."

"Oooh, look at her being all businesslike." Milla grinned, and the tension of the call eased. "Good job locking down those emotions."

I couldn't help but follow suit. My change of mood was a bit amusing, even to myself.

Arya sighed. "I suppose coming to New York makes the most sense, especially since we house everything and anything to do with MCD on the servers in the building."

I followed her sigh with an exasperated breath. "It's okay, Ari. I traveled by myself with seven-month-old twins across an ocean. I think you'll be fine on a thirty-minute helicopter flight to my place."

Milla busted out laughing and pointed to Arya. "She has you there. It's not as if Max isn't going to be with you."

"Whatever," she said, glowering. "I'm glad I'm available to lighten the mood."

"Okay, ladies, time for me to wake the sleeping tiger."

"Bye, love you. And remember."

I waited for Milla to finish.

"Trust him."

Nodding, I ended the call. I stood and walked over to the window that overlooked the harbor, and released a deep breath. No matter what I hoped, the past was always going to follow me, and now something new was sitting on my plate.

"Carmen, I taught you to deal with your childhood; now you have to learn to work through the pain all of us deal with as adults."

Natalie's voice echoed in my mind. She was right. I couldn't let the past dictate how I lived my life or worry about what I couldn't control. The first thing I had to do was talk to Thomas. If he accepted all the chaos around me, then I'd know there was real hope for a future.

CHAPTER SIXTEEN

Twenty minutes after my conversation with the girls, I walked toward the living room. The video chat with the girls and our discussion about Christof's message had left me exhausted and worried, so I decided to freshen up in my room before I faced Thomas. Midway through washing my face, I realized the girls were right. If Thomas and I were going to have a remote chance of getting to where Thomas wanted us to go, I needed to give him the trust that I expected of him.

My breath hitched as I rounded the corner and looked out at the balcony. Thomas leaned against the railings on the half wall, staring out into the distance at Central Park. He'd rolled his sleeves up and undone the two top buttons of his shirt. He talked on his cell and drank a dark-amber-colored liquid.

God, I wanted to lick him from head to toe.

He turned as if sensing my presence and stared at me

through the glass doors. His Dom gaze bored into mine.

All my worry and anxiety pushed to the back of my mind as arousal flooded my pussy. I pressed my thighs together, hoping to relieve the unexpected desire.

What was it about him that made my panties wet with one look?

The slight lift of his brows told me he knew what was happening to me.

He crooked a finger, telling me to join him, and without thought, I walked outside.

As I came up to him, he moved back, and I stepped in front of him. He caged my body and continued to listen to the person on the other end of the line.

"I said I've got it under control."

Thomas pushed me against the railing, rubbing his growing erection into the small of my back. He pulled the phone away from his head and whispered, "Hold on tight, and no matter what I do, don't let go."

What did he have planned?

I gripped the concrete ledge as the excitement of the unknown filled me. I knew I should stop this, I was the Mistress, I gave the orders, but the need to see what he would do overwhelmed me.

After I'd settled my palms against the wall, he placed the receiver back against his ear and spoke. "No, I wasn't aware of that. Give me the details."

He trailed his hands down my stomach and pushed my yoga pants down to my knees. I looked around and saw the balconies of other buildings. Various people were engaged in different activities, from breakfast to workouts, to others gazing at the city's skyline.

"Did you get a chance to watch it? What did it say?"

A hand came around my waist and slipped into my underwear. His fingers found my wet slit, and a hum rumbled in his throat.

Holy shit, he was going to fuck me outside, and anyone with a telescope would be able to see us.

"Send me a copy and any other information you discover," he said as he found my clitoral nub and pinched.

I held in a scream as my core contracted. I clenched the wall, trying to keep my balance. The sting vibrating through my body felt so good. No other man made me enjoy the pain as much as I loved inflicting it. He eased the pressure, giving me a chance to catch my breath.

But before I regained my focus, he pinched again, making my pussy quiver. I threw my head back against Thomas's shoulder. My chest heaved, and my mind clouded with nothing but the desire for more.

"That's new to me," Thomas said to the person on the line.

He ground his cock against me and repeated the motion a few more times until I couldn't hold up my legs anymore. His phone slipped, and he readjusted it on his neck and then gripped my body.

He slipped two fingers inside my weeping pussy and scissored them. I arched and cried out.

"Oh, that's nothing to worry about it. Carmen stubbed her toe. Tell me the rest."

What? Who is he talking to?

Before I could ask, he started working my pussy. My juices dripped out of me and down his hands. A spasm shot through me, and another followed.

Fuck. I wasn't going to be able to go over without screaming. The contraction ignited, and my orgasm washed over me. I bit my lip to keep from making a sound, but a loud moan escaped.

My chest heaved as I came down, and his hand slipped out from between my legs. He pushed my underwear down, and the sound of a zipper lowering reached my ears. The next thing I knew, the head of his cock was thrusting inside me.

My fingers dug into the concrete of the railing as he pumped in and out again. My sex sucked him deep, and the ridge of his erection rubbed the sensitive bundle of nerves inside my tender passage. Tingles coursed through my entire body, and I began to shake.

"So the three of them were up to something without telling us?"

What? The haze I was in cleared for a second. Was he talking about the girls and me?

He thrust back in, pressing me tight against the wall.

"Yes, I believe I need to have a conversation with your sister. I'm sure you can handle Arya, and Lex will have Milla covered."

Max? He's fucking me while talking to Max.

My temper flared, and I pushed him, but he gripped my hair, tugging it back, and the glare he gave me said he was pissed.

"Fine, let me finish what I'm doing, then I'll review the request with Alan."

Thomas tossed his phone on the lounge chair behind him and then slid a hand over my stomach and up to my neck. He held me immobile. His body stilled with his cock pulsing inside my aching, swollen pussy.

"Now, Ms. Dane," he gritted out. "You're going to tell me everything that's going on in your life or I will have so much detail surrounding you, you won't be able to piss without someone being there."

"Right now? I can't talk right now."

The throb of his cock in my pussy kept away any ability to discuss anything.

"I'm not moving until you tell me what's going on." He released my hair, and his hand came around my front. He slid a finger to each side of my screaming clit, pressing his digits together until I couldn't breathe from the delicious pleasure-pain holding my body in a torturous state of arousal.

"Please, Thomas, fuck me first. Then I'll tell you everything," I begged.

He slammed into me and we both grunted. "Why won't you trust me?"

"I'm trying," I cried, squeezing my pussy muscles to keep him inside.

He pulled out and then surged forward as the palm holding my throat tightened and his fingers clasped a little harder. "Why won't you give us a real chance?"

"I'm trying," I repeated as tears rimmed my eyes as my

skin prickled with fire, and all I could think of was his fucking me until I passed out.

"Bullshit. Prove it." He started pummeling my sex, not holding back any of the anger and hurt I knew lingered underneath. "I love you. It's my job to protect my family."

"I know," I conceded. "I'll tell you everything. Just fuck me right now."

We didn't have any more words as our bodies took over.

His hold on my throat intensified, and my mind clouded. "Is this what you want?"

"Yes," I gasped, and held on to the railing, letting him ride my body with abandon.

My pussy throbbed and demanded its release. I met Thomas thrust for thrust, pushing my hips back against him. All of a sudden, we both shattered, my pussy gripping his cock, milking it for every drop.

"Mine. You are mine."

"Yes," I moaned.

"Who is your Master?"

I didn't respond. I couldn't tell him that. I wasn't ready.

"Who is your Master?" he repeated as he pumped the last of his release into me.

"Please don't," I begged. I couldn't say it. I couldn't.

"Dammit, Carmen, why won't you submit, even when your body begs for it?"

Thomas pulled out of me, leaving me empty, and I sagged against the balcony. He walked away from me without a backward glance.

CHAPTER SEVENTEEN

I steadied my breath, trying to make sense of what had just happened between Thomas and me. I tugged up my thong and pants, ignoring the sticky wetness between my legs, and glanced through the glass doors behind me.

Thomas stared at me with a sadness that made my heart clench. One hand was in his pocket and the other held a braided keychain, which he rubbed back and forth with his thumb.

My lips trembled.

I'd given him that during the weekend in North Dakota where we'd conceived our boys. It was also the first time that I'd given him complete submission. I'd allowed him to take charge of all things, calling him my Master.

He'd offered me so much last night, letting me push him past anything he'd ever experienced before. I wouldn't lie to myself and say I wasn't frightened and excited by his reaction afterward. Deep down I desired to submit to him as much as

I enjoyed his submission, but by handing over that power, I was leaving myself open to having my world shatter again.

I turned, walking over to where Thomas had thrown his phone. I picked it up and turned it over in my hand.

If only Max had waited a little longer to call. Oh well, it was time to deal with the consequences of keeping Thomas out of the loop.

I moved to the balcony door, opened it, and stepped inside.

"Thomas. We need to talk."

He didn't acknowledge me, continuing to gaze out the window.

"Thomas. Do you want to hear about what's going on with me or not?"

He glanced to the side and glared at me.

"Stop scowling. I need you to stay calm when I tell you this."

"Stay calm! You told Milla to send orders to Alan about your protection before talking to me. The man in the very fucking next room. And on top of it, the request is for teams to monitor all properties belonging to you, Arya, and Milla, as well as doubling personnel to each of your private details. Something has the three of you scared shitless, and you didn't come to me. So don't you dare tell me to stay calm."

Well, I technically hadn't told Milla to do anything, she'd done it herself, but I was going to keep that to myself. I was almost positive she was in just as much shit as I was.

"Thomas, I promise I was going to tell you. Max got to you before I could come out here and start the conversation."

"Goddammit, Carmen. You're mine. Those boys are mine. It's my job to make sure you're safe. Do you know what could have happened to you at the gala if Christof decided to force you to go with him?" Thomas paced. "You should have told me about the incident, not Max."

"I'm sorry." I didn't know what else to say. This whole thing about keeping it quiet was a mistake from the beginning.

"That's not good enough. I will not let our boys grow up without a mother as we did. Now, if I were you, I'd start talking, and you better give me every microscopic detail."

I was willing to take the heat for keeping things from him, but the hell if I'd let him dictate to me.

I stalked over to where Thomas stood, and poked a finger into his chest. "I'm not your submissive or your child. You don't get to order me around."

Thomas grabbed my wrist. "When it comes to your safety, I am your goddamn dictator. Max shouldn't be the one telling me about this."

I tried pulling my hand free, but he held it tight. "Your brother is worried sick. While the three of you spent the last hour and a half plotting, twenty of my top men and women showed up at his estate. Not to mention the ones sitting one floor below us waiting for my instructions. Instructions I had no idea about."

I cringed inside. "I didn't expect security to move in so fast."

"How could you even question it after all that's happened these past few years? The minute a request comes from any of you, it's top priority." He glared at me. "Especially ones that come regarding the mother of my children." The vein on his forehead pulsed.

"Thomas, I'm sorry. I should have talked to you from the start. My only excuse is that I was trying to understand what was actually happening with Christof and didn't want to add more confusion to our relationship."

"The confusion is only on your part. I know where I stand and what I want. You need to catch up."

I scowled at his statement and then sighed. How could I fight about something when I knew I was wrong?

Thomas cupped the side of my face. "Now tell me about the money."

A lump formed in the pit of my stomach. "Max and his big mouth. I wanted to talk to you on my time."

"Too late."

I pulled out of his hold, pacing backward until I reached the couch and sat down.

Covering my face with my hands, I looked up at him. "You better sit down; this is going to be a lot to take."

As soon as he followed my instruction, I began. I told him about the initial finance discrepancies, the meeting with Christof, the e-mail. Then what the girls and I had concluded. He remained quiet for the most part, only asking questions when he needed clarification. By the time I was finished, I felt raw and completely exposed.

"Thomas, I don't expect you to believe me, but I had nothing to do with any of it."

There it was: something I knew was a deal breaker for

him. After what Dad put his family through, I wouldn't expect him to think I was innocent. Who would think the daughter of the man who stole over forty billion dollars from his clients would be anything but guilty?

I glanced up at Thomas. His face was unmoving and emotionless.

"Once the Boston gang gets here, we'll decide on next steps. Can you call Stacey and Natalie over to watch the five kids?"

I tilted my head and watched him with a bit of uncertainty.

"That's it? No reaction to what I just said?"

"What do you want me to say?" Thomas took my hand in his. "You aren't your father, Carmen. Despite what I said last year, you're so honorable, you'd sell everything you have to return the funds you used unknowingly for the foundation."

"How can you be sure?"

"Because I trust you."

I tried to pull free, but Thomas's hold on my fingers increased. "No matter how much I wish it, I can't take back the things I accused you of doing or being. All I can say is that I was wrong and ask for your forgiveness. Please, Carm, trust me to protect you and stand by you through this if nothing else."

I knew "nothing else" meant my submission. That night, of all the many painful things he'd said, telling me I forced him to be something he wasn't and that I'd faked my submission hurt me the most. I'd given him a piece of me that only he knew about. A part that solely responded to him.

"I don't know what to say to you."

"Say you'll give us a chance."

I stared at him for what felt like hours and then nodded.

He released a sigh and kissed the top of my head as he pulled me into his arms.

"I'm scared, Thomas. This situation is bigger than I could ever imagine." I wiped away a hot tear that slid down my cheek.

"Let me protect all of you. It's what I do. I'm good at it."

I inhaled deep and closed my eyes for a brief moment.

Please don't hurt me again. I don't think I'd survive if you did.

"Okay, I accept."

Thomas grunted. "As if you had a choice."

"Look, I'm letting you win this one, give me the illusion I made the decision."

"Like I let you believe that I'm not your Master." His voice deepened on the last word, and electricity shot to my pussy.

How does he go from serious to sensual in a matter of seconds?

Before I could linger on the thought, he had me flat on my back on the sofa. His amber eyes looked almost black, and he licked his lips, coming down and taking my mouth.

He pulled back for a brief moment. "I'll call in every favor I have to keep you safe."

"I know." I nodded, seeing the turmoil lingering behind the desire.

I drew him down, kissing him with the same passion I'd

tried to deny existed last night. Our tongues curled around each other, and the intoxicating taste of his embrace filled my body.

Thomas tugged up my shirt, his palm trailing up my rib cage and cupping my breasts. I instinctively arched up as my nipples pebbled tight, needing the harder edge of bite only he could give me.

"More."

"Yes, Mistress," Thomas crooned against my lips.

He pinched my aching bud, rolling it between his fingers. An exquisite sting tingled into the tip.

I shifted my face to the side and allowed his skilled mouth to move down my neck. "Why do you call me that when you want to be my Master?"

He unbuttoned my shirt and unclasped my bra, nipped the top curve of my breast, and then murmured, "One doesn't negate the other. Until you admit the truth, you'll never experience the freedom and exhilaration you're known for pulling from your submissives."

"Why can't it be simple?" I asked as I grabbed Thomas's head and brought it to my sensitized nipple.

Thomas took my not-so-subtle cue and sucked the tip into his mouth, pulling hard to a blissfully painful point and then shifted to the other side until it was in the same state as its twin. He released my swollen nub and rose above me. He unbuttoned his shirt, shrugging it off and then throwing it behind me.

"Carmen, you aren't a simple girl, and I'm not a simple man. Stop questioning what works between us." He unbuttoned my pants and started tugging them off. "Now, no more talking, we need to have makeup sex."

"What was the balcony episode called?"

"Angry fucking."

I giggled and he smiled back.

The last time we were silly while making love felt like a lifetime ago.

He rubbed his stubble along my stomach and over my hips, as he pulled my slacks free of my body. He pushed my knees up, settling in between and then licking the seam of my pussy through the fabric of my underwear.

"Thomas," I moaned, arching my body.

"I can taste myself on you. I like it."

I had a fleeting moment of shock, which disappeared when I saw how it aroused him.

"Kiss me."

Reaching down, I drew him to me. However, as he came over me, he captured my arms, pinning them above my head. He gazed down at me with a wicked gleam.

I licked my lips and repeated, "Kiss me."

He sealed our mouths, pushing his tongue in to rub and play with mine.

God, this man can kiss.

The taste of him, the feel of him, overwhelmed all coherent thoughts from my mind. I shifted, trying to create friction that would relieve the painful ache pulsing in my clit. But he wasn't having any of it and crouched over me, refusing my unspoken desire as he continued to devour me.

I wrenched my face away, panting for air. My body was on

fire. It was Thomas's job to satisfy my needs, and my desperate, sopping pussy required his attention.

"Give me what I want."

He lifted a sexy brow. "You're in no position to demand."

"Is that right?" I rubbed my leg against his thigh until I hooked my calf behind his. Shifting my hips to the side, I attempted to flip him, but he anticipated my move and flipped me to the other side of the couch.

"Tsk-tsk. That wasn't very nice. Your black belt skills are no use here. Did you forget I'm bigger than you?"

I snarled and bit his lip as he tried to kiss me. I drew blood but it didn't deter him. Clasping my wrist in one hand, he fisted my hair and ravaged my mouth in a kiss that sizzled my senses. Hot need tinged with a bit of anger at my inability to control this man consumed me.

His hand slid free of my hair and moved to cup my swollen breast. He pinched the tip and then released my mouth to cover my other nipple with his teeth in a grip that skated the line between pleasure and pain.

I moaned, my back arching into the sweet agony.

"More," I called out.

He repeated the exquisite torture on the other breast, only this time he followed by tearing my underwear and spearing his fingers inside me. He pumped his digits in a brutal pace, sending me over into a blinding orgasm.

"Thomas!" I cried out, riding the tide of spasms his fingers ignited.

"I love hearing my name on your lips."

Before I had completely come down from my climax, he

jerked up to sitting, freeing his hard cock. I'd barely caught my breath when he lifted me over him and thrust deep. He stretched my tight pussy with his thickness.

Gasping, I grabbed his shoulders and raked my nails over his bunched muscles. He shifted me onto my back and covered me, clamping my arms once more, his cock pulsing inside me. He gazed at me with so much emotion that, in this moment, there was only the two of us.

"I won't lose you. I can't lose you."

Tears clouded my eyes.

"Wrap your legs around me, *mi amor*."

The second I followed his instructions, he gripped my hip and began his assault on my quickening core. His cock slid in and out of my oversensitized muscles in deep, hard strokes, pushing me past anything but the feel of him. Ripples of ecstasy trembled inside me, pushing my orgasm to erupt, pussy spasming and clamping down until stars appeared behind my eyes.

I screamed my release, taking the pounding thrusts of his beautiful cock and demanding more until all that was left was satisfying our need. He brought me over the crest one more time before he bit the skin of my neck and poured into me.

CHAPTER EIGHTEEN

Three hours after my mind-blowing orgasms, I settled down in the living room with a cup of coffee. The "Boston gang" as Thomas called them were about to arrive, and I knew conversations I'd rather never ever have were about to take place.

Each of our laptops sat on my oversized coffee table, with room for the bombardment of electronics Arya would bring.

I smiled as Thomas entered the room with his coffee. "This feels very domestic, given the circumstance," I said.

"Would you really be opposed to making this permanent? I meant what I said. I want to marry you."

I want to marry you, too, but I'm scared.

"I want to take this slow. Make sure we're doing it for the right reasons, not because of Leo and Simon or the fear of what's happening with Christof and the embezzlement."

He remained quiet for a few moments. "What's it going to take for you to trust me?"

"I do trust you."

"No." He shook his head, setting his cup on the table, and turned to me. "You trust me with the boys and your safety, but nothing else. I want you to trust me with you heart and with our future."

What if he hurt me again? I couldn't deny my feelings for him. They remained the same as they'd been over a year and a half ago. He was the one, the man I wanted to marry, but I wasn't ready to risk it. Maybe once all the chaos settled, I'd revisit the possibility.

"I'm trying, Thomas."

He sighed. "Try harder." He reached out to cup my face, grazing his lips against mine.

The doorbell rang, signaling the beginning of bedlam. Natalie and Stacey came out of the nursery and headed down the hall, ready to take on three more hellions. They walked past us with the children in tow before the parents had the chance to turn the corner into the living area.

"Wow. They're awesome," Arya said. She unbuttoned her coat, throwing it over the back of the sofa. "Set the bags over there. We'll handle the rest."

Three of my personal security detail carried in four shoulder bags apiece with Max behind them with a large box.

"Are you planning on moving in?"

"You would think it looking at all the shit she insisted on bringing." Max set the box on the floor and walked over to the bar in the back of the living room. "I hope you realize how great a brother I am for flying back and forth from Boston in a matter of hours to help your ass."

"Yes, you're the best big brother a girl can ask for. It's such a hard life flying thirty minutes to and from your private estate to this building's helipad."

He poured two glasses of scotch, then walked over, handing one tumbler to Thomas. "You'll need this. These ladies tend to get into messes that drive their men to drink."

"Believe me, I know." Thomas lifted the glass in a toast of brotherhood.

Both Arya and I frowned, and then she grabbed a bag by her feet and started digging inside.

"I'm the one who needs the cocktail. I spent the last few hours chasing after two toddlers who won't stop running and getting into everything, while I packed for this visit." She pulled out three fifteen-inch monitors, setting them on the coffee table. "And for the record, this is the security shield for when we log into the server. This place is going to be harder to hack than Fort Knox."

I glanced at Max, who shrugged and took a deep swallow of his drink.

Arya was entering her general persona, and that meant either we helped her or became collateral damage from her tech insanity.

I looked behind her. "I thought Mil and Lex came with you."

"Mil's on a call, and with all the craziness, Lex is making good on his threat to stick to her no matter where she goes."

"I guess great minds think alike. I said something in the

same realm." Thomas glanced at me over the rim of his glass and smiled. "Wouldn't you agree, Carm?"

I lifted a brow, then couldn't help myself and smiled back at him. In our case, he was angry as hell with his cock buried deep inside me when he'd uttered similar words.

It was incredible how far we'd come in the last few weeks, hell, in the last twenty-four hours. My anger at him for the past was easing. Although my emotions were still all over the place, especially when it came to thinking about the future. One minute I wanted to jump in headfirst and the next I couldn't tell if I wanted him in my life or not.

This was why taking things slow was the best thing.

It's not going slow if you're banging each other every chance you get.

Thomas leaned toward me, tucking a stray hair behind my ear. "Remember that thought."

At that moment, Milla and Lex came around the corner of the hallway leading from the entryway.

"Good, everyone is here. Help me set this shit up." Arya continued her electronic invasion of my home, setting out cords and components. "I found something on the flight here that might connect everything together, but I'm not going to open anything until I know no one will track us."

"If you'd said this from the beginning, I wouldn't have taken the call."

"Shut up, Mil, and start working."

I shrugged and went to help a very agitated Arya before she bit my head off, too.

Fifteen minutes later, my large, spacious, and homey living room looked like a computer lab exploded inside it. Arya typed away with Thomas by her side discussing the software he developed while Milla and I sorted through who or what entity originated the accounts.

So far, every single one had my name or one of my privately held enterprises linked to it with conservatorship given to Dad. Some were opened around the time of Dad's murder, but the majority dated back almost twenty years, making me a freshman in high school.

None of this made sense. Why would Dad do this?

"Shit, everything we're finding leads to more questions. And I'm unhappy to report I am worth over forty billion in someone else's money." Just saying it made my stomach roll. All I could think about was the people whose worlds crumbled when they lost all their money.

One way or the other, I would get the money back to the right hands.

"Carm, don't freak out." Milla placed her hand over my knee. "We have agents at the CIA, MI6, and INTERPOL aware of what's happening."

My eyes nearly bugged out. "Have you lost your mind? All the evidence points to me."

"It's okay. I promise. Lex and Thomas convinced them you were the only person who could get the funds back for them without exposing the issues within financial institutions across the world."

"What issue?" How the hell was I going to expose issues?

Thomas answered. "That a well-programmed virus infiltrated entire banking networks to cloak accounts from detection."

"You should have heard him, Carm." Milla's eyes lit up. "He used all of these big tech words and made things seem a hundred times worse than they were. He pulled a signature Arya Rey move."

"Dane," Max interjected, making me shake my head. Arya still went by her maiden name in business dealings, and it annoyed Max to no end. Arya's excuse was that too many things had the Dane name, and she liked the one she was born with.

Not paying attention to Max, I glanced at Thomas, who stared at me.

Someone who'll believe in you and fight for you.

He'd defended me, protected me.

I wanted to get up and kiss him but stayed where I sat. "Thank you," I said.

He inclined his head, holding my gaze for a few more minutes before he frowned at Arya.

"If I get arrested for this, you're paying for every cent of my defense. I can't believe you, of all people, didn't let me know you were using this program. Do you know how much trouble we'd be in if you hacked the wrong person?" Thomas looked toward Max, who was reading something on his phone. "I hope you paddle her ass for this."

A grin cut across Max's face. "You could say that. I took a play from Lex's book. Arya's going to remember what happens when she doesn't take care of what belongs to me."

"If you're done discussing my private life, I'd like to

continue this search." She continued typing, but a red flush grazed her cheeks.

I returned to studying my spreadsheets and documents, and I said, "Don't get any ideas, Thomas."

"I wouldn't dream of it. Then again, you may enjoy it." There was amusement in his tone.

"I think I'm going to be sick." Max got up. "I don't want to hear about my baby sister's sex life."

"You're one to talk. Who's the one who converted my old homeschooling room into a sex dungeon?"

Max ignored me, scowling at Arya when she smirked.

"Here it is. I found a file hidden under a lot of encryption. Let's hope it's something substantial, otherwise I'm back to square one."

All of us gathered behind Arya and Thomas. They took turns inputting code, and after a minute, the document opened.

"Oh dear God. This is bad," Milla whispered.

Files containing all my private information appeared: fingerprints, social security number, passport, medical records, and pictures of Thomas, the boys, and me. It was everything needed to either steal my identity or open new accounts in my name or…Christof's words from the gala came to mind.

"Would you sacrifice your safety and reputation for your sons?"

A lump formed in my throat, and my skin felt cold and clammy. I rubbed my arms, trying to warm them up. I moved to the bar, made myself a shot of B&B, and swallowed it in one gulp. Then I turned back to Arya and Milla, who looked as bad as I felt.

Thomas stood, running a hand through his short, wavy hair.

"That's it. I've made the decision. There's only one way to make sure you're safe. We leave for the ranch first thing in the morning."

CHAPTER NINETEEN

W ell before noon the next day, we were on a flight to California. Thomas sat next to me, sipping a glass of cognac, and I nursed a B&B. We were both exhausted and thankful that Leo and Simon decided to take naps a few minutes after takeoff. Stacey watched over them in one of the sleeping cabins. With any luck, they wouldn't wake for at least two hours.

After Thomas had made his unilateral announcement, chaos ensued, with packing, planning, and reorganizing work commitments. Everyone agreed that the best place for Leo, Simon, and me was at Thomas's ranch.

During our past relationship, I never had the chance to visit La Cascada, but Arya and Max visited often and referred to it as an impenetrable fortress in the guise of a fancy vineyard and horse ranch. As of now, I'd be living there indefinitely, or at least until there was a solid plan to deal with the money or Christof.

Just thinking of his name made my stomach hurt. He was a dangerous man who'd slit a throat without a speck of remorse. Add in forty billion dollars, and the stakes jumped to an incomprehensible level. He wouldn't think twice about hurting my boys to get me to cooperate.

A shudder rocked my body, and the next thing I knew, I was tucked against Thomas's side.

"It's okay to relax, Carm. Staying on edge isn't going to help."

I couldn't deny that having him there to help me was nice. His presence brought a stillness to my psyche.

I took another sip of my drink, set my glass on the table in front of me, and then closed my eyes.

God, he smelled good, all male with a light scent of eucalyptus and sandalwood from the beard oil he used to soften his stubble.

In the pit of my stomach, I had an unshakable anxiety about what kind of reception was waiting for me with Thomas's family. I was expecting hostility from Diego. I'd avoid him and keep my mouth shut as long as he accepted my boys.

But I wondered about the rest of his family. His cousins, his aunt. Did they share the same opinion as Diego? It was going to suck if I had to spend weeks on end with people who hated me.

I guess I won't know until I get there.

"Do you still ride?" Thomas asked, pulling me from my thinking.

"I haven't in a long time. I couldn't while I was pregnant,

and after, I was too busy with the boys. The last time I went out was…" I trailed off and looked toward the window.

"When we went to Max's ranch," he said, finishing my sentence.

Before family complications and my insecurities. We were trying to figure out if what started as a one-night stand could be more, and we discovered it could. During those few precious months, we laughed so much, and the craziness of our sexual kinks wasn't something we focused on. We fell in love without pretenses. He wasn't the security-expert, nightclub-owning, rancher playboy, and I didn't have to be the uptight, never-show-your-emotions, cold Dane robot.

My heart hiccupped. Our last night there was the night we conceived our boys.

"Will you go riding with me while we're at La Cascada? It'll give me a chance to show you my land and also give us some time away from the house."

I glanced at him with a slight smile. He knew how I'd go riding to calm my mind during the chaos of my childhood. I loved horses, and he was offering me an outlet for the storm we both knew we'd encounter on the ranch. "Only if you promise to take me to the waterfall the ranch is named for. Arya's told me how breathtaking the view is from there."

He returned my smile. "Maybe we can engage in some extracurricular activities while there. There's a cave under the falls with ropes we use to swing into the lagoon at the bottom."

Ropes.

An excitement I hadn't expected sparked inside me. It had been so long since I'd practiced any form of *Kinbaku* or *Shibari*, the ancient Japanese art of bondage. Nothing could describe the experience of using hemp to bind and suspend a submissive while bringing them to a state of relaxation and euphoria and eventually release.

I licked my lips, picturing Thomas imprisoned with hemp, his muscles flexing and bulging, his gorgeous erection awaiting my attention.

He chuckled and said, "Are you thinking about what it'll be like when a seasoned rancher ties you up and makes you scream with pleasure?"

His words held humor, but the tickle in my stomach told me the fantasy he painted was what he wanted to do to me.

"No. I was thinking about what it would be like to bind said seasoned rancher to the wall of the cave and make him beg for release while he watches me make myself come over and over again."

"Is that a challenge?" He downed his drink and set his glass on a side table.

"No, it's a fact." I lifted a brow while running my tongue along my lower lips.

Thomas's gaze went to my mouth, and his eyes dilated.

Oh, I think it's time for a play session at thirty-five thousand feet.

"Come with me." I stood, extending my hand.

He slid his palm over mine and stood with a wicked grin. "Where are you taking me?"

"Somewhere to show you who's in charge." I led him toward the master bedroom. After what happened on the balcony, I had to get us back on level footing. I was his Domme and had to show him I was the boss.

Carmen, is this more for you or him?

"Now, that definitely sounds like a challenge."

Upon entering the room, I walked to the closet and pulled out the belts of the bathrobes.

"Are you planning on showing me what you would do if you had the ropes I mentioned?"

"You're about to find out." I glanced over my shoulders, quirking a brow.

Thomas lounged against the door and smiled. "I look forward to it."

"Strip and lie down on the bed," I ordered.

"Yes, Mistress." His voice purred, sending a flood of arousal and wetness to my pussy.

I kept my back to him, coiling the terry cloth sash in my hands and hoping to quiet my overactive libido.

"I'm ready, Mistress."

I turned toward him and couldn't help but admire his beautiful naked body. His erection stood rigid, pointing past his belly button and making me want to forget my plans for him and take him into my mouth.

I strolled to the side of the bed and climbed in next to him. I glided the end of one of the belts over his feet, up his thighs, pausing to circle his weeping cock, and then moving along his stomach to his neck.

I tied a loop around one wrist and secured it to the post

on the bed, making sure it wasn't too tight but would hold against his strength. I repeated the action with his other hand. Leaning back, I surveyed my handiwork.

"Perfect."

He smiled. Tied down or not he knew his strength and was comfortable with allowing me to control the scene. His beautiful corded abs flexed with each breath.

Damn, he's hot.

The taut muscles of his arms and shoulders bunched as he tested the bonds.

"You won't be able to untie those without a little help," I stated. "I did spend my summer vacations from school working on a horse farm."

"Something that seems to have come in handy with your subs."

I lifted a brow. "Any problems?"

"None whatsoever. But I should warn you. As a former military man, I know a few useful ones as well. You never know when a cord of rope can come in handy."

A tingle shot up my spine. I imagined Thomas binding me with rope, creating patterns that displayed everything he wanted to see and exposing nothing that he desired hidden.

When I looked at his face, his grin told me he caught my reaction to the words. I squinted my eyes. "I believe you're talking too much. I have plans for that mouth."

Stepping off the bed, I unbuttoned my dress, letting it slip to the floor while keeping my gaze locked with Thomas's. With slow, precise movements, I shimmied out of my panties and unfastened my bra. He ate up every shift of my body, his breath coming out shallow as his erection grew longer and harder, and the angry head at the tip bulged.

I reached down to slip off my heels, running my hands down my legs.

"Please leave those on, Mistress."

I tilted my head, studying him. It was a command in the form of a request. I toed the pumps off and straddled his thighs. "I decide what I keep on, and the shoes would hinder my plans."

The friction of the light dusting of hair on his thighs tickled my labia, and a moan almost escaped my lips. His hardness against my soft skin was an aphrodisiac I couldn't stop craving. I rubbed my pussy up his hips and settled over his throbbing cock. I pushed his head against my clit, grinding and sliding back and forth.

Thomas arched his head and pushed up his pelvis. "God, you're soaked. It feels so good."

His words pushed me forward with my plan. I crawled toward his shoulders, leaving a trail of my excitement along his abdomen and chest.

Thomas licked his lips, and his nostrils flared at the scent of my arousal.

"Would you like a taste?" I whispered, holding back a shudder as his breath grazed my bare pussy.

"Yes, Mistress," he murmured.

I brought my pelvis closer to him, positioning one knee above each shoulder. His tongue reached out to touch my weeping lower lips, but I pulled back.

"You have to ask, Thomas. Ask for what you want."

"I want you. I want to eat your pussy."

I shook my head and leaned against his chest. "No demands. Otherwise, I'll stay here, soaking your chest but leaving both of us in need. Ask me."

The muscles on the side of his neck clenched. "Please, Mistress, may I fuck you with my mouth?"

I lifted up toward him, but before I could shift, he jerked his head and fastened himself to my aching clit. His tongue dove into my pussy, and my body bowed in response, causing me to grab the headboard for balance.

I gasped, "Oh, Thomas. That's it. Keep going."

I closed my eyes, letting his well-trained mouth drive me toward the explosions slowly churning inside me. My nails dug into the headboard as the familiar tingle I only felt with Thomas intensified.

I opened my eyes and looked down at him. He watched me with smug satisfaction. He knew how to use his expertise, and I was the happy recipient. His arms pulled against his restraints, and a creak echoed from the tug of the belts.

He continued to devour me, bringing me higher and higher. All of a sudden my head snapped back, and a scream rose in my throat. I called out his name as my pussy contracted around his tongue and my essence flooded his mouth.

I was never going to survive without this man.

I pushed any rational thoughts out of my head as my orgasm continued to wave through my body. The sound of fabric tearing pierced my hearing, and all of a sudden

Thomas pinned me to the bed with my hands above my head. He used his thighs and knees to spread mine apart, and then he plunged to the hilt inside my tight, spasming pussy.

A surprised cry echoed from my lips at his invasion, and almost immediately, my body's need for him reignited.

"That's it. Milk my cock, *mi amor*." He covered my lips, and my salty-sweet tasted filled my mouth.

Our tongues dueled as he thrust in and out of my swollen core. One hand gripped my hip as the other continued to squeeze my wrists.

Oh God. It was happening again. His weight felt so wonderful. I arched up, rubbing my pinched nipples against the crisp hair of his chest.

"Please," I begged, not knowing what I wanted.

"Come for me," he ordered.

Before I could protest his command, my body responded, detonating around him. Exquisite fire scorched through my pussy as I clenched my jaw and thrashed against him.

"Once more, baby." Thomas's hand slid between our bodies to the throbbing bundle of nerves at the apex of my sex.

I tossed my head side to side. "I can't. It's too much. My body can't take it. Oh God."

He strummed my nub, sending another wave of need through my oversensitized pussy. "Yes, you can. Who's in charge, Carm?"

What?

I stared, shocked by his question.

The rhythm on my clit intensified.

"You heard me." He gritted his teeth. "Say it or I'll leave you hanging."

I closed my eyes, turning my face away. "Me." He couldn't win this. I had to hold the cards.

Fuck, this wasn't fair.

He stopped rubbing.

"No!" I called out, feeling the immediate loss of contractions in my pussy.

He returned to his ministrations, but at a pace we both knew would keep me on edge but never send me over.

"Say it," he ordered as he released my wrists and fisted my hair. He gazed down at me, plunging his pulsing cock inside me while his finger continued its torture on my tender clitoris.

"Please, Thomas. I can't. Don't make me." Tears rimmed my eyes.

"It's me, baby. I love you. Let go." He rubbed harder, and his breath became ragged.

"I can't. I…"

His pace faltered. "Fuck. I can't hold out anymore. You're so stubborn," he growled as he came, filling me with his ejaculation. He pumped a few more times until the last of his release emptied. He pulled his damp fingers from between my folds and gripped my thighs as he shifted to the side but kept his cock inside me.

We both remained quiet over the next few minutes. My body screamed for the final orgasm it never received, but more than that, my heart ached for what I'd almost revealed to Thomas.

I closed my eyes, letting Thomas's breath and weight soothe me. He loved me. He'd said it before on the balcony when he was so angry with me, but this time, it was raw and I knew from his heart.

What was I going to do? Could I believe he meant it?

I guessed the test would come once we landed in California.

Thomas lifted up on his forearms and peered down at me. "One day you're going to admit it. You know the truth deep inside. It doesn't make you any less, Carmen. You'll always be a Mistress. I have no problems saying I enjoyed your commands. Why won't you admit you enjoy my domination?"

My temper peaked, but I didn't respond to him except by pushing him off, dislodging his now-soft cock from my body. He handed me a tissue to wipe myself as I slid from the bed and went to the bathroom.

I leaned against the counter as my body shook. I couldn't do it. No matter what I wanted, I had to have some defenses left, until I could truly trust his commitment to me.

Thomas came to stand behind me, caging me with his naked body. His hands covered my grip on the counter.

"It's okay, *mi cielito*."

He kissed my neck as his palm slid up my arm and came to rest on my throat.

My pulse jumped, and I tried to pull away, but his hold intensified, bringing a need I couldn't accept to the surface.

"You can't deny your body's reaction, even if your mind wants to refuse." He held my gaze in the mirror. "I can admit it's different with you. I can only hope one day you'll accept the truth, that you can trust me with your submission." He slipped a finger over my lips. "Think about it, and when you're ready I'll be waiting."

He released me, shifting to start the shower. "Let's freshen up before we have to settle down for landing."

I stared at him for a few moments, then nodded and stepped into the stall.

CHAPTER TWENTY

After my shower, I dressed and added a few final touches to my makeup.

Thomas came out of the bathroom with a towel around his waist and stopped for a second to kiss me on his way to the closet.

I noticed red burn marks on his wrists, and guilt flooded me. I hadn't protected his skin. "Thomas?"

He turned and looked at me.

"Your wrists." I shook my head.

Walking toward me, he slid his hand around my waist. "I did it to myself when I tore the bonds." He grinned into my face. "Don't scowl like that. You'll get wrinkles."

"I'm serious. I'm sorry."

He kissed the tip of my nose. "If it bothers you so much, I'll tie you up at the waterfall, and we'll call it even."

A prickle went up my spine.

"We'll see," I grumbled, pulling out of his hold and walking toward the door.

"Where are you going?"

I glanced at Thomas over my shoulder. "To the lounge. I'll meet you there."

"Okay. I shouldn't be long."

I strolled to the bar in the main area of the plane, fixed Thomas and myself a drink, and took a seat by the window.

I giggled to myself as a thought crossed my mind.

I was an official member of the mile-high club. Arya and Milla would be so proud of me.

"What's so funny?" Thomas asked as he came in dressed in a casual button-down shirt, jeans, and cowboy boots and hat.

Holy shit!

I nearly swallowed my tongue. Thomas was sexy as hell in his suits, but damn. No, double damn. He was walking sex on two legs.

He grinned his knowing smile. "Like what you see?"

My cheeks flushed. "Possibly."

"I have something for you." Thomas crouched in front of me. "Give me your hand."

I hesitated but put my palm over his. Thomas pulled out a cushion-cut white and pink diamond ring from his pocket. My lip trembled. It was a replica of the ring my mother had worn.

"How…how did you get this in such a short time?" I looked up at him, not knowing what else to say.

"I had it made right after our visit to North Dakota and before I fucked everything up with us. I remembered you saying once that you would have loved to have your mother's ring. That it was your favorite piece of jewelry she'd worn. I wanted you to have the same design, but added the pink diamond halo to make it your own."

My hand shook as he slipped it on.

This is just pretend, Carmen.

"You keep telling yourself that, and maybe you'll start believing it."

Shit, I'd said that aloud.

I put a hand on his arm. "I'm sorry, Thomas. I shouldn't have said that. I...I..."

"Don't trust me. I get it."

"Please under—"

He cut me off. "I said I get it." He took a seat and strapped his belt. "We're about to land, take your seat. Stacey is with the boys." There was an underlying hurt in his tone, but he didn't say anything more.

* * *

Forty minutes later after landing at a private airfield and gathering our cranky boys, Thomas and I arrived at the gates of La Cascada.

"Let's stop here for a few minutes. This is the best vantage point of my land."

I was thankful for the short respite. Leo and Simon weren't happy their naps were cut short and only after a lot of soothing did they calm enough for us to focus on anything other than them.

I stepped out of the car, and chills prickled my arms. There weren't enough words to describe the beautiful vineyard and ranch. From what Thomas told me, his family owned the land as far as the eye could see. Only a few miles northwest of Napa Valley, this area of California held a unique microclimate, perfect for creating Cabernet and Bordeaux blends.

"It's beautiful, but all I see are rows and rows of grapevines. Where are the stables?"

Thomas shook his head. "I had a feeling the vineyard wouldn't impress you, especially since you have your own."

I rolled my eyes. "As a winemaker, I can appreciate the land. So are you going to answer me?"

"On the other side of that hill. The climate is less humid and more suitable for the stables and the animals."

The security gate beeped as three horse riders exited through the gate and inclined their heads. I noticed a gun strapped to one of their ankles and then watched them scan the area for any safety threats. These weren't ordinary cowboys or ranch hands. They protected his land and the people on it.

Their presence reminded me I wasn't here for a casual visit, even if I'd pushed it to the back of my mind for a minute.

He pointed in the direction east of the main house. He touched my lower back. "I know what you're thinking. And I haven't forgotten our conversation from before we left.

Come. Let's get to the house before the boys lose their minds again. One more thing, don't say anything to anyone about the real reason we're here. The fewer people that know, the better."

I nodded, and we returned to the car as a slight uneasiness settled in my stomach. The threats posed by Christof weren't going away just because I'd left New York. Sooner or later, Christof was going to contact me again. I just hoped I could handle whatever he'd expect me to do.

I pushed the worry aside and focused on the view outside my window.

As we drove through the land, I couldn't help but welcome the stark change from urban life to the country. If I'd had a choice, I'd never live in the city. The noise, crowds, and lack of space became overwhelming at times. That's the reason I loved the Hamptons so much. There the pace was slower and more relaxed.

The car pulled up to a two-story sprawling ranch house. It resembled a vintage nineteen twenties estate house painted with bright colors indicative of Thomas's family's Mexican heritage.

Gathering all of the boys' things, I prepared to get them, when I noticed they'd fallen asleep on the five-minute drive from the gate.

I sighed. "Figures. Their schedule's turned upside down. Hopefully, in a day or two, they'll be back to normal. Stacey, will you stay with them and let me know when they wake?"

She inclined her head in agreement, and I scooted toward Thomas.

"I tried to tell them that Mommy likes to control things and sometimes it's easier to submit than test their mother's will, but our boys are independent and just wouldn't listen," he joked.

I frowned. "You're so not funny."

He leaned over and kissed the top of my head. "I'm just trying to get you to relax, *mi amor*."

I inhaled deep and followed him as he stepped out of the car.

Here goes, into the lion's den. I squared my shoulders and slipped my arm into Thomas's.

As we approached the front porch, I noticed the woman from Travis's party. She had the same frown marring her face that she did at the party.

She'd never gotten a chance to talk to me then, but it looked like she was going to talk to me now. I'd thought I'd get at least past the front door before my first hostile encounter.

Thomas noticed my hesitation. "She's a family friend. Sophia's harmless. If she says anything, I'll handle it."

Of course he would.

"Sophia, what are you doing here?" He spoke casually, but his tone was that of a Dom speaking to a submissive who'd stepped out of line.

"I heard you were coming back. I wanted to welcome you home." She ran down the steps and threw herself into Thomas's arms, jarring me away from him. "Did you miss me?" She kissed him on the cheek and then rested her head on his chest.

A low growl formed in my throat but thankfully, I held it back. This bitch was groping my man.

Did I just say my man?

I guess he was. There was no point in denying it, at least to myself anyway. Now to rein in my urges to hurt Sophia. This was Thomas's territory and I had to let him handle it.

Thomas pulled out of her hold and tucked his arm around me, gathering me to his side. "We're here to see Abuelo. When I texted Tia Isabella earlier, she said he wasn't feeling well."

"Yes, he's here and resting." She glared at me, and the venom in her stare told me I'd made an enemy of her for something I had no idea I'd done. "Are you sure about bringing her to the ranch, when Diego isn't well? You know how he feels about *gringas.*"

"You'll show her respect, Sophia. I don't know what's gotten into you. Carmen's the mother of my children, and I won't have you talking to her that way."

"I was only stating the facts." Her eyes bored into mine. "I can't believe you'd pick her over me. Someone you've known for a short time versus a person who's been in your life for twenty years." She turned and ran inside.

"Well, that was awesome. If this is any indication of what to expect, I can't wait to see what happens next," I muttered and allowed Thomas to guide me into the house.

"Tia Isa," Thomas called, and within seconds, a beautiful, auburn-haired woman came out of a side room.

"Oh, *mi'jito.* I'm so happy you're home." She cupped his face and kissed each cheek.

She turned to me and smiled. "You're Carmen? I'm so happy to meet you." She surprised me by hugging me and kissing both my cheeks. "Let's go inside. You must be tired. Where are the *gemelos*?"

"The twins are sleeping. The nanny will bring them in once they wake up," I answered.

"We're so happy you're finally here."

"I'm not sure if everyone will agree with you, considering our families' history."

She touched my hand. "Never forget the sins of the father aren't the sins of the child." Then I thought I heard her whisper, "I should know."

"Come. Let me get you something to drink. I made Thomas's favorite, watermelon agua fresca."

She guided us to the kitchen and poured two glasses and passed them to us.

We stayed in the kitchen for twenty minutes chatting and getting to know each other. I genuinely liked Isabella. She had an easy manner about her that drew you into conversation. Thomas sat back, smiling at me and enjoying his refreshment as Isabella and I talked away. I learned she was the same age my mother would have been and that she was a widow with a son in Texas and a daughter in Florida who both ran local vineyards. I told her about mine in Cape Town and promised her a case of our newest vintage.

"Isa!" a loud voice yelled, causing me to jump and both Isabella and Thomas to sigh. "If they arrived, it is your duty to bring them to me first."

"Time to go pay our respects," Thomas announced.

I nodded, stood, and followed Thomas into a large living room. Tapestries and paintings of fields and horses filled the walls of the giant room. There was a large crucifix on the back wall and an antique mirror framed by dark wood. In the center of the room, there were four oversized three-seater couches, one holding Diego as he rested.

"Hola, *Lito*." Thomas crouched in front of him. "I heard you're overdoing it in the fields."

He grumbled, "Someone has to do your job when you run off to play in your dance clubs."

Thomas ignored his comment and glanced at me. "*Lito*, this is Carmen, and we've brought our sons home to meet you."

Diego turned to Thomas without acknowledging my presence. "*What have you done?*" he asked in Spanish as his face flushed to a beet red.

"*Nothing. I have brought my family to see you, to meet you,*" Thomas responded, glancing my way and pleading with his eyes for me to remain quiet.

He knew I was fluent in Spanish and would understand everything that was about to be said. I sighed inside.

An ache formed in my heart as I realized Thomas's standing up for me meant a rift was about to form between him and his grandfather.

You wanted him to put you first. What did you expect would happen?

I remained where I stood and waited for the storm to unleash.

"How dare you bring her here? I raised you better than to bring the likes of that woman into our home. Do you know what her kind did to our family?"

This was not going to go well. I'd encountered his wrath before, and I was sure Thomas had as well, but something told me what was about to happen, would hurt Thomas deeper than anything he'd experienced with Diego. It didn't matter that Diego wasn't feeling well; he would make his opinion heard.

"She did nothing to us." Thomas's voice grew angry. *"Tia Liliana brought her troubles on herself. She should never have slept with another man when she was married."*

"How dare you say that to me? It is because of her father" — he pointed at me — *"that she died."*

"You mean killed herself after murdering Carmen's father?"

I closed my eyes trying to push away the memory of the scandal that I lived through after my dad's death.

"The bastard deserved to die for what he'd done to Liliana and hundreds of others."

"That wasn't her call to make. You read her diary. She wanted revenge for ending their relationship. She was happy the money was gone. She called it blood money for being forced to marry Tio Fidel."

I couldn't believe what I was hearing. Dad's murder had nothing to do with his embezzlement. My lip trembled, and my chest tightened.

In a sense, it would have been better to think his death was the result of his crimes. At least then there was some understanding of justification. Knowing he'd died for another reason made me feel like I didn't understand the past as I thought I did.

I didn't want to hear anything more.

"*That's not true.*" Diego grew somber and pulled his blanket from his lap onto his chest. "*I don't want to discuss this anymore. I made my position clear the first time you came home telling me you planned to marry her. Your obligations are to this family. Without us, you wouldn't be the man you are today. I thought you understood this last year and now she's grabbed onto you again by claiming you fathered her children.*"

I remembered the devastation I'd felt when he told me he refused to turn his back on his family, his heritage. The pain still lingered but now that I understood the no-win situation he'd found himself in, it no longer festered.

I wanted to reach out to comfort Thomas, to ease some of the resignation and pain etched across his face.

"*Lito, give her a chance.*"

He shook his head. "*How do you know those boys are yours? I heard about all the perversions she enjoys. She has clubs dedicated to them. Only a slut would behave in such a manner.*"

That was it. I couldn't hold my tongue anymore.

Before Thomas could open his mouth, I responded in Spanish. "*This slut is willing to have a paternity test to prove Thomas is their father.*"

Diego stared at me in surprise, then frowned at Thomas. "*You stood there and let me think she didn't understand anything I said.*"

"*She speaks eight languages and Spanish is one of them. I*

will only say this once. There will be no paternity test. If you saw the boys, you'd have no doubts. And what happens in our bedroom has nothing to do with you or anyone who wants to spread rumors."

"So that is how it's going to be. You're choosing a gringa over your family. Don't come begging for my help when she ruins your life."

"Lito, don't do this. I don't want you to miss the chance to know your great-grandsons."

"You made your choice. Now I hope you can live with it."

Thomas sighed and rubbed a hand over his eyes. "I think we should check on the boys," he said in English as he walked over to where I stood, cupping the side of my face.

I swallowed and nodded, trying to hold back tears. Thomas defended me.

He tucked a stray hair behind my ear and lifted my left hand, kissing the top. "I told you, I won't let anything come between us again." The diamond on my ring sparkled, making him smile. "This is real, Carm."

Before I could respond, Sophia stalked toward me, grabbing my hand out of Thomas's, and shouted, "You can't marry her. You're promised to me."

CHAPTER TWENTY-ONE

How could you do this to me," Sophia cried. She looked over at Diego, who remained quiet. "You promised he would come around. I waited all these years for him."

I jerked my hand from her grasp, causing her attention to return to me. "I think you need to calm down and gain some perspective."

"Perspective! You stole the man I love. You seduced him, knocked yourself up, and trapped him into marriage. What more is there to see?"

The hell I trapped or stole him. I'd know, wouldn't I?

I remained quiet for a few seconds, taking a deep breath and steeling myself against the questions I wanted to ask Thomas. At this moment, I had to focus on Sophia and her accusations. No matter her pain, I wasn't responsible for her feelings toward Thomas.

I responded in the coldest tone I could conjure and glared down at her. It was the first time I'd ever been thankful for my five-foot-ten-inch height. "I cannot steal someone who never belonged to you in the first place."

Sophia flinched at my words and clenched her fists. "You are a *puta*. You…"

"Enough." Isabella rushed in, pulling her toward the kitchen. "I could hear your screaming from the other end of the house. This is not the time or the place. They're a family whether you want it to be true or not. Thomas was never yours to claim."

"But…" She jerked out of Isabella's hold while staring at me with pure hate. "You'll never make him happy." She spat in my direction and ran out of the room.

A small part of me hurt for her; I stood between her and the man promised to her.

I wasn't sure what was worse, having a father who couldn't care less about my future or one who thought he knew everything that was good for me and tried to arrange my marriage to the right girl, like Thomas.

I glanced toward Thomas, studying him. His face held sadness as he looked toward the kitchen.

"Did you have a relationship with her?" I asked, not caring that both Isabella and Diego could hear us. I had to know if I'd been the other woman.

"No, *mi amor*." He traced a finger down my cheek. "I never viewed her as anything other than a family friend. I only noticed her interest in me after my discharge from the army. At the time, I'd assumed it was a crush. "

"To her, you're more than a crush. She still wants you."

"It doesn't make a difference. It shames me that anyone

would put hopes in Sophia's head of anything more." He glared at Diego, who clenched his jaw at Thomas's words. "Didn't you learn anything from forcing Tia Liliana into a marriage you arranged?"

"If your father hadn't run off and married your *gringa* mother, Liliana would never have sought someone outside of our heritage."

"*Lito*, you can't keep blaming everyone else for your mistakes." Thomas took my hand again and sighed. "Let's go. I think we're finished for now."

I allowed Thomas to guide me out of the room, but before we entered the hall, Stacey came toward us holding two upset boys.

"I couldn't calm them," a frazzled Stacey said.

I took Leo and Simon in my arms, and they immediately rested their heads on my shoulders. "What's all the fuss?"

"Ma…ma…ma," called Simon as he hiccupped.

"Let me have one." Thomas offered his hands, and Leo reached for him.

"Are those the babies?" Isabella hurried toward me with excitement lacing her voice. She stopped midstep with a gasp. "*Ay Dios mío*, they look just like you and your papa, everything but those beautiful green eyes." She came toward us, trying to take Simon's hand, but he pulled it back and burrowed into my neck.

"It's okay," I cooed. "This is your Tia Isa." I wearily smiled at Isabella. "They do look like their papa, don't they? This shy fellow is Simon, and the other one over there is Leonardo. We call him Leo."

Isabella's eyes clouded. "You named him after my brother. Leo would have loved it. Wouldn't you agree, Papi?" She turned toward the sofa, but Diego was gone.

A pang of disappointment filled me. I'd hoped if Diego had seen the boys, then he'd accept them as Thomas's. Oh well, it was wishful thinking.

Isabella shook her head. "I don't understand him. What more proof does he want?"

"It's okay, Tia Isa. *Lito* is stubborn. He'll come around," Thomas reassured his aunt, who nodded.

I wasn't going to hold my breath. Diego was so locked in his anger that he couldn't see what was in front of him.

"Isabella, would you mind showing us to our room? I need to give the boys a bath and feed them before we put them down for the night."

"Oh, please don't hide them away upstairs. I want to spend time with Leo and Simon."

I smiled at her and patted her hand. At least someone wanted us around. "I'll bring them down as soon as we're cleaned up."

She nodded and led us through two hallways and up a flight of stairs. Isabella paused outside a pair of double doors. "This suite has enough space for all of you, and the nursery is next door with another bedroom for the nanny."

"Are you sure, Tia?" Thomas asked. "We can take the one down the hall."

She frowned at him. "This is your ranch and vineyard, no matter what Papi thinks. You will have the room that rightfully belongs to you and your family. Do I make myself clear?"

Thomas nodded and opened the door. We stepped in, and I gasped. "Wow. I feel like I stepped into the Victorian era."

"It is. This was my parents' room. My mom was an architect and restored the house."

"It's beautiful here."

A knock sounded on the door, and Thomas went to answer it. He brought over the boys' day bag and set it on the bed. "Tia Isa sent it up. She said Stacey put two bottles in there for them."

"Okay. Here we go. Time for Bath Time for Twins 101."

For the next thirty minutes, Thomas and I bathed, lotioned, and dressed the boys. I couldn't help but laugh at the stress on his face at the constant movement of the twins.

"Are they always this active?"

"Yep. Well," I thought aloud, "today they're a bit extreme. They do this whenever we have a long flight. You should have seen Simon and Leo when we returned from Italy. Spazzy was an understatement."

I pulled out the milk, and the boys started screaming within seconds of seeing their bottles.

I laid Simon on the bed. "Put Leo next to him. They settle down faster if they're next to each other."

Thomas complied, and I fed the babies their evening meal. I held a bottle in each hand while they kicked and played with my fingers.

"How do you do this all the time? They seem to want the same thing at the same time."

I smiled and looked over at him. "I'm used to it. I

wanted to give them what my mom gave Max and me when we were babies." I glanced at the ring on my left hand. "I don't have a single memory of her that doesn't make me happy."

"We're lucky that we had loving mothers, even if it was for a short time."

"Yes, we are. I used to wish every day for an extended family around. It was so lonely growing up. Somehow or other, Dad alienated us from everyone."

I grew quiet, swallowing the lump forming in my throat. What would my life have been like if Dad had been the father he was before Mom's accident? Would he have chosen the same path?

"I'm so sorry, Carm. For everything. I'm not going to let anything happen to you or our babies." Thomas sat down behind me on the bed and rubbed my shoulders, while Leo and Simon continued to drink.

I closed my eyes and let the warmth of his hands sink in.

Before I lingered too long on the past, the boys finished their dinner, spitting out their bottles, burping simultaneously, and then turning to each other to play.

I smiled. "Such gentlemen."

"I mean it."

I glanced over my shoulder, surprised by his somber tone.

"If I'd been there for you from the beginning, you would have confided in me when all your issues with Christof started."

The regret in his eyes tore at my heart. I couldn't hold on to the hurt anymore. He'd stood up for me downstairs with an immeasurable cost to his relationship with the man who'd raised him.

I grabbed one of his hands from my shoulders and brought it around to thread his fingers with mine. "We're both at fault in this. I shouldn't have kept them from you. I was so hurt." I shook my head. "I couldn't see past it, and you were trying to do your family duty."

"I want you to trust me again." He kissed my neck and drew me back into his arms.

My skin prickled, and I whispered, "I want that, too."

He deserved to understand my hesitation. "I've never been as vulnerable as I've been with you. You made me feel emotions I don't even want to acknowledge. You still do, and it scares me."

Then I remembered something one of the Dommes I trained with had told me. *"A Domme can find strength in vulnerability with the right submissive. He will love her unconditionally, giving her the freedom to be herself without consequences."* She then laughed. *"I can't wait to see the man you commit to. Your submissive will have balls of steel."*

Except Thomas was no submissive. He was all Dom. I knew, without a doubt, he was the one topping me.

Shit, was I lying to myself about who I was?

"It's the same for me. Until I met you, I'd never considered letting any woman do the things I've done with you. We fit, Carm. I believe it. Now you have to believe it. I meant what I said. I'm not going anywhere. I'm here for the long haul."

At that moment, Simon decided to flip onto his stomach,

nearly falling off the bed before Thomas's fast reflexes caught him.

"Why don't you get freshened up before we head down to dinner? In spite of Diego's attitude, Tia Isa is excited you're here and has made a welcome feast."

I nodded, slipping off the bed and walking into the bathroom. I touched up my makeup and distracted myself enough feel strengthened against any more emotional upheaval.

Right now, an encounter with Christof might be easier than one with Diego.

That was a stupid thought. Christof was bat-shit crazy, and I doubted he thought of anything other than his end goal.

I'd deal with him sooner or later. I squared my shoulders and opened the bathroom door.

As I stepped into the room, Thomas scanned me from head to toe. "You're not facing a firing squad."

"Very funny." I glared at him as I grabbed a few items for the boys to keep them calm until Stacey took them to bed. "I'm an unwanted interloper in the lion's den. It's better to appear cold and heartless."

"You aren't cold or heartless. You use your demeanor like an iron shield. Even downstairs with Sophia. The instant something hurt you, your walls go up, and you revert to the perfect, emotionless Domme."

"It's safer to be perceived like that than weak and vulnerable." I pinched the bridge of my nose, inhaling deep. "I've never been allowed to believe otherwise."

Natalie taught me to never let anyone see my weaknesses. I'd become an easy target for others' anger toward Dad. If I wasn't easy prey, then all the predators would find other targets.

He moved behind me and rubbed his hands down my arms, sending a calming warmth into my body. "Let me be your safe place. You can trust me. You can trust us."

I placed my hands over his. "I'm scared, but I promise I'm trying."

He kissed the back of my head. "That's all I ask."

* * *

"I bet you got into so much trouble doing that as a kid," I said as Thomas slid Simon down the staircase railing.

He gave me a heart-stopping, wicked grin. "I'll admit, Tia Isa smacked me with a wooden spoon a time or two."

I laughed as I envisioned a rambunctious boy who looked like an older version of mine, causing chaos in this house.

Our happy mood vanished as we reached the living room and heard a loud argument in Spanish between Isabella and Diego.

"She doesn't deserve his wrath because of me." I moved to enter the room, but Thomas put a hand on my lower back.

"Don't worry. It doesn't matter what he thinks."

We walked toward the threshold of the room, not announcing our entrance.

"Papi, look with both your eyes, they look exactly like Thomas. This hate you have for the Danes is making you blind."

"If you want to live in this house, you better understand one thing, I make the decisions. I put up with it when Leonardo brought that woman here, and look where that got me. My son is dead. I won't do it again."

"But…"

"No, I have made my decision. They leave today, and if you don't like it, go with them. This is my home."

"You have it wrong, *Lito*. The house belongs to me, not you. My mother's money bought this land and the vineyards surrounding it. If it wasn't for her, the ranch would be half its size." Thomas strolled into the room, surprising Diego by stepping between him and Isabella. "You will never threaten Tia Isa again. She's only telling you the truth."

"This has nothing…" He trailed off when he caught sight of Simon in Thomas's arms. "*Dios mío*, he looks like Leonardo." Diego stumbled back and sat on the couch. His eyes clouded and he glanced toward me and Leo. "They're ours?" He couldn't hide the wonder and surprise in his voice.

Thomas came to me, taking Leo from my arms and brought both boys to Diego. "These are your *bisnietos*."

Diego took one hand from each baby and ran his thumbs over their fingers.

"Do you still need a paternity test? Do you accept them?" Thomas asked, but Diego remained silent. "*Lito*, I…"

Diego cut him off. "I still want a test. I won't pass down any of this." He gestured to the room around him. "If I'm not positive they belong to us."

Hurt flashed across Thomas's face, then it turned to anger. "I have no need for anything more, *Lito*. The house and the land already belong to me. The vineyards, which you say you work for the future, my mother bought. The woman who you never accepted into this home. The reason Papa was able to make such a great fortune out of what you and he started was because of Mama."

He stood up with the boys and walked over to me. I took Leo and Simon from him, remaining quiet, and thankfully so did the boys. They seemed fascinated by the animated discussion happening around them.

"Are you saying I am not welcome here?" Diego demanded.

Thomas sighed and shook his head, walking back over to him. "No, I never said anything like that. This is your home for as long as you wish. But understand this. I don't need your inheritance. Papa gave me more than any man can spend in a lifetime. Something Leo and Simon will inherit after me. My family will always come first."

Thomas glanced at me. "Let's go. I don't think there's anything more to say."

I nodded and waited for him to approach me.

"You are just like him. A disgusting Dane," Diego shouted. "You steal everything that doesn't belong to you."

I bit my tongue, trying to hold back a retort to put him in his place. He was hurting, and I was the best target for his pain. I'd take it for Thomas.

"You and your kind are the reason this family has suffered so much. You've perverted his mind to your ways. Instead of standing up like a man should, he hides behind your skirt."

His words were a direct hit to my heart. Was I using my

will to push him into submitting when he didn't want to? No, what we did was freely given, even if we were still trying to figure out the dynamics of our relationship.

Thomas opened his mouth to respond, but I shook my head.

"Diego, this is my family now. You can hate me all you want, but don't hurt them because of me. Please don't miss the chance to know your great-grandsons."

With those last words, I walked out of the room.

CHAPTER TWENTY-TWO

The next morning I rose early and headed to the stables. I strolled down the pathway, letting the crisp air soothe my senses and ease the tension from the day before.

After the argument with Diego, I'd lost all desire to eat and went upstairs to tuck the boys in for the night, and then to my room. I hated to miss the grand dinner Isabella had prepared, but I couldn't sit through a long meal where I'd be the target of Diego's fury.

I'd felt like I was reliving the isolation of my childhood. I was an outsider here as much as I was with the Boston elite, all because of the crimes of my father.

What did I have to do to prove I was worthy?

I wiped a stray tear from my cheek with the back of my hand and checked around me to see if anyone was awake. The only people I saw were a few ranch hands and kitchen staff who waved to me as I passed.

Thomas was still asleep with the boys, who'd decided they

had had enough of Stacey around midnight and wanted their parents, crashing the minute their heads hit our pillows.

I took in the fresh air surrounding the vineyard. Thomas was so proud of his home and all his family had accomplished. If only I could make this tension with Diego easier.

When Thomas joined me in our room a little before eleven, I was exhausted and falling asleep. He didn't say anything, stripping out of his clothes and climbing into bed. I'd kept my back to him, hoping he didn't notice I was still awake. There was no point in adding my emotional turmoil to the drama he'd most likely dealt with at dinner. But instead of allowing me to pretend I was asleep, he'd pulled me against him, tucked my head under his chin, and said, "Don't even think about freezing me out."

We didn't discuss what happened with Diego but held each other, talking about safe things such as wine, horses, and the various aspects of the ranch he managed.

His love and pride for his family's legacy were easy to hear in his words. I learned about the program he developed with Arya that tracked all aspects of the ranch, from the age and health of the grapes in the vineyard, to the projections of stallion and mare birth rates and the price cycles for stock auctions. The number of hats Thomas wore amazed me. The cool confidence he handled them with spoke to a deeper part of me, telling me he was truly the dependable and dedicated man I'd believed he was when we first got together.

Right before I dozed off, he told me to go riding in the morning, and he would help Stacey take care of the boys.

He'd somehow figured out that I needed to regain my bearings in a place where I didn't quite fit in.

He understands more about you than you do, Carmen.

I pushed the thought to the back of my mind and selected a beautiful black-and-gold colt. As I laid a blanket over the horse's back, Elonso, Thomas's cousin, appeared.

"Good morning, Mistress."

I jumped, not expecting anyone to be around, and then checked behind me, making sure no one heard. "Don't call me that here. I don't want my lifestyle discussed."

"My apologies, Mistress." He smiled a sheepish grin. "It's a term of respect on the ranch. No one will think anything of it."

"You're so not funny." I couldn't help but smile back. "When did you get here?" I asked as I selected my saddle.

"Last night. Whenever we have an auction planned, the family comes into town to help prepare the stock." He attempted to take the saddle from me. "Mistress, why are you doing that? If you'd let any of the hands know, we'd have prepared one for you."

I nudged him out of my way. "Elonso, I grew up around horses. I know what I'm doing."

"No, I insist," he said as he plucked the saddle from my arms.

His stocky six-foot-five frame was too strong for me to win a tug-of-war, so I shrugged my shoulders and relented, allowing him to take over.

"It figures you'd pick this one out of the entire herd." He laughed.

I cocked a hand on my hip. "And why is that?"

"Because Misu is Thomas's favorite colt, and since you and the horse belong to him, it makes sense that you're drawn to each other. Thomas is Master to you both."

The thought of belonging to Thomas sent a shiver down my spine.

I shook my head at the craziness of his logic. I'd picked the horse because it reminded me of my favorite Arabian in New York.

Laughing, I tried pretending that his words didn't worry me. "I think you've got a few screws loose. I have no Master."

He grinned at me. "If you say so. Make sure Thomas doesn't hear you say that. No man wants to think that his woman doesn't believe he's Master. Especially a Dom like him."

"Why do you submit, then?"

Elonso looked up from fastening the belt under the horse's flank. "Mistress, there are very few who know what I enjoy in the clubs or the dungeons of my Mistresses."

I nodded, understanding what he was saying. "It's no different for me. Those outside our lifestyles would never understand the desire to submit or dominate."

"Or switch," he stated with a gleam in his eyes.

"It isn't like that," I insisted, too afraid to accept that what was happening between Thomas and me had a name.

Was I a switch?

When I looked back on our relationship, I couldn't deny the truth. Thomas had topped me from the bottom all along. He allowed me the level of control I needed without forcing me to be something I wasn't.

Do you keep telling yourself this, hoping the answer might change?

Elonso walked the horse over to me and lifted his hand to help me climb onto the colt's back.

"May I please give you a piece of advice, Mistress?" Elonso looked up at me as I settled into the saddle.

I sighed and inclined my head.

"There's nothing wrong with what you and Thomas share. The world doesn't need to know you submit to him. Only he does. If you love him, don't hold back or deny a part of you exists out of fear. He needs your trust as much as you need his."

I stared at him for a few seconds. Elonso knew only a limited amount of information about my relationship with Thomas, but he had better insight into it than I did.

I inhaled deep. It was time to accept I wasn't the Domme I had made myself out to be. With the right man, with Thomas, I could hand over my control and accept my desires.

Until that horrible day when he'd ended our relationship, he'd never made me feel any less for my sexual cravings. In fact, he pushed me to explore them. Now all I had to do was to stop fighting against my fears and let Thomas know I accepted the unusual dynamics of our relationship.

"Thank you, Elonso. I understand what you're saying." I steered the colt forward, out of the stables, and towards the cliffs overlooking the vineyard.

After the house was no longer in sight, I guided Misu into a full gallop. My heart raced, and for the first time since I left the Hamptons, I felt at peace. Here away from everyone with the land, the wind, and the colt, there was no judgment. There were no mistakes or living under the shadow of past sins or the worry over what was in store for me when I returned home.

I tugged the reins, bringing Misu to a trot. We arrived at the edge of the cliffs, and I stared toward the valley. The beauty of it reminded me of the vineyard I'd inherited from my mother, tucked away in a small village outside of Cape Town.

One day I'd take the boys there. However, it would have to wait until all the chaos with Christof and my life was behind me.

I glanced at my watch. I had three hours until my conference call with the girls. Hopefully, Arya and Thomas's software detected something new. I knew it had been less than forty-eight hours since we discovered the file on me, but something told me staying on the ranch wasn't going to keep me off Christof's radar.

A group of birds chirped as the wind picked up, and my focus returned to the area in front of me. I smiled into the breeze, letting it tickle my face and push my worried thoughts away. This land held an almost fairy-tale beauty. Rows and rows of grapevines lined the hills, and a rich, earthy scent of soil filled the air.

Given my reason for being here, I couldn't think of a better location to hide out.

Mama would have loved it here.

Her family, who were German winemakers, had settled near Cape Town during the early nineteenth century, creating one of the country's first vineyards. Even to this day, the winery produced some of the top Shiraz vintages coming out of South Africa.

Thomas's family vineyard was known for its Cabernet blends that held a hint of citrus and apple, a beneficial result of the apple and lemon farms nearby.

The sound of hoofbeats echoed behind me, and I turned my head in time to see Thomas approach. He wore his cowboy hat low, shielding his face from the sun.

He brought the horse to a stop alongside Misu and smiled, causing my heart to skip a beat. "Hi."

"Hi, yourself. How are the boys doing?"

"Surprisingly well. They're charming their tia Isa. I think we're going to have many visits from their great-aunt in the future."

I smiled. "The boys are going to be spoiled rotten. Not like they aren't now, but it's…nice."

Could this be our future? Going back and forth between families on both coasts?

"*Mi amor*, what's got you thinking so hard?"

"Thomas, is this really going to work? I know what I said, but your family needs you."

In the short time I'd been on the ranch, I realized how everyone depended on him, from Diego and Isabella to the ranch hands who organized the stalls. Committing to me meant possibly giving up the ranch for a life in New York.

I wasn't sure if I could bear it if he chose me and then had regrets. He loved his family, his horses, his land, and taking any of that from him would cause me more guilt than keeping the boys from him.

He studied me for a few moments before he responded. "I know you don't want to believe it, but I'm not going anywhere. Nothing will change how I feel about the people here on the ranch. What you have to understand is that I made my decision about us long before I learned about Leo and Simon. You are my future."

I swallowed the lump forming in my throat. In the back of my mind, I'd had a fear he was pushing for a relationship because of our sons and his traditional values. Now, it was as if a weight had lifted from my shoulders.

Sensing the thoughts running through my mind, he cupped the side of my face and sealed my lips with his, stealing all thoughts from my mind but the desire to deepen our embrace. He savored my mouth with slow strokes of his tongue, sending a shot of arousal straight to my pussy.

I loved the way he kissed, enjoying every nip and taste.

Our horses shifted, forcing us to separate. Thomas held my gaze as he released his hold on my flushed face while his fingers rubbed a line down my throat, making my breath hitch.

He pulled his horse to the side. "Follow me. It's time."

CHAPTER TWENTY-THREE

I tightened my grip on the reins. "Time for what?"

I knew what he meant, but I asked anyway.

He glanced over his shoulder. "Time, Carmen," he said in a deep tone that sent butterflies to my stomach.

Oh hell. The voice.

I kept Misu where he stood as my heart began to beat a heavy drum in my chest.

He was right. It was time to give him what I craved to do. No more holding back out of fear. No more focusing on past hurts. No more expecting him to fail me.

I rubbed the back of my neck with shaky hands, taking a deep breath.

Following him meant giving him everything, not only my heart but also my power. The side I'd promised I wouldn't give anyone again. This time he'd push me to limits I'd never reached before.

Thomas paused his horse, turning to look at me.

"Carmen," he ordered as he held my gaze. Then his face softened. "Come, baby. I'll take care of you."

He was right. He'd shown me I mattered. It was time to gift him with my trust.

"I'm coming, Ma-Master."

Thomas's eyes clouded with desire, and then he turned. "Follow me."

My heart jumped with every step of the horses. I trailed behind Thomas, steering Misu in the direction of a path I hadn't noticed on my way to the cliffs. We wove through lush brush until the roar of water echoed around us. A half mile later, we reached the waterfall Thomas had told me about, the one the ranch was named after.

He dismounted and tied his horse to a metal loop attached to a boulder near a cave. He then walked over to me, gripped my waist, and lifted me off the saddle.

The contact was like a shot of electricity through my system. I gasped as goose bumps prickled my skin. Thomas made sure to rub the juncture of my pussy against his growing erection before he set me on my feet.

"Stand over there while I take care of the horses." He pointed to the entrance of the cave.

I followed his directions as my nerves jumped into overdrive. Excitement and anxiety ran havoc inside my body.

He tied Misu next to his stallion. He returned to me, taking my hand in his, but not moving.

"Breathe. This is your choice, Carm. I won't take what you aren't willing to give me. Whatever you decide won't change how I feel about you."

I remained quiet as I stared at him. He was giving me an out.

One that I didn't want.

"I made my decision when I followed you here." I touched his cheek with the back of my hand.

A smile touched his lip, making my heart skip a beat.

He leaned down to give me a light peck and then turned, guiding me along a path into a cavern that opened up underneath the waterfall.

The cave wasn't a cave. It was an outdoor living room of sorts. Antique Mexican art decorated the wall furthest from the water, with a small kitchen underneath.

The wall closest to the waterfall held a variety of loops and hooks and ropes and a small table with a metal box. This was an outdoor dungeon. Everything in the space was brand new, as if he'd designed it for us.

My heart jumped. I knew what he'd planned.

"Strip."

My head jerked from the wall toward Thomas. He'd removed his hat, shirt, and boots and sat in a wicker chair sipping a drink of some kind.

"Don't make me repeat myself or you'll be punished."

My breath accelerated. "Sorry," I whispered.

"Sorry, what?"

My pussy contracted.

"Sorry, M-Master."

I untucked my shirt from my jeans and then brought my fingers to the buttons. A tremor ran through me as I worked the fastening open. I pulled the shirt off and began folding it.

"Let it drop to the floor."

Down it went.

"Now the rest. I want nothing between my gaze and your beautiful body. There's no more hiding from me, Carmen. Today I will learn all your secrets."

Inhaling deep, I reached down to tug off my boots.

"Let me do that." Thomas rose from the chair and walked over to me. He trailed a finger from my collarbone, between my breasts, down my stomach. He stooped toward the ground, and his palms glided lower until he reached the bottom of my jeans. "Lift your leg."

He removed each of my boots, placing them on the side. Then he unfastened my jeans, sliding the denim down my hips. He remained crouched with his face was a hairbreadth from my aching pussy. I watched him lick his lips. The urge to demand he use them was on the tip of mine, but I held it back, knowing that today I wasn't in charge.

Hell. With Thomas, I'd never been in charge.

Thomas stared at my swollen labia, licked his lips, and then stood, returning to his armchair.

I closed my eyes and prayed I could go through with this. Was I strong enough to hand over my power for my pleasure?

"Keep going, Carm," he urged. "Give me what I want."

"Yes, Master," I whispered as I opened my jeans and lowered the zipper. With slow, precise movements, I shimmied my pants past my hips to the ground and stepped out of them. I left them in a pile and waited.

"I said strip. That means everything."

A crease formed between my brows.

"*Mi cielito* isn't used to submission. She's used to giving the commands." He picked up his drink, sipped, and set it back on the table. "This is your choice, Carmen. As you showed me, there's freedom in submission, in letting someone you trust take the reins. Can you do it? Can you let go and allow me to give you what you most desire, or are you too afraid to ask for it?"

I didn't respond. He'd never truly submitted to me. It wasn't in his nature. The submission he'd showed me was for my pleasure more than his.

Nevertheless, what he said was right. Submission never meant that I lost power. I was giving control as a reward for my faith in him.

I unclasped my bra, sliding it off, and then pushed down my underwear.

A cool breeze grazed my naked skin, making my nipples pebble and elongate. As he stared at me, not saying anything, my breath started to come in shallow pants. I wanted to fidget, but I held still. My submissives weren't allowed to twitch a muscle until I was finished with my perusal of their bodies and had given them permission to move. Now I was on the receiving end of this scrutiny, and it both frightened and excited me.

After a few minutes, Thomas walked over to me, circling me as he studied my every curve. I squeezed my eyes closed, not sure what he was thinking and how he saw the changes in my body after having the boys. Even though we'd made love since my pregnancy, he hadn't examined me the way he was doing now.

I wanted to cringe. I no longer had the perfect body I once possessed. There were signs of loose skin and stretch marks.

"God, you are exquisite." He ran his fingers just below my belly button. "This beautiful body created my sons."

He trailed up my stomach, stopping to cup my breasts and causing my nipples to pebble harder on contact. "Open your eyes. I want to watch your every reaction to what I'm doing."

Lifting my lids, I stared into beautiful desire-glazed amber.

"Today, I want you to trust me."

I started to respond, but he raised a brow, and I kept my mouth shut.

"I'll take care of you and keep you safe."

Coming here was my first step in accepting what Thomas was offering me. I had to give him what he'd given me. A submission that spoke of my complete trust in him.

A calm settled into my mind.

He's my Master. Today I am not a Mistress. I am his slave.

A sharp pain fired through my nipples as he bit one and pinched the other, bringing my attention to Thomas.

"Stop thinking and focus on me," he murmured against my breast.

My legs buckled and he held me up by the waist, his mouth never leaving my aching nub. My palms came instinctively to his shoulders, gripping them tight.

He sucked and laved the peak as his fingers tweaked and strummed the other bud. My head fell back, and I couldn't think of anything but the beautiful pleasure he was giving me.

All of a sudden, he dropped to one knee, spreading my legs apart and fastening his lips onto my aching pussy.

"Thomas," I moaned.

He growled in response as he delved deep with his tongue into my swollen and wet folds.

"Master," I corrected myself.

His arm anchored me, keeping me from falling while the fingers of his other hand slid into my passage. He pumped in and out and continued to feast.

I gripped his hair as my mind whirled.

Yes. Almost there.

There was no holding back my want, my desire. There was no need to. Thomas controlled this. My pleasure was his pleasure.

"Please," I begged, surprising myself. I had to hold back until he gave me permission. I needed his permission.

"Come now," he commanded without stopping his ministrations on my weeping pussy.

Everything imploded. My orgasm tore through me, and I arched into him as my legs lost all ability to stand. I screamed out his name. My wetness flooded his hand, my core squeezing tight around his pumping fingers.

He tore his mouth from my pussy. "That's it, baby. Give it to me."

I continued to convulse and floated down with a few lingering spasms. Thomas gathered me into his arms and carried me to the sofa.

He held me against his chest, allowing me time to steady my breath. I lay on him like a rag doll, not saying anything until he took my hands and fastened a cuff on each wrist. He made sure to keep a finger-width opening between my skin and the soft, buttery leather. With a clasp, he connected the bonds together.

"Close your eyes. Now we begin."

CHAPTER TWENTY-FOUR

My heart jumped at his words, and tingles prickled my body. I could do this. I knew I could.

I lowered my lids, and a mask slipped over my eyes. My senses immediately fired. The sound of the waterfall and our breaths became more pronounced. And the cool breeze coming from the cascading water glided over my skin.

"I want you to feel what I'm doing to you. I want you to enjoy every sensation. I want you to show me every true reaction without you anticipating anything. Do you understand?"

"Yes, Master."

"What is your safe word?"

In all my time in the lifestyle, I never thought I'd need one. I usually asked for a safe word. I knew Thomas would push me today, but he would never hurt me. He would protect me with his life.

"Carmen, I asked you a question. What's your safe word?"

I almost said that I didn't need one, but I'd never allow an untried submissive that kind of leeway with their safety. Moreover, as much as this was about my faith in Thomas reading my body, he had to trust me to let him know if I was at my limit and couldn't take any more. It was the give and take of any D/s relationship.

"Cabernet."

"Good. Now give me your hands."

As I lifted my bound wrists toward him, he grasped them and guided me forward. My heartbeat accelerated. I knew where he was taking me. The sound of the waterfall intensified. We were near the wall and ceiling with all the hooks, ropes, and chains.

Oh God, this was happening. He was going to bind me to the stone. I could do this. It was Thomas. He was the only one who could give me what I wanted.

A chain clinked, and my anxiety peaked. Thomas stretched my arms above my head, attaching them to the metal. My body pulled taut, with my hands high over me and my bare feet holding my weight on the ground.

I hiccupped, trying to hold in a cry of worry.

"Breathe, baby. You'll enjoy this. I promise." He kissed my lips, deepening our embrace until I opened my mouth to demand more. Then he pulled away.

"Now to dress you in hemp, the way you envisioned doing to me."

My heartbeat jumped.

Rope.

"I'm going to tie you so that your beautiful breasts are the centerpiece of the dress. Today, you will experience the exhilaration you enjoy giving your submissives."

I scowled. Was he reminding me of them to taunt me?

"Why do you bring up the men I've played with? Doesn't it bother you to know what I've done with them?"

Thomas leaned his forehead against mine.

"I'm not naïve to think a renowned Mistress hasn't had the same number of slaves as I've had."

I growl escaped my lips at the thought of anyone else being with Thomas.

He chuckled, kissed me, and drew back. "What I know is that there is and will be only me between these legs." His hand cupped my weeping pussy, then slid up to rest between my breasts. "And in this heart for the rest of our lives."

"Thomas, the one slave I slept with was Andrew. The only other person I've been with is you."

He traced my lips, and the urge to lick them overwhelmed me. "I'm very pleased to hear that. There will never be anyone else."

Thomas moved away from me, and the sound of him unzipping and shuffling through a bag reached my ears.

A brush of his hands on my abdomen told me he'd returned, and anxiety hit the pit of my stomach.

Holy shit. I'm about to get my first experience in Shibari.

A knot slipped around the back of my neck, making goose bumps prickle my skin and wetness flood my pussy. The ends draped over my shoulders and hung between my breasts. The abrasive material against my body brought forth a sense of desire I'd never experienced before.

I'd enjoyed watching my submissives' skin flush and redden with anticipation and excitement, but now I felt the same euphoria.

"You're so beautiful. I love how your nipples strain for my attention, not to mention the glistening between your legs."

The weight of three more knots brushed my breasts, belly, and the folds of my pussy lips.

"Spread your legs. I want the position of these knots to be perfect before I start my masterpiece."

He repositioned the bottom knot against my clit, causing me to jump a little.

"Steady," he murmured as he brought the rope ends to the sides of my labia, around my butt cheeks, and up to loop to the knot at the back of my neck. Each shift of the binding rubbed my pulsating nub in a torturous rhythm, providing enough stimuli to quicken my pussy, but not enough to send me over.

He continued threading the rope around the front of my body, weaving a pattern across my stomach and breasts, and finally ending beneath my rib cage.

By the time he tied the final knot, the stimulation of the rope against my labia caused a sheen of sweat to coat my skin and a pulsing deep in my core. I needed relief. If only I could rub my thighs together, I'd come. But the binding kept my thighs apart.

Besides, this wasn't about me, it was about pleasing Thomas.

My Master.

Why did calling him that intensify the throbbing in my pussy? Was this what I wanted? A Master? Logic told me I'd always be a Domme, but something about Thomas called to a part of me that I was scared to release.

You can do it, Carmen. He's yours. Let him give you the freedom you crave.

"Tilt your head up and open your mouth."

I did as he commanded as a glass touched my lips and an icy liquid poured down my throat. I swallowed the water and let it cool my overheated body.

I opened for more, but he denied me by pulling the cup away.

"Not too much, *mi amor.*"

He set the water on the table, and the next thing I knew, cool gel slid down the crack of my bottom as Thomas spread my cheeks apart.

I clenched, knowing what was about to happen.

"Relax. I'm going to prepare you."

"For what?"

"You know what. I told you what I planned the other night." He pushed his pinkie in, working my hole until my tight muscles released.

A protest escaped my lips when he pulled out, but almost immediately a lubricated object pressed at my puckered entrance. "Relax and push out. It will help the plug go in."

No one had ever fucked my ass. Even before our breakup, the closest I'd gotten was Thomas fingering me during sex.

Could I do this? I sighed inside. He was only preparing me.

I calmed my muscles, and the plastic slid in a fraction. The plug pushed past my tight bundle of nerves, lodging in until the wide base sat against my bottom. My ass burned from the invasion, and I felt full but not uncomfortable.

Thomas's touch left my body, and all I could hear was running water.

Moments later, a swish of a cat-o'-nine-tails snapped in the air, and what felt like fingers glided up my thighs and stomach.

"Do you know what that is?"

A chill went up my spine. It was my instrument of choice. The one I'd used on Thomas that first night so long ago when neither of us was looking for anything more than a submissive to pass our time but instead found something that frightened and satisfied a deep part of us.

CRACK!

I flinched, seeing stars as pain shot across my thighs, slowly dulling to a sting.

"I asked you a question."

"A cat," I hissed, and my wetness slid down my legs, soaking the rope between my thighs. My craving for more negated my momentary pain.

"That's right. Do you remember what you told me the first time we met?"

My skin prickled. "I asked you if you were strong enough to give me everything I desired, even if it went against what you thought you knew."

Thomas trailed the wisps of the leather over my shoulders and across my breasts, sending goose bumps over my skin.

"I accepted your question as a challenge, and by the time

our night was over, you pulled out a side of me that no other woman even knew existed."

The image of Thomas bound, with manacles holding his arms above him and his feet clasped to the floor, popped into my mind. That night he'd shown me a man, stronger than anyone I'd met before, who could gift me with the pleasure I needed to calm the turmoil in my soul.

Deep down, even now, I knew he submitted as a gift to me, not because it came naturally to him. The least I could do was the same. But with me...a part of me needed to submit.

CRACK!

"Fuck," I called as my body arched into the fire branding my breasts. I breathed through the discomfort and let the adrenaline course over me.

"Are you paying attention, love? I want you to focus on my voice, not the ones in your mind."

"Sorry," I whispered as my skin heated from the tendons of the leather cat-o'-nine-tails and the tug of the rope. My pussy flooded with desire and screamed for more.

"Sorry, what?"

I turned my head in the direction of his voice. "Sorry, Master."

"Today I ask you the same question. Will you give me everything, even if your mind tells you that you're not a submissive?"

I'd come to him willing to give him what he wanted from me. But was it for him or me? Could I give him all of me?

Will I still be Carmen at the end of this?

"Carmen, does it scare you to admit that you enjoy submitting to my touch?"

I remained quiet. He knew I was scared. Why did he want my answer?

"What are you so afraid of losing if you let me in?"

I still didn't respond. My bound body cried for me to admit what he wanted.

CRACK!

"Please," I called out, squeezing the plug tighter and feeling the sting on my ass. My sensitive center contracted and quivered.

"Tell me what I want to hear. What you want to say."

Carmen, he's given you the proof of his love. He put you first. Now give him and yourself the words.

He struck, again and again, crisscrossing all over my thighs, stomach, and arms. I arched into every slap of the leather, rejoicing in the singe left by the talons. I couldn't get enough. My nipples ached for attention as my pussy swelled and screamed for release. The more I thrashed against the ropes, the more the friction in my core intensified. But it couldn't send me over.

"Thomas, let me come," I begged, feeling the tears soaking the blindfold and dripping down my cheeks.

"Master," he commanded.

"Master. Please." My body was on fire. I wasn't sure how long I could last without shattering.

"No, not until you admit why you're so scared to let go. I know the answer. You know the answer. Now, say it."

"Don't do this," I sobbed as my pussy wept and throbbed.

Thomas cupped my face with one hand as the other grazed my clitoral nub. "Say it, baby. I won't let you fall."

I panted out short breaths and then bit my lip. By coming here, I knew he'd want me to say it. I accepted it, but now actually uttering the words meant someone else held the reins to hurt me again.

Thomas tugged my blindfold off. My eyes adjusted to the light and I stared into his. What I saw crumbled any last resistance I had left.

"Depending on your means, you can hurt me again. By giving you everything, I am risking who I am." Tears streamed out of my eyes, and his thumb wiped them to the side while the other strummed my clit, causing my body to bow. "Don't you understand? I won't ever be that weak girl who'd let everyone around her dictate her life. But with you no matter how hard I try, I…I can't…"

"Can't what?" His stubble grazed my wet cheeks.

"I can't control anything with you. Why can't I do it with you? Why do I need you to be in charge so much?"

"Because of who I am to you," he crooned, not taking his gaze from mine and continuing to strum my clit. "I made mistakes with you, but I'm not your father. I'm not one of the bastards who turned their back on you."

"Then who are you?" I asked, my breath coming out in shallow pants.

He sucked my bottom lip it into his mouth, intensifying my body's needs. "You tell me."

My heart knew the answer. He knew the answer. I could trust him. I had to let go of the past.

Say it, Carmen.

"You're my Master."

His fingers plunged deep into my sopping pussy, and his thumb's rhythm intensified.

My mind clouded as my orgasm grew inside me, but I kept my eyes locked with his.

"Who do you belong to?"

"You. I belong to you," I gasped.

"Come now."

Thomas scissored his digits, making my pulse pound in my ears and my back arch. Heat poured into every part of me, nearly driving me insane, and my pussy convulsed around his fingers.

"That's it, *mi cielito*. Let go."

I closed my eyes and rode the waves of pleasure detonating inside me. I threw my head back and thrashed against the hemp, letting the friction of the rope prolong my release.

I wasn't aware of Thomas removing the plug until the crown of his lubricated cock nudged at the puckered entrance to my ass. He held me close at the waist and slipped a vibrator into my pussy as he pushed in a little further.

"God, you're so tight."

He slowly worked his cock through the resistant ring of nerves, letting me adjust to the burn and bite of his girth and length. He stilled once he was fully seated.

I breathed through the discomfort as a gentle tingle reignited inside my core. I threw my head back against his shoulder.

"I have to move, baby," Thomas gritted out.

I nodded, and before I knew it, Thomas was fucking my ass. He clicked on the vibrator and worked it in the same rhythm as his cock.

My mind whirled from all the stimuli. I couldn't focus on anything but the ecstasy flowing throughout my body. The force of his thrusts pushed us against the wall. Thomas released the vibrator and looped his hand around the chain holding my wrists.

He continued his assault on my senses and my ass until another firestorm erupted inside me. My heart pummeled out of control, and all I knew was that in Thomas's arms I could fly.

A few seconds later, he pulled out and yelled his release, coating me with his cum.

CHAPTER TWENTY-FIVE

A few last tremors shook my body as my orgasm waned and my breath calmed. Nothing I'd ever experienced or done had prepared me for how I felt at this moment. Thomas unlatched my arms and carried me to the sofa. He massaged me from my shoulders down to my elbows and ended with my hands. Once he finished making sure I'd regained circulation, he left me on the sofa to clean up.

I relaxed into the couch and closed my eyes. A sense of relief and uncertainty panged my stomach. Was I a submissive pretending to be a Domme? No. I wasn't like Arya or Milla. How would this work?

I shifted, and a whimper escaped my lips at the pleasure from the bite of discomfort in my ass.

"Easy," Thomas murmured, coming to crouch in front of me.

He slowly untied each of the knots on the front of my

body. He kissed and caressed the skin the rope had covered. "Here, let me sit you up." He gently lifted me and pulled the remaining hemp from under me.

He picked up a warm wet towel from a bowl on the side table and cleaned me from front to back, making sure to remove any remnants of our scene from my body.

Thomas ministered to me, not saying a word. When he finished, he set the cloth back in the bowl, sat behind me, and gathered me into his arms, holding me close while running circles with his fingers over my arms and thighs.

I knew we had a lot to discuss, but I couldn't decide where to start. The loss of control had given me the most intense orgasm of my life. What did that say about me? Would Thomas expect me to submit every time we were together? I wasn't sure I could do it. Deep down I knew I still needed to dominate, even if Thomas took over in the end. Fuck, I was making no sense. Fuck, fuck, fuck.

Until I met Thomas, I accepted my desires as an ingrained part of me. Now I hadn't a clue what I wanted.

I moved to get up, but Thomas's grip on me tightened. "Where are you going?"

"I…I have to go. I need to check on the boys." I struggled to get up.

"They're fine with Tia Isa and Stacey. I'm not letting you run away. We need to discuss why you're so upset."

I couldn't talk about it. I bit my lip trying to hold in tears. What did it say about me as a person if I wanted him to submit but freaked out when I gave myself over to him for the same thing?

Oh God. This isn't me.

"Please, Thomas. Let me go. I…" I shook my head. "I just can't. Let me go."

I shoved out of his hold and stood. I rushed toward my clothes and haphazardly put them on. I had to get out of here. I tugged on my jeans and tried to zip and button them, but my fingers shook too much.

"Carmen."

I froze in place as Thomas's Dom voice washed over me.

Dammit, he shouldn't affect me the way he does.

"Look at me."

I kept my gaze on my hands, not trusting myself to see the disappointment on Thomas's face. My vision clouded and tears fell in fat drops down my cheeks.

"Baby, it's going to be okay."

Thomas's hands gently gripped my shoulders, making me flinch, not because he hurt me, but because I needed his touch so much.

"This isn't me. I don't think I can do this. I'm a Domme. I'm the one who has control." My fists came up as he turned me to face him, and I hit his bare chest. "Why did you make me feel this? I don't know who I am anymore."

Thomas pulled me against him, imprisoning my arms between us. I struggled against him, but he wouldn't release me.

Exhausted from fighting to free myself, I leaned my head against his heart and sobbed. I screamed and demanded to know why he made me love him so much. I blamed him for not protecting me from Christof and bringing me to the ranch. I said so many things that made no sense. All I knew was that I had to get it out.

Thomas held me until I spent the last of my tears. I raised my head to look at him and realized I wasn't standing anymore. I was curled against his naked body as he sat on the floor.

He cupped my face in his palm, giving me a knowing stare. "I know exactly what's going through your mind, and I'm not going to let you run. I won't let you make the same mistake I made. I'm not going to let you give up because it's easier."

A part of me was ready to do exactly that, run back to New York and pretend this had never happened. The knowledge he would fight for me gave me comfort. Maybe there was a small glimmer of hope we could make this work. But how? I couldn't think about that right now.

"I won't," I whispered, knowing my words contradicted my instincts, and then hiccuped.

"*Mi amor*, trust in us. Trust in our love."

From the first night we were together, he'd seen deep to the secret part of me and had given me the submission and the domination I needed.

"Thomas, I trust in you more than any man before." I looked up into his face. "Thank you."

"A few moments ago, you were panicking, so what are you thanking me for?"

"For understanding my needs better than I do. You allowed me to top you and gave me your submission when you'd never allowed anyone else to do it to you."

He lifted a brow and gave me a wicked grin. "I don't recall any of it being a burden."

I shook my head, but before I could say anything, he placed a finger on my lips. "Carm, what we share is unique and special. Submitting didn't mean I gave up an essential part of who I am. I did it because I enjoyed it and wanted to. I gave you the level of control you needed while maintaining mine."

I replayed all the different scenes we'd engaged in over the past two years, and the one common thread was that Thomas knew what I needed even before I did. Every time he submitted to me, there was an aura of power that I'd ignored. There was no doubt he enjoyed what we'd done, but it wasn't who he was. His core persona was to dominate, and if I was honest with myself, he dominated even when I thought I was in charge. He allowed me to set and dictate the scene, even when everything inside him said he should be in total control.

A sharp grip clenched my heart. He submitted knowing how raw it made a person, even when it wasn't his nature. He did it for me.

What more proof do you want, Carm? The man loves you. No Dom plays a submissive for any other reason.

I bit the tip of his finger and spoke. "You've got it all figured out, don't you?"

"*Mi cielito*, you're easier to love than figure out."

"Back at you." The turmoil that churned inside me only moments earlier eased.

He kissed the top of my head and then sighed as he

glanced at his watch. "We need to get back. Both of us have conferences in less than twenty minutes."

I nodded, wiping my face against the sleeve of my shirt.

We dressed and rode back to the stables in silence. It was as if we both had to sort through all the thoughts running through our minds.

I shifted in the saddle, trying to relieve the tenderness in my nether regions as my mind continued to reel from the scene Thomas and I shared.

Could I be a Domme and a submissive? It made no sense. Maybe I was what Elonso said. A switch.

Thomas brought forth a part of me I'd never wanted to acknowledge. The part that I thought made me too vulnerable.

Logic told me submission wasn't a sign of weakness. It was a position of power, where a person was strong enough to hand over their control to another. But my emotions warred with the logic.

Could I be a Domme in the world and still be Thomas's submissive?

I glanced at Thomas, who rode alongside me. His face looked calm. However, the hard press of his full lips said he was in deep thought. His six-five frame maneuvered the stallion with relaxed grace. He was the most versatile man I knew, security specialist, nightclub owner, and rancher/winemaker.

I rubbed the ring on my left hand with my thumb. I wanted the engagement to be real. I loved him so much. He and the boys were my happiness. Now I had to find a time to tell him what was in my heart.

I opened my mouth to say something, but at that moment, a crew of ranch hands, at least twenty, greeted us. They were corralling and loading the stallions and foals for auction.

We said our hellos and made our way to the stable. I moved to slide off Misu, but Thomas jumped down from his horse and grabbed me by the waist, slipping me down the front of his body. My nipples peaked on contact.

He held me a few inches above the ground, so we were eye level. "I meant what I said. I'm not going to let you run. I will come after you the second you think about it."

I rested my hands on top of his shoulder, peering into pools of golden brown. Apprehension and uncertainty gazed back at me. He gave off a self-assured and confident vibe, but inside he was as worried and unsure as I was. He wanted me but didn't know how to keep me.

"I'm not going to run," I said. "I'm trying, Thomas. I trust you. I really do. I want our relationship to work. I just have to get used to depending on someone other than myself. I'm going to make mistakes, just don't give up on me."

He lowered me to the ground, kissing my forehead.

I slid my hands around his waist and pressed my face into his chest. We stood like that for a few minutes until the sound of footsteps echoed behind us.

We walked hand in hand out of the stall and down the corridor. Thomas brought my fingers to his lips and kissed my knuckles. "I know you're scared, Carm, but you're not alone. I'm your family now."

"Thomas," a voice called from outside the stables.

"Thomas. Diego wants..." Sophia stopped talking and gaped at Thomas and me, then her eyes narrowed. "What's she doing in here?"

I opened my mouth to respond, when Thomas tugged me a little behind him as if shielding me from Sophia. This was his fight, even if I was the target. Until I came to the ranch, I'd never had anyone fight my battles, but now having someone step in to protect me meant the world to me.

"Why wouldn't she be? She's my fiancée."

"It can't be real. I thought it was only because of the boys." She shook her head with her hands against her temples. "But she isn't one of us. She doesn't belong here."

"This is her home as much as it's mine." Thomas sighed. "Sophia, *Lito* shouldn't have led you to believe anything would happen between us. We aren't right for each other."

"It's not true. We're..." She stopped midsentence, and then anger flashed across her face. She walked around to stand in front of me. "How could you? He isn't a submissive. You horrible woman. You turned him. There's a place in hell for someone like you."

What the hell was that about?

I looked over at Thomas and noticed the deep red welts on the wrist of the hand he was using to hold mine. He'd done that to himself while we'd made love on the plane.

"Sophia, tread carefully," Thomas warned, his face going cold. "You have no idea what you're talking about."

"No, I will not keep quiet." She jerked my hand from Thomas's. "You will not let her make you into something you're not. Diego's right. You don't belong here. You're poison."

She raised her hand to strike me, but Thomas blocked her slap, squeezing her wrist. "Don't ever try to lay a hand on her again. Do you hear me?" The cold anger in Thomas's tone told me he was past calm with Sophia. "If you want to remain a welcome guest here, you'd better get your act together."

She flinched, and tears spilled down her face. Her shoulders slumped, and she turned, running out of the stables.

We both remained still for a few moments, letting the scene that had just played out before us soak in. Thomas again protected me. I didn't have to say anything. I peeked at him and found him watching me.

"Has it sunk in how much you mean to me? I'm not going to let anyone hurt you. Not my family or Sophia, and sure as hell not Christof."

I winced inside. Thomas mentioning Christof's name reminded me of what I'd have to face once we returned to New York, but right now, I was safe, here with Thomas. He deserved to know how I felt.

My lips trembled, and I reached up, cupping his face. "Thomas, I l—"

"Mistress Carmen."

I pulled my hand back and turned toward Elonso as he rushed into the stables and abruptly stopped, taking in my private moment with Thomas.

"I'm so sorry to disturb you, but you have an urgent call from Ms. Erickson. I told her you were out riding, but she insisted she get in touch with you."

What could Jane want? Why didn't she call my cell? I

searched my jeans for my mobile and realized I'd never picked it up before leaving the bedroom.

Shit. Something important must have happened for Jane to call the ranch.

I glanced at Thomas.

"Go. Take care of business. We'll talk after your call with Arya and Milla." He drew me toward him and then whispered in my ear, "If it's about Christof, I want to know immediately."

I pulled back, saluted Thomas, and then grinned. "Yes, boss."

"Smart-ass," he responded, and turned toward a group of waiting ranch hands. I followed Elonso to the house.

CHAPTER TWENTY-SIX

After a brisk walk, I entered the house to hear happy squeals and laughter coming from the living room. The boys had taken to their tia Isa with excitement. My heart warmed.

Family.

My boys had family.

"Stop hogging the boys. Give me one."

My skin prickled. That was Diego. With gingerly steps, I tiptoed to peek into the room and saw the boys playing on the floor with Isabella and Diego.

"Come to *Lito*," Diego said to Leo, who grabbed his grandfather's beard and pulled hard. "You are a handful."

Simon, not wanting to be left out, crawled to Diego and climbed onto his legs.

The joy on Diego's face brought tears to my eyes.

He played with Simon's fingers and hugged Leo against him, kissing his chubby neck. "You boys are lucky. You have your papa's good looks and your mama's jewel eyes. What more can anyone ask for?"

At that moment, Diego looked up, and surprise flashed on his face. I inclined my head, and he did the same.

He'd accepted the boys.

We still had a lot to work through, but at least where it came to Leo and Simon, he was trying. Maybe one day he'd grow to like me.

I glanced at my watch. Shit. I needed to call Jane back fifteen minutes ago.

I rushed up the stairs to the bedroom. I grabbed my phone from the bedside table and dialed Jane's number.

Jane answered on the first ring. "Carmen, we have a big problem."

"Well, hello to you, too. What's going on?"

"Someone tried to break into your penthouse, and four of our satellite offices were burned down."

A chill went up my spine, and my hand shook.

"What? When did this happen? Was anyone hurt?"

"No, no one was hurt. It happened about two hours ago. The incidences occurred simultaneously. Lex said the arson at the buildings was to distract from the break-in at your apartment."

I didn't have anything but basic household items there. What would be the purpose of trying to enter my apartment in the headquarters of the company? They had to have known it wouldn't be easy to get up there.

"Did they get into the penthouse?"

"They only made it into your private elevator, but it

locked down when the fingerprint reader didn't recognize their fingerprints. The moment the elevator doors closed, the system shut down and alerted security."

Thank God that Arya and Thomas had installed extra protection measures last year. After all the run-ins with Christof, we couldn't be too secure.

An overwhelming urge to find Leo and Simon and run came over me. I clamped down the thought, taking deep breaths. I had to think of a plan, but first I needed all the details.

"Jane, I need you to make sure that all the staff for the satellite offices are taken care of and get Arya to call her friends at the FBI and INTERPOL."

"Carmen, you're taking this a lot calmer than I expected. I'm worried. Do you think we should shut down the head-quarters until we resolve this?"

"We can't afford to fall apart, Jane. You're stronger than you think. We can't let whoever did this win."

Christof was behind this, I had no doubt. No one knew I'd left town. As far as anyone was aware, I was in my pent-house recovering from the flu.

My stomach dropped. That meant the break-in was meant for me.

"Do we have any details on the robbers?"

"The men refused to give any information. But Lex told me security found three vials of sedatives, two with children's dosages and one for an adult. They were expecting you to be home."

I swallowed, trying to calm my body, but my mind kept racing.

There was no returning to New York for the boys. It wasn't safe.

The safest place for them is here, Carmen. There's more security on this ranch than Fort Knox.

"Does Thomas know?"

"Max and Lex were conferencing with him a few minutes ago."

"I guess that saves me from telling him," I muttered to myself.

"I tried to contact you first, but I couldn't reach you."

"It's not your fault."

It was mine for losing track of time while getting my brains fucked out.

At that moment, Thomas walked into our room. His gaze told me he knew everything.

"Jane, I have to go. Keep me posted on what the investigators say. Make sure you keep your security with you, no matter what."

"I learned my lesson once. I don't need another one. Make sure you follow your own advice."

"I will." I stared back at Thomas.

I hung up, and before I knew it, I was in Thomas's arms.

"Do you realize what could have happened if you'd stayed in New York?"

I buried my face in his shirt. "I'm scared. Christof needs me to access the funds and…" A shiver shook my body.

"He can use Leo and Simon to get you to cooperate. He knows you'll do anything for them."

The thought of anything happening to my babies

paralyzed me. I had to leave. I was the target, and keeping them near me made them one, too.

"Thomas." I stepped out of his hold. "I can't stay here anymore. I have to put distance between me and our sons."

"The hell you're leaving." He ran a frustrated hand through his hair. "You've lost your ever-loving mind if you think I'm going to let you take a step off this property."

"Thomas. Please try to understand. My being here is endangering everyone."

"And you leaving here only increases the possibility of our boys growing up without their mother."

I wanted to argue, but both of our phones beeped with a text from Arya.

Get on the line now. I just discovered something that is bad, really bad. And make sure it's a secure line.

I looked at Thomas, who was walking to the door.

"Let's go. We'll call her from my office."

I followed Thomas to a series of doors near our bedroom. He slid a panel to the side, pressed his thumb to another panel, and then leaned down for a retinal scan. The door opened with a loud click.

"Nice office." I shook my head as we stepped into a technology lab that could rival the one Arya had at her estate. "You're just as bad as Arya with all the gadgets."

There were rows of computer banks and terminals along one wall. The dark-gray-painted room gave off a bit of a spooky vibe with all the video and surveillance equipment positioned throughout.

"They come in handy."

I walked over to a computer with a series of programs running. Line after line of code filled the screen. As I read the script, I looked over at Thomas.

"This is the virus Arya planted on Christof's computer. How has he not detected you on his server?"

"You can read that?" The surprise on his face made me laugh. "I thought you didn't have an IT background."

Just because I hadn't gone into a profession with computers didn't mean I knew nothing about them. I was proficient enough that Arya had tapped me as tester during the trial phase of Arcane.

"Who do you think proofread the code Arya wrote for the MI6 project?"

"I assumed it was Mil. I know one of your master's is in computer science, but I thought your focus was architecture."

I scowled at him. "You assumed wrong. Architects use computers, too. Unlike Mila, I actually enjoy the programing side of things."

Thomas walked over to me, studying me.

"If I weren't already in love with you, I'd fall in love right now. My sexy Mistress is a secret computer geek."

"Funny. Now answer the question."

"Because this program is proprietary and illegal, and outside of our small circle, no one knows it exists. That's why I was so mad when I found out Arya attached it to the hacker's computer."

"Has it revealed anything?"

"Not the last time I checked. Arya is supposed to contact

me if she finds anything from the analytics she's running."

That wasn't what I wanted to hear, but I guessed with all the activity at my penthouse and facilities, it was better to take Christof news in smaller doses.

I moved to the conference screen and logged onto the conference server. "We should call Arya before she has a heart attack."

"One thing before we call her." Thomas cupped the back of my head. "I haven't forgotten about our conversation from a few moments ago. From this point on, I'm going to be with you every second of the day and night."

I frowned. "Thomas, despite what happens between us in private, I'm not a submissive. Don't for one minute think I'm going to let you walk all over me. I won't take security lightly, but I still have a business to run."

Before Thomas could argue, the conference screen began to ring. I answered the call and Milla came on screen with Lex, Arya, and Max in the background. She took a seat next to Lex and ran a weary hand over her face.

"Hey, Mil. What's the emergency?"

"Carm, we're in a major shit storm over here. Not only are we dealing with the media frenzy around the facility arsons, but word leaked that someone tried to break into your place. And then on top of that we had a security breach on MCD servers."

I pinched the bridge of my nose. That's what I got for thinking I'd get bad news in small doses. The media was something inevitable when a high-profile company had fires, but the security breach was my main concern.

"When did the breach occur? Jane never mentioned anything about it."

"We thought it best to kept it to ourselves. The fewer people who know, the better. Arya's software blocked all access and routed it to the fake server but…" She paused. "You aren't going to like what I'm about to say."

"Keep going."

"Whoever did this knew we'd intercept it. They left a trail in the form of an encrypted video file in the historical files for MCD. Arya's already contacted the security agencies. It's bad, Carm."

I glanced to the side as Thomas rolled two chairs in front of the screen. I took one and he the other.

Arya tinkered on her laptop, then looked up. "I'm putting the file on the screen."

Christof's face appeared. Thomas took my hand in his as we waited for the video to start.

"*Hello, krasivaya dama. I am sorry to disturb your time away from New York. You can't know how disappointed I was to learn you weren't available for the appointment I'd scheduled for you.*" A slight smile touched his lips. "*I'd never have guessed you for someone who runs when faced with adversity.*

"*I know Mrs. Dane and Mrs. Duncan are watching this with you. I was surprised to learn that all traces of Ms. Dane's financial impropriety over the past decade have been removed. As you can guess, this news has resulted in significant losses for my organization. We can just add that to the list of transgressions that require restitution. But remember, there is always a trail. Otherwise, you wouldn't have discovered the fund lost over ten years ago."*

What the hell was he talking about? I glanced at Milla, who cringed, and then at Arya, who wouldn't look in my direction and continued typing on her laptop.

"I wanted to let you know that your lovely faces are always in the back of my mind. I've viewed our interaction as a sort of sparring for the past few years, and now it is time to collect. In forty billion ways.

"Ms. Dane, I will contact you with instructions, and remember what I said when we met: do not mistake politeness for weakness. There are five children involved, after all. Do svidaniya, Ms. Dane."

The video ended, and all I could think about was that if I didn't get Christof the money, he'd come after Arya, Milla, and me through our children.

We had to protect our babies.

Thomas stood, walked to the back of the room, poured himself a shot of something, drank it deep, and returned. "What would the four of you say about bringing your families here to the ranch?"

Max looked over at the people in the room with him, and they all nodded. "We'll be there by nightfall."

CHAPTER TWENTY-SEVEN

Around ten in the evening, I made my way up to my bedroom. Arya, Max, Milla, and Lex had arrived by late afternoon, and from the moment they stepped foot in the door, we were making calls and preparing for whatever Christof had planned for us.

Arya had taken over Thomas's lab while Milla and I handled the daily ArMil and MCD tasks to make it seem as business as usual. With the auction preparations still in full swing, Lex and Max decided to help Thomas finish up so he wasn't distracted when we met with agents from various agencies who were coming to the ranch in the morning.

I closed the door to my room and walked straight toward the bathroom. A hot shower would help calm the uneasiness in my stomach. Something about this whole thing still didn't make sense to me. Deep down I was positive Christof was part of the embezzlement, but nothing in any of the financials or hidden accounts Milla and I scoured pointed to anyone with Russian ties. How was Christof able to hide any connection to my father?

I stripped and stepped under the scalding spray. The water soaked my body and washed away the grime from the day. Once my skin began to turn prunish, I quickly finished my shower and dried off. If Thomas wasn't back from the auction preparations before I went to bed, I'd call him and tell him to wake me as soon as he got home. I needed touch to calm this turmoil.

We'd come so far. I still feared what would happen in the future, but he'd shown me over and over what I meant to him. He'd stood up for me and protected me, as no one else had before. Most of all, he believed me when I'd told him about the money missing from the foundation and wanted to help me prove my innocence.

I had to let Thomas know that he was what I wanted, that I chose him.

I wrapped a towel around my head and another around my body and stepped into the bedroom.

"You took a long enough shower."

I came to an abrupt halt and glanced at the bed. Thomas sat on the end, wearing only his lounge pants. His hair was damp, and a few stray drops of water sprinkled his shoulders. A hoof-sized bruise marred the left side his beautiful corded abs, and the scent of his shampoo lingered in the air around him.

"I didn't know you were waiting for me," I said.

"Come here."

I narrowed my eyes at his command, but I moved toward him. I had so much to tell him, and all I could think about was jumping his delicious body.

"Please. I need you tonight."

The plea in his voice sent a shiver down my spine and kindled a throbbing between my legs.

I came to stand between his thighs and rested one hand on his bare shoulder as the other gripped my towel. He peered up at me and smiled, making my pulse jump.

Not saying a word, he slipped his arm around my waist and tugged me forward.

"Oh," I exclaimed, dropping the towel.

A second later, Thomas's lips covered a nipple. I threw my head back and arched against him. He bit and laved the straining bud, sending exquisite pleasure tingling throughout my body. A deep need for more ignited. He shifted to the other breast as his hand kneaded my ass.

He lifted me, and I found myself straddling his cotton-covered erection. He cupped my face as I gripped his shoulders, and he stared into my eyes.

What I saw in his made my heart contract. Love, worry, anger. We shared the same uncertainty. For the first time in my life, I had someone who was mine to lean on.

God, I love you.

His eyes seared into mine, and his hold on me tightened for a brief second, making me realize I'd said the words out loud.

"Tonight it's only us, no fighting for control. Just two people in love."

My lips trembled and I nodded my head. I could give him this. I could give myself this.

He sealed my answer with a kiss, teasing my lips at first, then devouring moments later. We savored each other's tastes as a low purr escaped from my throat. The tingle inside my core flared into a raging fire, making me rub my pelvis against his cock for relief. One of his hands slid down the cleft of my ass to my soaked pussy.

I was desperate for him. I needed to feel all of him.

"Please," I murmured against his lips.

Thomas shifted our positions by turning and pinning me beneath him on the bed. He gazed down at me with a wicked smile.

"I like tossing you around like my personal rag doll."

"No one's ever thought of me like that."

He growled. "And no one else ever will. You're mine. Say it."

"Yours," I said, threading my fingers through his hair and drawing him to me. "Only yours. You're all I want."

He bit my lower lip and then sucked it into his mouth. I lost track of anything but the feel of Thomas against my body. He slowly pulled back and then kissed down my neck, between my breasts, over my stomach. He settled between my spread knees and blew on my swollen labia. I bowed up from the cool sensation on my burning flesh.

"I love how your pussy glistens for me, hungry for my cock." He took a swipe down the center with his tongue and then blew again. "And I especially love your honey taste."

My skin prickled, craving more of his touch.

With slow licks, he began an unhurried feast of my pussy. He positioned my legs on top of his shoulders as my fingers dug into his scalp. My body shook as everything inside me tightened. I jerked upward, crying out.

"That's it, *mi cielito*. Let go."

"Thomas," I screamed as my body flooded with ecstasy. I arched my head back, squeezing my eyes and my pussy tight. I rode the crest of my orgasm until I couldn't focus on anything but the beautiful pleasure running through every part of my body.

He slid back up as the last of the tremors contracted inside me, and took my mouth again. My essence exploded on my tongue, mixed with the mint of his toothpaste.

He deserved some of the same pleasure he'd just given me. I tucked my feet under his thighs and flipped him onto his back, repositioning myself on top of him.

I leaned over and gave him the same wicked grin he'd given me. "My turn."

He lifted his arms and tucked them behind his head. "Who am I to argue?" He tilted his pelvis up, making his cotton-covered cock rub against my aching, soaked pussy. My core instinctively contracted, wanting more.

"Tsk-tsk. I'm not going to let you distract me with your magic cock," I jokingly admonished as I slid down Thomas's body. I cupped his rock-hard erection. "Besides, would you want to deter me from my mission?"

He shook his head and closed his eyes as I pulled out his cock and licked the throbbing vein running along the base of his beautiful pulsing shaft. I glided and squeezed my hand along his length, and then, when he wasn't expecting it, I engulfed his weeping head in my mouth.

"Oh *Dios*," he called, pushing up further into my mouth.

I grabbed the base, making sure I wouldn't gag. I hollowed my mouth as I bobbed up and down, enjoying his freshly showered scent and the salty-sweet taste of his pre-cum.

His fingers slipped into my hair as his hips jerked upward to meet the need I'd stirred in his body. I swallowed seconds before he reached the back of my throat, causing him to throw his head back at the tight squeeze of my mouth.

"Carm, stop. When I come, I want it to be in you."

I released him with a pop, sliding up his body. Before I reached the top, he flipped me onto my back once again and sealed our lips together. He consumed me like a man starved. I cradled Thomas's body against mine as our kiss went on.

Thomas pulled back with a sharp bite to my lower lip. He spread my legs further apart and lifted up to get a proper angle. As his cock probed my slick waiting sex, he asked, "Who do you belong to?"

I stared at him through a desire-clad haze. I wanted to laugh if my pussy wasn't screaming for him. No matter what he said, the Dom in him was always lying under the surface. I reached up to trace his jaw.

"You." I lifted my hips, trying to draw him to me, but he held still.

"Do you believe this is real? That what we share will last."

His gaze continued to hold mine, and I knew I had to tell him the truth. This was it. There was no turning back.

"It's real, Thomas. It will last. I...I want it all, a family, more children, marriage, everything."

"About time you caught up." He thrust deep, and I cried out at the invasion.

I wrapped my legs around him, tugging him close, bringing him deeper into my swollen, aching core. "More," I called. "Harder. Faster."

His control seemed to evaporate, and he started pummeling my pussy. I gripped his shoulders as my sex gripped his thick cock.

"Almost there, please," I begged.

Thomas's hand slid between our bodies, slipping into my folds and pinching my clit. "Come now, *mi cielito.*"

I called out his name as my orgasm washed over me. I couldn't think of anything but the glorious free fall Thomas had thrown me into. My fingers dug into his skin, and my back bowed. This was the best orgasm I'd ever experienced. I was with the man I loved. The one I planned to spend the rest of my life with.

Thomas continued to pound my pussy, not letting me come down.

"One more time."

I didn't think it was possible, but before I could respond, I was going over again, only this time, Thomas followed.

CHAPTER TWENTY-EIGHT

Around three in the morning, I gave up trying to sleep and settled down with a cup of tea in the palatial living room of the ranch house. I should have been exhausted from the number of times Thomas and I made love, but no matter how hard I tried, I was restless.

We'd held each other, never speaking of the worry that was plaguing both of us. Every time I'd opened my mouth, I lost my nerve to talk about what we were going to do about Christof. I was scared to ruin the intimacy of what we'd shared. The same seemed to be true for Thomas. In all the times we'd made love or played, it never felt as desperate as it had last night. As if it would be the last time we'd be together.

God, I hope that isn't true.

The only time Thomas mentioned anything about his worries was after he'd woken me to make love again.

"You will take care of yourself. I know you, Carmen. Don't take any unnecessary risks. Promise me?"

He'd held me on the cusp of orgasm until I agreed. A promise I wasn't sure I could keep.

I sipped my tea and thumbed my necklace. It was a cross, a replica of the one on the wall across from me. I'd gone to bed with only my engagement ring on and woke wearing the necklace. A smile touched my lips. Thomas must have slipped it on me while I slept.

He thought he was slick by placing a tracker on me.

I still felt like I should put some distance between the kids and me by leaving the ranch. Eventually, Christof was going to find out where we were. It didn't matter that Milla and Arya had changed planes and routes three times before taking a three-hour drive to get to the ranch.

I set my mug on the coffee table, tucked my feet under me, and reached for a blanket. After I got comfortable, I picked up my notepad. Christof had said something that didn't sit well with me. *There's always a paper trail.* Initially, I thought it had to do with how Arya had erased all traces of embezzlement from the foundation accounts and replaced the transactions with those from her personal foundation.

When I told her I was worried about someone linking her to the changes, she blew it off, telling me what she'd done was untraceable, and she was the current expert on this type of programming.

All of a sudden it hit me. Christof kept looking into the files from the time of the indictment because something in there led to him, and whoever hid his information hid the money.

I pulled out my phone. It was time to call in reinforcements, but before I could send my text, Arya came into the living room, carrying her computer and a bunch of other equipment.

"I'm glad I'm not the only one who can't sleep." Arya dropped a bag in my lap.

"What's this?"

"A secure laptop. Thomas has it linked to his encrypted network. I want you to go through the files I marked from your dad's time at the company. Something in there links Christof to this whole thing."

I gaped at her, turned over my notepad, and showed her the line I'd written on it. "I guess great minds think alike."

A few minutes later, as I finished signing into MCD's system, Milla came down with her laptop and sat next to me without saying a word.

"Let's get to work. I know you bitches are thinking about the same thing. I'm not letting that monster win."

I glanced at Arya over the top of my screen, and she shrugged. We worked for the next hour looking for traces of anything that linked Dad to Christof.

"Ari, the only files left are the ones containing Dad's e-mails, and the feds scoured them. This is hopeless." I ran a frustrated hand over my face.

"Look through them again; maybe they missed something since they didn't know him personally," Milla suggested.

"Mil, I didn't know the man who raised me. The man I knew died with my mother."

"Look anyway."

I sighed and opened the files with the thousands of e-mails Dad had written during the time leading to and after his indictment. Where was I supposed to start? I decided to go through the draft folder since it was the smallest.

I scanned through the subject lines and stopped at the one addressed to me and titled *Max and Carmen's party*. In all the years since Mom's death, he'd never planned a party for me. This was for our twenty-first birthday. The e-mail contained information on vendors and guests to invite to the party with their phone numbers. Everyone on the guest list were the people who'd turned their backs on me and Max and couldn't get far enough away from us after the embezzlement news became public.

"Come look at this. It's a party list for my twenty-first birthday. But we never had this party."

Milla scooted next to me, and Arya sat down on the other side.

"Holy shit, Carm. Those aren't phone numbers. Those are account numbers." Milla pulled the laptop from my hands. She scrolled to the bottom of the e-mail and my heart sunk.

There was a message to me.

Hey, butterfly,

If I don't get to it, make sure you send out the invites in time for the party. I have to go out of town for a few days and will be back in time for the party. Sorry, your old man tends to get carried away and allows work to overtake his life sometimes. I promise to make it up to you and Max. Be good and don't open your gift until I get back.

Love you,
Dad

Tears streamed down my face. This was two weeks before the news broke. Before my world turned upside down.

Why hadn't he sent this? All I ever wanted was a glimpse of the dad I'd lost. He'd written the letter in the exact way he'd talked to me when I was younger.

I might not have hated him so much if I'd gotten the e-mail. He'd loved me after all.

"He called me butterfly." I hiccupped. "He hadn't called me that since before Mom's funeral. He'd nicknamed me that when I was four and kept asking to wear my mom's butterfly pin."

"Carm, I know this is a lot of news to take in one sitting, but we need to look at what's actually in the e-mail." Milla put my laptop next to hers on the table. She pulled up the file containing all the hidden accounts.

"Holy shit," I exclaimed as I read over Milla's shoulder. "You're right. The numbers next to the names match part of the account numbers on the list."

I couldn't believe I was looking at a list of potential people involved in the scandal. Every name and "phone number" had an account with the same digits in it.

Dad was leaving clues. He wanted me to know who was part of the scheme.

I glanced up with tears clouding my eyes. "Do you think Dad was innocent? That he took the blame for others?"

Arya shook her head. "No, Carm. He was involved up to his eyeballs. I researched everything I could when we discovered the hidden accounts. He signed a confession. It was obvious others were involved, but all the evidence pointed to your dad. Why he didn't name them, we'll never know."

I wiped the wetness from my face with the back of my hand. I couldn't accept this. He could have made his life easier if he'd named people. He could have made our lives easier.

"There has to be a reason for what he did. He wouldn't have just ruined our family legacy. We have to keep digging." I closed the e-mail and searched the rest in the folder. "This one is to Max. It's dated a few days later and has the subject 'your hiding place.'"

I opened the e-mail, but the only thing in it was a picture of a house. I examined the image. Where had I seen this before?

"Let me see that." Arya took the computer to get a closer look. "That's the back of the Hamptons house before the renovations."

I scrunched my brows. "How would you know that?"

"I see that painting every day when I walk down the stairs of my house. It's Max's favorite picture. He says it reminds him of his childhood and all the secret passageways hidden inside the mansion."

"Oh my God, Dad was leaving a paper trail. Max was the only one who lived at the estate at the time. He'd come home for the summer after clerking in a state judge's office. I don't understand why Dad never sent the e-mails and they were buried under a hundred drafts of other e-mails, but I know he wanted us to find them."

I had to go back to Boston, to the estate. Something was behind that painting. My gut said it would answer every question I had about Dad.

"Carm. I think you need to hold on a minute. You could be jumping the gun."

I stood up and paced. "I'm not. I know it. Deep down I know it. I've spent so many years trying to understand why he would steal all that money when we had plenty of our own. I hated him for what he did to our family. I have to find out the truth."

"What if you find out you're wrong? That he is, in fact, the bad guy in all this?" Arya stepped in front of me, grasping my shoulders. "I'm worried about you. There's only so much a person can take, and I think you've reached your limit."

"Ari. This is about Max, too. Our children will always have this cloud over them. You saved me from adding to the same fate, and I can never thank you enough, but I have to do this. All of us deserve to know the truth. Whether I'm wrong or right, I need to end the questions."

"What about Thomas? He's not going to let you leave half-cocked on the off chance you find out anything about your dad. Especially with the video Christof sent."

I'd been so caught up in what happened with Dad that I forgot Christof needed me to access the accounts.

My heart hurt to leave, but I had to go back. I only hoped Thomas would understand why I was leaving. Now I had to get these girls to help me break out of my gilded ranch cage.

"Thomas knows that what happened with Dad has affected me my whole life. Now, which one of you is going to let me borrow your plane?"

The girls stared at me as if I'd lost my mind.

"Carm," Milla said. "Didn't you learn anything from my mistake last year? Did you forget we ended up hostages?"

Her words killed my fight to leave the ranch and took me back to the fear I'd felt for Milla and me and my unborn babies.

Little boys who I'm fighting to protect now.

"What do I do, Mil? I know the answers are there. If there's an off chance I can prove Dad was going to do right by us in the end, I have to do it. " I closed my eyes and inhaled deep. "I have to find out the truth. Please help me."

Milla and Arya released a collective sigh.

"This has to be a twenty-four-hour thing only." Arya pulled out her phone and began texting. "If I were you, I'd go change. Once everyone wakes up, you're not going to get a chance to leave."

Relief washed over me. My girls had my back.

"Ari," I said. "This place is locked down tight. No one gets on or off the property without security knowing about it. Hell, I can't even organize my own detail without Thomas knowing."

"I have my ways. I've called in a favor." Arya's phone beeped with a reply. After she read the message, she looked at me. "You have exactly twenty minutes before the helicopter arrives. Get moving."

* * *

My plane landed in Massachusetts a little before three in the afternoon, just shy of seven hours after leaving California. I would have arrived sooner, but after my dramatic helicopter escape, we landed at a private airfield and then drove three hours to San Diego. There I boarded a private flight chartered by Milla's cousin Ian.

The security detail Arya had arranged for me were former CIA and INTERPOL agents who provided personal protection for select clientele. They took their assignment so seriously that they confiscated my phone, saying it was a security risk and they would return it once we landed.

I glanced down at myself and laughed. They'd even made me change my clothes. What I wore looked like something Arya would pick for the days she locked herself in the lab. Baggy linen pants, hoodie, baseball cap, and sneakers made up the outfit. With my hair tucked into the hat and dark sunglasses, no one would know who I was.

"Ms. Dane?"

I glanced up at the flight attendant, who came into the lounge area of the plane.

"The captain has informed me that the ride Mrs. Dane arranged for you is waiting at the end of the tarmac. You'll be taken to a drop-off location, where another car will take you to your family's estate."

"Thank you, Maureen." I smiled at my flight attendant/ bodyguard/INTERPOL agent and then turned back to look out the window.

A lump formed in my stomach along with a large dose of nausea. I rubbed my hands together, when my fingers grazed over my engagement ring.

Thomas.

I was afraid to think about how he'd reacted when he saw the helicopter land and whisk me away.

With my phone with the agents, I couldn't call him and explain. God, I hoped Arya was able to calm him down. I'd call him when I got to the house.

Logic said I should have waited to talk with him and then go, but I knew Thomas wasn't going to budge. And I had to do this. I was willing to chance an encounter with Christof to find the answers that had haunted me for most of my adult life.

Maureen came into the lounge. "Ms. Dane, your security lead, T. J., has just sent word you will head straight to the estate. Remember you will go by your alias, Mrs. Thomas, from the moment you step off the jet until the moment we return you to California."

I nodded, and Maureen spoke into a communicator on her wrist.

I shook my head inside. I knew it was Arya's version of a sick joke to pick Thomas's name as my alias. I gazed out the window, watching a small propeller plane taking off.

"Mrs. Thomas, we're free to descend. Your lead is waiting for you and will take over from here."

Here we go. Time to get some answers. Well, at least I hoped I would.

"Thank you for all that you've done."

She inclined her head as she led me down the steps of the jet. I tugged my cap lower over my face, just in case anyone recognized me.

As I moved toward the waiting car, a new level of anxiety erupted inside me. Standing before me was Thomas. He stared at me as someone would watch a stranger. He scanned the area, said something into his wrist communicator, and then waited for me to approach.

You are in so much shit, Carmen.

He stretched out his hand, clasping mine in a shake. "Hello, Mrs. Thomas. I'm your security lead, T. J."

CHAPTER TWENTY-NINE

A shiver ran down my spine hearing him say my name. "Nice to meet you, T. J. Please call me Catarina."

Thomas's thumb slid over the ring he'd given me. He raised a brow and then released my hand to open the car door. "Please make yourself comfortable. We'll arrive at the estate in about ninety minutes."

"Thank you." I slid into the limousine, scooting to the other door. I closed my eyes and leaned back against the headrest.

This was bad.

Thomas was too cool.

Yes, he was in work mode, but I felt it under the surface. The moment we were alone, he was going to lose it. At least I'd have an hour-and-a-half respite before the confrontation.

The door closed, and within seconds, I found myself on my back, hands pinned above my head, and an angry Thomas over me.

"Do you know how pissed I am at you? Do you know the hell you've put me through over the past few hours? Do you have any idea what it felt like to see you get on that helicopter? If it were that important, I would have brought you here. Why do you have to fight me at every turn?"

I struggled against his hold, but the only thing that did was rub my body against his, causing my core to spasm.

Shit. I'm mad at Thomas for manhandling me; why the fuck am I aroused?

"I'm sorry," I said as I gazed into his burning eyes, filled with both anger and lust. "I can explain. Let me sit up."

"Your explanation can wait; right now I need you." He sealed my mouth with his. I remained stiff for a brief second, but the desire overpowered any restraint I tried to muster.

A moan escaped my lips as our tongues curled around each other. The insatiable craving I had for him roared full force to the surface. One of my hands slipped through his grasp and I threaded it into his hair.

Thomas groaned, then whispered against me, "I'm not going to let anything happen to you. I couldn't bear it. You should have come to me first."

"I know," I said between kisses. "No more talking. I want you inside me."

He broke the kiss, his lips swollen and breath coming in pants. His erection rubbed against my aching clit, sending a flood of arousal between my legs. He tugged me to sitting. He grabbed my baseball cap from my head and tossed it behind him, followed by my shoes, then came my hoodie, shirt, and jeans.

"Remind me never to let Arya dress you again. That outfit is hideous. She takes covert to a completely new level. At least you had this hidden underneath." His fingers trailed along the edge of my bra, dipping into the cups to glide along my nipples, causing them to stiffen to tight peaks.

It wasn't fair to be the only one naked. I leaned up to reciprocate, but he shook his head. "No, Carmen, you don't control this show." He pulled a scarf from his pocket and held out his hand. "You with me, *mi cielito*?

He's not your sub. You're his.

I nodded as I swallowed and then slid my palm over his. My pulse accelerated, drumming into my ears.

A slight smile touched his lips as he wrapped a loop around one wrist with the soft fabric. As he finished, he threaded the silk through the grab handle inside the car.

"Now give me the other."

Once he had me restrained, he leaned back to admire his handiwork.

"Now, Mrs. Thomas." He chuckled. "I do like the sound of that, but Mrs. Regala rolls off the tongue better."

I swallowed and licked my lips, and a slight pang of fear crept in. "Thomas…I…I've never done anything like this."

"I'm well aware of that," he crooned as he ran his fingers up one thigh, over my stomach, and down the other.

"When you touch me, it's like nothing I've ever felt before." I bit the inside of my mouth. Why had I admitted that?

"Are you willing to give yourself to me? To take what I give you?"

"Yes," I answered through a husky breath.

An image flashed behind my eyes, of me in the playroom, bound, helpless, arching into the pleasure and the pain of a cat-o'-nine-tails.

"What're you thinking? Your skin has taken on a beautiful flush." He grazed his five-o'clock shadow against my jaw, and without thought, I tilted my head, giving him access to my neck.

Dear God, how does he do it? How does he make me crave submission?

Because to him, you aren't the cold Domme everyone knows. With him, you can relinquish your control and know he'll cherish the gift you're giving him.

"I don't understand why it comes so easy, with you."

"It's simple. You belong to me. Whether you fight it or not, you can't change the fact it's true."

I closed my eyes for a brief moment, letting his statement sink in. He was right.

When I opened my lids, I stared into beautiful pools of gold. My breath quickened. I knew what Thomas planned. It's what I'd have done to my submissive.

"Are you going to punish me?"

He sat back, watching me, his face not giving away any of his thoughts.

"What would Mistress Carmen do?" He hummed the question, and then waited for my answer.

I remained quiet. Thomas wanted me to give him the consequences of shutting him out. He wanted me to accept my place in his life.

When I finally spoke, I barely recognized my voice. "She'd punish her submissive for holding back, for not trusting."

"Does Mistress want to decide her punishment, or should I?"

This wasn't a choice. I knew the correct answer. It was no longer my place to decide.

I shook my head, staring at him with weary eyes. "You pick."

"Good answer."

He opened a cabinet and selected a few items: clothespins, a flexible ruler, and a ball gag.

He turned back to me, lifting the gag, and asked, "Do you trust me?"

My breath came out in short pants as I eyed the object. I'd used the item on my subs in the past. By agreeing to this, I'd give up my voice and complete control. I'd be helpless, relying on Thomas to read my body and to know how much I could take.

"Yes."

He fisted my hair, drawing me to him and sealing our mouths in a bruising kiss.

As he pulled back, he lifted the ball. "Open."

I complied, biting down on the black latex ball. Thomas fastened the straps behind my head, making sure it wasn't too tight.

"I wish you could see how gorgeous you look. Make sure to breathe through your nose. I won't hurt you, baby." He ran the pad of his thumb across my stretched lips. "And if at any time you can't take what I'm doing, snap your fingers. I'll stop, no questions asked. Do you understand?"

I nodded my agreement. My mind fired, taking in everything around me, from the clean leather scent of the new limousine to the anticipation of the unknown prickling my skin.

"Now we begin."

He pushed my legs apart, and fully clothed, he settled between them. He reached behind him and brought forth two clothespins. He glided the ends over my collarbone, across my shoulder, and then between my breasts.

This light touch of the small pieces of wood puckered my nipples into buds, making them ache for and dread the pleasure-pain awaiting me.

"I love how those emerald eyes went from calm and observant to dilated and aroused."

He tugged the lace of my cups down, exposing my breasts to his gaze. Leaning down, he sucked one straining peak into his mouth, biting and laving. My back bowed as a deep throbbing ignited in my core, soaking through my underwear. I moaned and bit hard on the rubber.

He slowly brought the pin toward my breast and fastened the clip to the end. White-hot agony fogged my mind and then dulled to a gentle ache. He repeated the pleasurable torture on the other nipple.

By the time he took the ruler in hand, all I wanted was for him to fuck me. The weight of the clothespins and pulsing of my pussy were making me insane. I couldn't voice my desire. I had to wait until he was ready.

I moaned, trying to compel him with my eyes, but he shook his head.

"I know what you want. I'm not going to give it to you." He smacked the ruler in his hand. "It's time to see how long you can hold out on your orgasm."

No, he wouldn't. He planned to do to me what I'd done to Samuel.

"Let's see if you can handle your own type of ministration." Thomas smiled as he leaned down to kiss my forehead and then grew serious. "You know the rules. No coming until I give you permission."

The first two strikes landed across each aching nipple, and I cried out under the gag. I held my breath until the fire on my buds eased.

"Breathe, *mi amor*. Let the endorphins come."

The next five strikes seared over my stomach and thighs. If I could have spoken, I'd have asked for more, specifically on my swollen pussy.

I waited for the next series, but nothing came. I opened the eyes I hadn't realized I'd closed and gazed at him.

Thomas was trying to steady his own breathing. This scene affected him as much as it did me. He unbuttoned his shirt, pulling it off, followed by his shoes and pants.

"Are you strong enough to take more without coming?"

The challenge in his words cooled some of my hunger to go over.

"Because as soon as you are, I'm going to fuck you senseless."

Before I could respond, he began another set of smacks,

across my breasts, along my hips, and to the sides of my sopping silk-covered folds.

I wasn't going to last. The quickening in my pussy was too much to hold back. Goddammit. I wasn't a pain junkie, but all I wanted was that last strike to send me over.

Thomas's hand slid up my stomach and up to my breast. "Ready? Let's see who's stronger." He released the pins from each nipple in tandem with the slap of the plastic ruler across my labia. I screamed as my orgasm took over.

I couldn't control it anymore. I couldn't take any more. I thrashed my head back and forth. I needed him inside me now.

Immediately, he unfastened the gag, throwing it on the floor with my clothes.

Tears clouded my eyes from the overload of sensation. "Thomas, I need…"

He covered my lips with his finger. "No talking. Right now I want to fuck."

The telltale sound of my underwear ripping reached my ears. In the next second, Thomas's cock pushed into my throbbing pussy, slamming to the hilt.

We both groaned, and my head fell back against the door window. My arms remained taut against the grab handle, and my back arched. He pummeled into me, setting a relentless pace. One I couldn't control, even if I tried. He was laying his claim, and I was helpless to do anything but let him.

He slid his fingers up my throat, and with a slight squeeze, he brought me to the cusp of my orgasm. "Who's your Master?"

"You are," I breathed out.

"I can't hear you." He pulled out and slammed back in. One hand squeezed the tender flesh of my thighs, making my mind cloud with pleasure.

Why was he doing this? I had to come again. Damn him and his magic cock. I was about to lose my mind.

"Please, Thomas. Let me come," I begged.

"Not until you scream it."

"You are my Master. Will always be my Master," I shouted. "I have to come. Please let me come again."

"Come now, *mi amor.*"

Thomas's hand squeezed tighter around my throat, and he bit the skin on my shoulder. I detonated, pushing back into his thrust, contracting around his rock-hard girth. I called out his name as sensations of ecstasy cascaded throughout my body. I continued to ride the waves of bliss until Thomas called out his own release.

CHAPTER THIRTY

Thomas released me from my bindings, making sure I regained feeling in my arms, then gathered me against him. We were silent as the car continued its journey to the family estate.

"Carmen, this won't work if you can't trust me or lean on me. I shouldn't be the last one to find out what's going on in your life."

I inhaled, enjoying the comfort of his scent. "I'm sorry. I'm trying."

"I don't believe you." His gentle tone couldn't hide the anger under his words.

I lifted up. "I do trust you, Thomas."

He slid me onto the seat next to him and then leaned his arms against his knees as he raked his hand through his hair. "Bullshit."

I jumped but kept quiet.

"I've done everything you've asked of me. I've defended you, told my grandfather to fuck himself. I've put you and our boys before everyone, even allowing others to believe I'm your submissive. All I asked is for you to stop keeping me at a distance."

I couldn't defend myself; everything he said was true. "I'm sorry. There's nothing I can say to justify how I reacted. I should have waited to talk to you. My only excuse was that I had to find out the truth about Dad, and I was scared you wouldn't let me leave."

He turned to me. "When will you get it through your thick skull that I won't let you down? Yes, I would have argued against it, but you weren't a prisoner at the ranch. I would have come with you or sent someone to check out your theory. What more can I do to get you to depend on me?"

"Thomas." I touched his knee, but he jerked away from my touch. "I should have trusted what we have. Please forgive me. I'll make it up to you. I want us to be a family."

"How can I believe what you're saying when you're hell-bent on doing things on your own? If I meant anything, you would have woken me, not have my heart torn out thinking someone kidnapped you when the helicopter landed. Then I had to find out from Arya and Milla what was going on. What did you think would happen if you depended on me for once?"

"I'm not only doing this for me. I don't want our boys or Max's to suffer the way we did with the taint of embezzlement. There are answers behind that picture. I have to find them."

"You aren't the only one who's lived with that kind of stigma. What do you think happened when my aunt killed your father? The press, our community, even family turned their backs on us. I was the nephew of the woman who cheated on her husband and then murdered her lover, one of the richest men in the country."

A lump formed in my throat. I'd never viewed it like that. Thomas had dealt with the same type of shame. I covered my face with my hand as tears seeped down my wrists.

"I don't know what else to say, but I'm sorry. Give me another chance."

"We'll have to discuss the future after we get you back to the ranch." He gathered my clothes and tossed them to me. "Put these on. We're about to pull through the gates. We have exactly forty-five minutes to get in and out. Max and Arya are supposed to be on a vacations, and we don't want anything to look suspicious."

We quickly put on our clothes and waited for the door to open. Thomas stepped out first, making sure the area was secure, and then I followed.

The estate was quiet, with the bare minimum of staff around. As I walked up the steps, memories of my childhood hit me. From running down the hallways to sitting in the reception room and Natalie telling me of my mother's accident, to sitting on the front porch wishing for anyone to come visit me in the grand house.

I entered the two-hundred-year-old building and realized for the first time since Mom's death that it wasn't just a house but a home. There were toys in the foyer, flowers on every tall table, and the smell of cookies and baby powder in the air.

Arya and Max had turned the cold and museum-like residence into something warm and inviting. No, it was all Arya. Max lived here for years, and it never changed.

I glanced behind me to find Thomas watching me, not saying a word. He knew how I felt about the mansion.

"Arya's turned this place into the home it was before Mom died. It's not a lonely here anymore." I set my purse on the entryway table. "Better get this over with, so we can go back."

I moved to climb the stairs, but Thomas stopped me with a touch to my arm. "Let me make sure the team has the house secure." He scanned the room and whispered into the mic at his wrist.

After a few minutes, he nodded and guided me to the picture. The beautiful painting of the Hamptons house hung against the wall at the top of the stairs. It wasn't in a place of honor, where everyone would notice it. In fact it was in the middle of a series of landscapes.

Thomas lifted off the frame, and a crease formed between his brows. "There's nothing behind there."

He stepped back to let me see. It was a smooth, decoratively papered wall. I couldn't be wrong. There was no way I risked so much and came all the way here for nothing.

The wallpaper looked untouched with no sign anything was behind it, but I had to be sure. I ran my fingers back and forth over it. "This place has tons of hidden compartments." I felt around and found what I was looking for, a small divot under the wallpaper. "Arya's going to have to forgive me for doing this. She has a thing for antique wall paper."

"I'm sure she'll be fine."

I paused for a minute. "I thought you were angry with me. Why are you being so supportive when I know you'd rather I'd stayed on the ranch?"

"Because you're mine. No matter how angry I am with you, it won't change that. Like I said in the limo, I would have eventually come with you."

"Yeah, kicking and screaming," I muttered.

"What was that?"

"Nothing." I poked my finger into the dent and tore the paper to the side. "I knew there was something here."

A flat panel appeared without a handle or any obvious way to open it. I pressed all around until a door pushed open, revealing a safe. There was an electronic keypad with a thumbprint scanner.

"I'm not going to be able to open it, if the plate is programmed to Dad."

"Give it a try. Your bigger problem is figuring out the code."

"I know what it is. It's the code Dad used for everything. My parents' anniversary."

I pressed my finger against the scanner, and a screen appeared, asking for an eight-digit code. I typed in my parents' anniversary with two digits for date and month, and a four-digit year. Within seconds of entering the last number, the safe opened, revealing a deep sixteen-inch box crammed full of files and hard drives.

"Hold on. I want to take some pictures before we get anything out. Just as backup." Thomas pulled out his phone and snapped pictures of the safe. He took off his jacket. "Put everything on here."

One by one I took out stacks of files and seven book-sized hard drives. In the back of the safe was a taped envelope with *Max and Carmen* scrawled in Dad's handwriting.

I reached in and retrieved it, sitting down on the stairs.

My hands shook as I turned the envelope over and over in my hand. Did I really want to read what was inside?

One way or the other, this is going to give you closure.

I inhaled deep and tore the seal. I tilted the envelope and out came a letter, my mother's butterfly pin, and my great-grandfather's cufflinks.

"Oh God." I picked up the pin, ignoring everything else. "I thought he buried her with it."

Tears streamed down my face as I looked at Thomas. He reached over and thumbed the wetness from my cheeks. "Read the letter, baby. We don't have a lot of time."

I unfolded the letter, and a new wave of tears started. It was dated two days before his murder.

To Maxwell and Carmen,

If you're reading this, you know what I've done and used the clues I left to find the safe. The two of you were always so bright and clever beyond your years.

When this all started, it wasn't supposed to go this way. I'd made a few bad investments and hoped to recover. I was arrogant and thought to take the easy way, a way that wasn't how a gentleman conducts business. I joined a group of investors who laundered money they'd accumulated through various means. What I didn't realize at the time was that once I entered this assembly of men and women, there wasn't any way out.

When you read this, whether I'm sitting in jail or dead, I want you to know I was trying to make things right. If it weren't for my fear of what would happen to the both of you, I would have turned myself in long ago. They took your mother from me. I couldn't lose you, too.

The files in this box reveal every scheme I took part in as well as those I wasn't involved in but knew about.

On the hard drive, you will find everything you need to piece together the program I used to hide the funds from detection, and as with everything, you know the code to activate the software.

Do what I couldn't do and make this right with all the people I hurt.

Lastly, I hurt a woman I grew to love. She was young and desperate to leave a suffocating marriage. She didn't deserve what I did to her. I seduced her and took her money, but in the end, I was the one who fell in love. Not since your mother have I felt this way. Find her and give her back her inheritance; we have plenty of money.

You both are paying for my mistakes, and I under-

stand why you've cut ties with me. I can't imagine what either of you is going through. I can only hope one day you'll forgive me.

Dad

My hands shook as I lowered the letter. My brain felt overwhelmed by what I'd read. He was guilty like Arya said, but he wanted to make things right.

There was so much he never said to us. He had loved us. God, I'd hated him for so long, and it turned out he kept doing it to protect us. A hiccup escaped my lips, followed by a whimper. The next thing I knew, I was sobbing.

Thomas lifted me into his arms, rocking me until I had no more tears left.

"*Mi cielito*, we have to go. It isn't safe here, especially with what we've discovered. Go freshen up. I'll wait for you downstairs."

I nodded. "Okay."

Thomas helped me stand. He closed the safe, then returned the painting back to the wall. No one would know anything was out of the ordinary when looking at the landscape.

"Thomas, will you send Max a picture of the letter? He needs to see it."

"Consider it done. Go, we have to get these files to a safe location."

"Give me five minutes." I went up to the second-floor powder room to wash my face.

I had barely turned off the faucet when a knock came from the door.

"That was quick. I still have another two minutes," I said, glancing at my watch.

As I exited the bathroom, a hand grabbed me from behind as another closed over my nose, and everything went dark.

CHAPTER THIRTY-ONE

My stomach turned as a horrible scent invaded my senses. I tried to push the nausea down, but it intensified. I waved my hand, hoping the scent would disappear.

"She's waking, sir." A man spoke with a slight English accent.

"Good. Make sure she's unharmed."

I jolted up as I recognized the owner of that voice, but the headache throbbing to life had me lying back down.

"Not too fast, *myshka*."

I blinked, trying to clear the haze from my vision. "Christof," I whispered.

"At your service, Ms. Dane."

The last thing I remembered was going to the bathroom. "How did you...I don't understand. I was in my family home. Where's Thomas?"

My heart sunk. What if something happened to him?

Please God, don't let anything have happened to him.

"Slowly, *pchelka*. Drink this. It will allow the chloroform to exit your system faster."

"No, tell me what you did to Thomas." I tried to push the glass way, but Christof forced me to drink it.

"He is as you left him, waiting for you. We didn't want to call attention to ourselves, unlike your escape earlier today. When you decided to visit your family estate, the opportunity to acquire you presented itself and we seized it. Take a few more sips."

I followed his direction, and a few minutes later, both my mind and my stomach settled. As I tried to sit up, I realized I'd been lying on a bed in what appeared to be a brownstone.

Fuck. My predicament was getting worse by the second.

"Where am I?" I asked, but he didn't respond.

I blinked a few more times, and then slowly Christof came into focus. He sat on the bed next to me, his handsome face giving the impression of concern.

"Why am I here?"

His lips curved into a deceptively beautiful smile. "We both know the answer to that. Your fiancé wasn't going to let you out of his sight. Needless to say, I had to make sure you are available for an appointment I've scheduled."

He reached over, pushed my hair to the side, and ran a thumb across the bruise on the side of my face. He turned, looking at the man. "Mr. Ellsworth. When I said bring her to me unharmed, that meant I don't want a mark on her body."

"Sorry, sir. Ms. Dane woke during transport, and my men became a bit overenthusiastic."

I turned in the direction of the voice. In the corner of the room stood a tall, golden-skinned, impeccably dressed man. He wore a tailored suit, which I knew without a doubt was custom made for him.

Is it a rule or something that the bad guys have to look like they walked off the pages of a fashion magazine?

I shook the thought from my head and refocused on Christof.

His gaze went to my wrists, and I rubbed them without thought. "Was this done to Ms. Dane before or after you took her?"

"They were on her when we left the estate," Ellsworth answered.

"Interesting."

I didn't want him to linger on my relationship with Thomas. Christof was a known sadist who had a reputation of pushing limits beyond what was acceptable. "Why am I here?" I asked again. "If this is about Arcane, then you might give up now. I have no access to any aspect of it."

"Ms. Dane. Arcane isn't the program I need your help with."

Oh shit. He thinks I can access the software Dad used.

Okay, Carmen, pretend ignorance.

"Mr. Christof, I have no idea to what you're referring. I think you're wasting both our time."

Christof moved closer to me, and before I knew it, he had his hands clenched in my hair and my head arched back.

I gritted my teeth against the pain and glared at him. "Let me go."

"I have tried to be a gentleman, but it seems that method

doesn't work with you. Let me put it this way. Eric Dane hid the money he owed my father. It is my duty to collect. You are the key to activating the program he used to swindle us."

His hold tightened, making my eyes water.

"You're hurting me."

He released me, making me wince as the circulation returned to my scalp.

"Apologies. Abuse to women is not my style."

Telling him he was full of shit was on the tip of my tongue, but I held it back. He'd allowed Milla's torture at the hands of one of his men and then used images of her abduction to torment her. He may not get his hands dirty in the traditional sense, but he wouldn't think twice about hurting me to get what he wanted.

"Eric was a very smart man. So smart, he fooled me into allowing him complete access to the cloaking software. He hid what belonged to my family and then thought to use his access to the program as a bargaining chip. He should have known. I don't bargain."

"You were behind his indictment."

"Very good. It wasn't me directly but my family. It was a shame Eric's lover killed him before we were able to procure the passwords needed to reactivate the software."

I closed my eyes for a moment, this new information overloading my still-fuzzy brain. Christof wasn't the mastermind behind all the crimes he'd committed as everyone assumed. He was just the mouthpiece.

I tried to remember what I'd learned during the MI6 operation. All information we'd found said Christof's father and brothers, with the exception of Abram, were killed when he was a teenager. I never could understand how an orphan had the means and education to create the empire Christof had built. I recalled questioning the agents about this, and they blew it off as meeting the right people at the right time.

Now it all made sense. Christof was the front man for his family's activities.

"All these years, you terrorized Arya, Milla, and me, saying it was because of the MI6 project, and it turns out that had nothing to do with it the whole time."

Christof tilted my chin up. "Your involvement with the MI6 project was just a small inconvenience for our operations, but it gave the perfect excuse for my interest in the three of you."

I glared at him, trying to move my face out of his hold. "All the crap you put Arya and Milla through for Arcane was a ruse as well?"

"No, my interest was genuine. I planned to reprogram Arcane for my purposes. The auction for the government aspect of the application was an added bonus. Since Arcane is now out of the question, we are revisiting previous options."

"I still don't understand how I can help you."

"I believe you're the key to activating the software your father used to cloak the transactions he made on our behalf."

"I'm not the computer genius of the group. You've got the wrong girl."

Shit, I shouldn't have said that. If Christof went after Ari again, I'd never forgive myself.

"I know all about you, Ms. Dane. One of your master's

degrees is in computer science and you were integral in the MI6 project. Your specialty is code breaking. According to one of my sources, you were the clandestine tester for Arcane."

Only a handful of people knew about that. Fuck.

I scooted to the end of the bed and stood, making me almost eye level with Christof. I wasn't comfortable having him tower over me anymore. "What incentive do I have to help you?"

A disingenuous smile touched his face. "I know where your children are, Ms. Dane. Remember when I said you'd have to choose between your reputation and the safety of your family? With one phone call, I can have the children apprehended in the same way you made your escape from your fiancé's ranch."

Oh God, the helicopter tipped him off. I was such a moron. If I survived this, Thomas was never going to let me out of his sight. I couldn't blame him, either.

"I've spent a considerable amount of time and energy arranging access to your father's modified software. Now it's your turn to do your part. And don't think I haven't learned from your friend's tricks. This time I have Arya Rey Dane's European counterpart monitoring you. There'll be no corrupting my system again."

I cringed inside. That was exactly the thought that had flashed in my mind. I wasn't a pro like Arya, but I was proficient enough to create a few glitches here and there.

When Christof had kidnapped Arya, she'd installed a tainted version of the Arcane software. The moment she activated the program, Christof's whole system went down. It resulted in exposing all aspects of his operations, from arms deals and drugs to human trafficking.

I rubbed the back of my neck, trying to rub the tension in my muscle when my fingers connected with my necklace. My heartbeat accelerated.

The tracker. It had a GPS chip. Thomas had a way to locate me.

I had to find a way to stall Christof. But how? Hell, I didn't even know where we were. It could be in the middle of the desert for all I knew.

"What do you expect me to do? No matter what you believe, I can't reprogram the software. I don't have that level of skills. If your expert can't active it, I'm not going to be able to do it."

"Your task is simple. I need you to break Eric's passcode."

"And how am I supposed to do this?"

"I remembered a conversation I had with him years before your mother's death."

"You mean years before you killed her."

He shrugged his shoulders. "One does what they need, to ensure cooperation. Your father thought he could end our association. My father sent me to remind him that wasn't possible."

I grew up thinking it was a simple accident that killed Mom; now I wasn't sure how to feel knowing she was murdered to keep Dad in line.

They took your mother from me. I couldn't lose you, too.

Dad went through all the effort to protect us even after

he was under investigation. The software was his insurance policy nothing would happen to Max or me.

"Now back to the subject at hand. Eric Dane said his young daughter could memorize codes, numbers, and passwords without ever needing to write them down. I'm hoping your memory is as sharp today as it was in your youth."

All of a sudden, I understood what he wanted me to do. "You think something from my childhood is the code to unlock the software?"

"Yes, Ms. Dane, we are going to put your recall skills to good use. We begin in fifteen minutes." Christof turned and left the room.

I stood staring at the door for a few moments, and then noticed Mr. Ellsworth was still standing in the corner.

His gaze connected with mine as he spoke. "Would you like for me to step outside while you freshen up? Mr. Christof has provided a change of clothes, more suitable to your style."

I glanced at a pair of fitted leggings and a black embroidered tunic sitting on a chair near the bathroom. That definitely wasn't my style. I preferred jeans and a T-shirt. However, I wasn't going to argue; I'd worn the same clothes for God knew how long.

"Yes. Thank you."

He moved to leave, but paused. "I would suggest you get your head in the game. Mr. Christof's family does not practice the level of restraint Mr. Christof does. Do not waver when speaking to him. He discards anyone he deems weak."

Wait a second. Did he say family? Christof's father and

brothers were alive? Oh, shit, this was getting worse by the minute.

"Why are you giving me this advice?" I studied the bodyguard.

"Because I'd be remiss in my duties if I didn't prepare you." His voice changed, giving way to a slight American inflection. "Your safety is of the utmost importance to my employer."

Did his accent change?

I couldn't believe what I'd heard. I almost asked him about it, but he turned, leaving me inside the room.

Let's add that to the list of things that didn't make sense.

I swiftly washed my face and donned the clothes laid out for me. I opened the door and waited for Mr. Ellsworth to lead the way. He took me down a set of stairs and around a corner toward the front of the house. I took a quick peek outside and saw the ocean, but nothing distinguishing to give any clue to where I was.

As we approached a large reception room, I heard an intense argument in Russian.

"Wait here until you're called. It is better not to disturb them," Ellsworth said.

I paused outside the entryway. Dad had insisted I learn Russian as part of my education when I was younger, and now I understood why.

"Vladimir, you are useless. I asked you to follow simple directions. I've disposed of men for less."

"Do not blame me for your mistakes, Papa. You ordered the hit on his wife. It was Ivan and Serge who carried it out.

Because of you, he spent the next decade orchestrating his plan."

"You dare to blame me! Your carelessness has led to the mess we're in now." Papers smacked a table.

"It has been over ten years. How was anyone to know that Dane had copies of all the files? I searched their house from top to bottom years ago."

Could Thomas have used the files we'd taken from the safe? I knew he'd do what was necessary to help me.

"Bring her here. If she isn't useful, you'll suffer the consequences. I am tired of cleaning up after you and your brothers."

I inhaled deep and prepared to meet the Russian dragon.

CHAPTER THIRTY-TWO

Let's go." Mr. Ellsworth nudged my back to move into the room. "Remember what I said."

I didn't acknowledge his words, just entered the room. To my right stood two men, who from the family resemblance I could assume were Christof's brothers Ivan and Serge.

Dmitri Christof sat in the corner of the room. He had the identical features that made Christof so handsome, except his had a more distinguished edge brought on by age. He stood as I approached.

His gaze bored into mine with a predatory gleam. This man did not have the polish Christof used to cover his ruthlessness. Dimitri remained quiet, staring at me.

Ellsworth said not to let him frighten me.

Here goes.

I hadn't spent years as a Domme to be intimated by just anybody. Until Thomas, there hadn't been a man alive who could make me submit to him.

"Tell me why I shouldn't end you for what you did to Abram."

My eyes held his, not flinching at the depth of his scrutiny. If Thomas didn't find me, I'd end up dead anyway. I'd never see Leo or Simon again.

No, I couldn't think like that. I had to do whatever was necessary to make it back to my babies. Even if it meant helping these bastards embezzle the funds Dad had taken from them.

"Because you need me. I'm the only one between you and forty billion dollars," I answered in the coolest voice I could muster.

"A confident woman." A smile touched his lips. "I like that. Now deliver what my son has promised. Don't fail me, Ms. Dane. As I told my son, there are severe consequences for those who disappoint me."

Christof stepped between us before I said something in response. "Come." He led me to a table covered in various types of computers.

As I walked around the couch, I noticed the front page of a national newspaper.

The headline read:

THIRTY-TWO ARRESTED AS
CO-CONSPIRATORS IN THE DANE
EMBEZZLEMENT SCANDAL

I came to an abrupt stop, and for the first time since I entered the room, my hands shook.

"Now you understand the urgency behind what we require of you," Christof said as he maneuvered me to the table.

A woman stood upon my approach.

"Ms. Billings is here to monitor your actions while logged onto the server."

I glanced at her for a second as I sat down and then did a double take. I knew her from somewhere. I thought back to anywhere I'd interacted with a British IT expert, and then I remembered. She was one of the MI6 agents I'd worked with during graduate school.

A brief moment of hope sparked to life, and then it disappeared. If she was here, then either she was a plant, or she worked for Christof. There was no point in getting ahead of myself.

She pretended she hadn't seen my reaction and stretched out her hand for me to shake it. "I'm Veronica. I'll log you in and then once I confirm we're on a secure network, you can begin."

"You're the one who hacked my computer."

Veronica shrugged in response as she connected to various networks all over the world, routing and rerouting until she was comfortable with the level of encryption and traceability of the network.

"Now we can begin, Ms. Dane. I've tried all combinations of you, your children, and your brother's personal information without any luck, so you can leave those out of the possible number-letter combinations." Veronica repositioned the screen toward me.

As I adjusted the laptop, I noticed the screen flicker, and a small window appeared and then disappeared. Instantly, I knew Veronica had connected the laptop to something outside of Christof's server.

My heartbeat accelerated. I wasn't alone. She still worked for MI6.

I placed my fingers over the keyboard.

"One more thing. If you enter the wrong password five times, the system will lock down. It will take at least a few hours for it to come back up."

"Ms. Dane, I suggest you don't make too many mistakes," Dimitri said from behind me.

I released a deep breath. "No pressure whatsoever."

I had to make sure I made mistakes on the first three, or they'd grow suspicious. I typed in two combinations I knew would fail, then peeked at Veronica, who seemed to be taking notes. She gave me no sign as to what to do. I looked around, and all focus in the room was on me.

Then, out of the corner of my eye, I noticed on Veronica's pad the words *sign in* underlined three times.

Here goes, I was about to either help out the authorities or knowingly become an embezzler. I keyed in my parents' anniversary and pressed enter.

I held my breath, and a red screen appeared that read *one attempt left*.

"Oh dear God, it has to be it." I couldn't hide the quiver from my voice.

What was I going to do? Every bit of confidence I had in knowing the password disappeared. I'd wasted three chances on the careless assumption I knew all of Dad's passwords. I ran a hand over my head and rocked. The next thing I knew, Christof had my head pulled back and a gun pointed against my temple.

"Ms. Dane, you have wasted four chances. We don't have the time to wait for a second go at this. Do I make myself clear?"

"Y-yes."

He released me, and I fell forward, catching myself with my hands against the edge of the table.

I closed my eyes and thought back to my childhood, what words it could be. I disregarded all nursery rhymes and household passcodes. Those were too obvious.

Dad had to have left some hint somewhere. If the best hackers in the world couldn't figure it out, how was I going to do it? It has to be something straightforward, something so simple no one would expect it as a password. All of the sudden, it came to me.

"I know what it is." The clue was in the safe the whole time.

I carefully typed in *BUTTERFLY CUFFLINKS* and then hit enter.

Immediately the system activated, and all the air left my body.

I sagged back against the couch, closing my eyes. Immediately, buzz sounds surrounded me and glass flew everywhere.

I couldn't understand what was happening. Veronica looked as surprised as I did, but it didn't last long and she threw me to the floor, covering me with her body.

"Keep your head down. This isn't part of my operation. I don't know who the fuck authorized this. Go now."

I crawled to the hallway, crouching behind a half wall near the stairs. Shots continued to ring out around me, then all of a sudden they went quiet.

Tears clouded my vision as the true fear of never seeing Thomas or my boys hit me. I'd done all this and now was going to die in this house.

"There you are, Ms. Dane. I was looking for you." Christof towered over me. Blood covered his face, and what looked like a bullet wound bloodied his shoulder.

He hauled me toward him. "Are you part of this?"

I shook my head. "I…I don't know what happened. I did what you said. You're the one who brought me here."

"If you deceived me, I will kill you, but before I do that I will make sure you suffer more than you ever knew you could handle," he gritted out. He looked behind him at Ivan and Serge, who lay dead on the floor. "They thought to kill me would win them favor with Papa. They should have known he'd never pick the children of his whore over the one from his wife."

Ellsworth came up behind him, holding Dimitri's limp body. "Sir, we have to leave now."

"My father?"

"Gone, sir. I didn't want to leave him here."

Christof's face dropped, and then he nodded. He pushed me toward the back of the house but came to an abrupt halt.

Thomas stood before us, with a gun pointed at Christof's head. "Go ahead. Give me another reason to kill you."

"We are at an impasse, Mr. Regala. You want Ms. Dane, who I don't plan to release, and I want to leave, which you don't want to accommodate."

"You have five seconds before I put a bullet in your head." Thomas cocked his revolver.

At the same time, two identical clicks echoed behind me. "It looks like you're outnumbered, Mr. Regala."

"I wouldn't be so sure," Ellsworth said as he pressed the barrel of his pistol against Christof's temple and shoved me to the side.

Surprise flashed across his face two seconds before Ellsworth knocked him out with a blow to the back of the head.

I looked back and forth between all of them. I couldn't believe what had just happened. I had to have imagined this.

"Thomas," I gasped, trying to brace myself against the kitchen table, but I lost my balance.

Thomas caught me before I hit the floor. "Easy, baby." He cradled me against his chest. "We aren't leaving the ranch for at least a year after we get back home. You're going to be the death of me."

I curled into his hold. "I knew you'd find me."

He kissed the top of my head and turned to Ellsworth. "I don't know how I'm ever going to repay you."

"You've saved me enough times. We'll call it even."

Ellsworth leaned down, made sure Christof was still breathing, and then clasped hands with Thomas. "It good to see you again, man." His British accent had turned into full-blown Southern country boy. "It's time I took out the trash. The cleanup team will be here in ten."

Thomas nodded to him and carried me to a waiting van. Before the door closed, he buried his face in my hair. "Don't ever put me through that again."

"I promise. No more crazy adventures." I closed my eyes and soaked into the heat of his body. "I'll make it up to you. Tell me what you want, and I'll do it."

He took my hand and rubbed the engagement ring he'd given me. "You can marry me."

I looked up. "I thought you said the engagement was real."

"You never said yes."

"Ask me."

His eyes lit up. "Will you marry me, *mi cielito*?"

"Yes." I slid my fingers into his hair and drew him toward me. "I'll do anything you ask of me, Master."

EPILOGUE

Who's in charge?" I asked while running my nails down his shoulders and arms.

His skin prickled. "You are, Mistress."

"Do you want me to continue?" I pressed my fingers against the base of his spine.

"Yes, Mistress." He groaned and then moaned, pushing his restrained body back into my caress.

"Naughty, naughty. I said no movement."

Stepping away, I strolled to a table positioned at the far end of the room and glanced over my shoulder.

My lover clenched his jaw and kept his gaze down. His muscles bulged from the shackles holding his arms above his head.

"I'm sorry, Mistress."

I smiled at his apology. This man submitted to no one, but he kneeled before me, offering me everything for a moment of my attention.

I turned back to the table, flipped my black hair from my shoulder, and then selected a leather-braided crop from my favorite selection of instruments. Pivoting, I returned to my slave. Sweat trickled down his muscular shoulders, honed from work in the field and not the gym. He nuzzled the inside of my thigh, and it took all of my strength to hold back my own desire to moan.

His cheek twitched as I shifted away and around him. He smelled my arousal.

"I'm here to relieve your discomfort, Mistress."

I snapped the crop against his back, making him flinch. "Not a sound or you will wake the boys," I ordered.

He didn't respond so I flicked the crop again, but this time over his beautiful, firm ass. His wrists tugged against the manacles attached to the ceiling, and a growl escaped his lips.

I dropped the rod and crouched in front of him. I reached out, gliding my hand along his leather-covered thighs and stopped once I reached his straining erection. I cupped his cock, running my palm up and down, squeezing with each stroke.

The feel of him under my fingers sent a prickle down my spine. I expelled a shallow breath and licked my lips.

All of a sudden I realized he was watching me.

"Did I give you permission to look at me?"

"My Mistress craves her release?"

In response, I pinched his nipples, and his hazel eyes immediately dilated. I cupped his face, kissing him with all the desire the past hour had brought to a peak. Our tongues dueled, but I pulled away. I had to regain control of myself. A Mistress remained in charge at all times, sacrificing her pleasure for her submissive's.

I stood up and moved back to the table. I closed my eyes and bit my lip.

Get it together, Carmen.

I wasn't sure if I could hold off much longer. Wetness pooled between my legs, dampening the crotch of my bodysuit. I steadied my breath and then jumped as hands clamped around my wrists, pulling me back against a firm chest.

"Now it's time for the Mistress to become the slave."

My heartbeat accelerated, and excitement coursed thought me. "How did you get free?" I peeked at the floor behind me and found the shackles open and on the floor.

"You're no longer in charge, Carmen," his raspy voice murmured in my ear. "You always smell wonderful, *mi amor.* Like gardenias."

He slid his palm down my stomach to my fabric-covered crotch and rubbed, starting a steady rhythm.

My head fell back, and I moaned aloud.

"Time for the orgasm you've denied both of us for the past two hours."

His pace increased.

"Please," I cried out as the first wave shot into my aching pussy.

My mind clouded.

"The boys," I reminded him.

"They won't hear anything. They sleep like their mama."

He tugged my arms a little harder and continued his torturous onslaught. "Now come for me, *mi cielito*."

Tear prickled my eyes as I crashed over. "You…you're my world, too."

"More. I want more."

"I…oh God…"

"Carm."

Huh?

"*Mi amor*, wake up."

What?

I glanced around me and realized I was clutching the armrest of my beach chair. I squinted my eyes against the sun as Thomas came into focus.

"Sorry, I must have fallen asleep."

A smile touched his beautiful face, and he leaned down, caging me against the lounger and grazing his stubble against the side of my face.

"I know what you were dreaming of," he whispered into my ear while running a finger down the curve of my throat and between the V of my cover up.

I turned my lips toward his, grazing his mouth with a quick kiss.

"Hey, none of that, there are kids present." Arya laughed from behind me.

"Yeah, keep the PDA to a minimum. My innocent eyes can't take it."

I turned and glared at Laurel and Hardy. In return, Milla stuck her tongue out at me while rubbing her very pregnant belly.

I shook my head at my comedian best friends and then turned back to Thomas. "Whose idea was it to take a joint vacation with these two?"

Thomas kissed the top of my forehead and answered. "Yours."

"Next time talk me out of it," I grumbled.

Max walked up with two dripping toddlers, setting them on the chair next to me. "Grab one before they get sand everywhere."

I slipped out from under Thomas's arms, capturing a wiggly Ashur before he made a beeline for the water. I quickly wiped him and handed him a sand shovel. "Go play with Leo and Simon."

He ran off and began flipping little grains of sand in the air.

"That boy is a handful," Lex said as he settled a sleeping Bri against his chest. "This one on the other hand is a perfect angel, unlike her mama."

"Hey, I heard that." Milla threw a towel at Lex.

"Just you wait," Max said, pointing at Milla. "That one cooking in there will give you more hell than all our four boys put together."

"That's just mean, putting a curse on your future nephew."

"That's not fair, Carm. You never let me have any fun. I think I'm going to go spoil your boys and hop them up on candy so they keep you up all night." Max left in a pretend huff, grabbing Leo and Simon, who squealed in laughter.

Dream forgotten, I couldn't help but laugh at the madness of our conversations and life.

Exactly a year ago, Thomas rescued me from Christof's crazy house in Maine. So much had happened since then, including a brand-new embezzlement scandal. Thankfully, the Dane name was nowhere associated with it.

The thirty-two who were arrested after Thomas handed over the files I discovered in Dad's safe were not only found guilty of conspiring with Dad but also were involved in a new scheme Christof and his family had initiated.

Christof was sentenced to life without parole at a maximum-security prison in the mountains of South Dakota. A prison monitored by a security system Arya designed and donated.

"This is great, isn't it?" Milla slipped her arm around my waist.

Arya came around to my other side, resting her head on my shoulder. "We got our happily ever after."

"Yes, we did."

Did you miss Arya and Max's love story? Then see the next page for an excerpt from *Rule Breaker*!

CHAPTER ONE

Look at me, baby. I want to watch you as you come."

Opening my eyes, I stared into unending depths of green. The love gazing back at me brought tears to my eyes.

He used his thumbs to wipe away the drops and leaned down to kiss me. "You are mine, Arya, never forget that."

My body clenched around him as he slid into me. He moved with agonizing slowness, denying me the orgasm he'd been building up for hours. I lifted my hips, trying to urge him to move a little bit faster. Frustrated, I jerked on my arm restraints and struggled to free myself.

"Please," I begged, "I need to touch you. Release my wrists." The force of his thrusts increased and my body responded with tiny spasms.

Oh yes, right there.

"Not yet, not until your core ripples around me, squeezing every drop from me."

His hand moved between our bodies, toward my swollen, aching nub. He rubbed back and forth as his pace quickened.

That's it, oh God, almost there.

The burning need inside my body increased to an unbearable level. My hips rose up and down to match every thrust. The convulsions started.

Yes, at last.

"Arya, can you hear me?"

What?

"Arya, wake up."

Where am I?

Sweat ran down my body as my heart pounded out of control, and my body ached for an orgasm that seemed unattainable. I jerked my arms, expecting restraints, but found nothing. I relaxed back onto the bed.

Only a dream.

"Are you listening? Wake up! They're talking about us on the news." Milla's excited voice blared into my bedroom.

I rolled over, taking a quick peek at the clock. Four thirty a.m. Wasn't it against the girl code to wake someone up too early? Why couldn't Milla let me sleep a little bit longer?

"Did you hear me? We're big news."

"Go away, I don't care," I moaned. "I have ninety more minutes until the alarm goes off. Why are you in my penthouse anyway? Don't you live across the hall?" Maybe if Milla left, I could fall back asleep and finish my orgasm.

"Scoot over and listen to the report. There should be more info right after the commercials."

Nix the extra sleep idea.

"Fine," I grumbled and shifted over, making room for my oh-so-bossy and chipper best friend.

She grabbed the remote from the bedside table and turned on the broadcast. I squinted as the blaring light from the giant TV lit up the room. Why did I put a sixty-inch plasma in my bedroom? The damn thing was too bright. As my eyes adjusted, I took in Milla's appearance. She still wore the plum Valentino suit from last night, but her hair was wet and slicked back into a bun.

"Did you even sleep? When I left, you and Carmen were busy downing shots with the rest of the team. Don't tell me you just got home."

Please have a hangover.

"Okay, I won't. After the party, I went back to Carmen's and spent the night working out last-minute details of the merger. I came home as soon as the statement went out."

Totally unfair. Even during graduate school at MIT, she drank like a sailor and still woke up at the crack of dawn for classes.

"I'm so happy that the three of us are back together. I missed her."

"You and me both. Having our resident dominant around will keep us in line."

"Isn't that the truth?"

We had been known as the three musketeers while at MIT, but I'd pushed her away when my life had fallen apart.

She was living in New York now, and returned to Boston

only for the merger. I sighed. I should have reestablished the friendship we'd lost five years ago. She deserved better than my distancing myself from her because of her brother.

Wait. Did Milla say something about a statement?

"What statement?" I pinned Milla with a confused glare.

"Shush, the commercial's over. Listen."

"Breaking business news.

"It's official. MDC won the bidding war for the security technology think tank ArMil Innovations. An undisclosed sum was negotiated, with all parties remaining tight-lipped about exact figures, but analysts estimate it to be in the area of $150 billion. Our sources say negotiations were settled late last night with a celebration following.

"Many of you may recall the buzz surrounding Arya Rey when she hacked MI6's security database after a direct challenge from the chief of the Secret Intelligence Service at the Def Con Conference in Las Vegas. The brainchild she created as a result of the competition, ArMil Innovations, became the highest-valued security technology development company in the world.

"Thirty minutes ago, a joint statement was released by Milla Castra, cofounder of ArMil Innovations, and Carmen Dane, technology CEO of MDC International, through MDC representative Grant Mills.

"'We are proud to announce the joining of ArMil Innovations with MDC International. Together, our companies will harness our unique talents to develop new, innovative, and affordable technologies for all your security needs.'"

I turned my attention back to Milla. "You have been a

busy girl this morning. What happened to taking a few days off to unwind and bask in our success? I think this decision requires a poll. I vote for relax. I'm going back to bed." I laid back down and pulled the covers over my head. "Make sure you switch off the television, and close the door when you leave."

Milla ignored my less than subtle hint. "Before we take our well-earned vacation, we need to meet with the new team Carmen assembled." She paused. "Ari, are you sure you're going to be okay with this? It isn't too late to delay the merger, at least until you've had a little more time to adjust. I'm worried about you."

Milla's now somber voice caught me by surprise. I tugged the covers off my head and peered at her. We might not share any blood, but she loved me, and without question, she would fight any of my demons for me.

"I'll be fine, Mil. It's been five years. I survived the darkest days of my life and came out on top. I'm not twenty-three anymore. I can handle it. Besides, he's in charge of the whole organization. He won't bother with us." If only I believed the BS flowing from my mouth.

Ever since Lex Duncan, my other best friend and adviser, suggested selling the business aspect of our company to allow me more time to focus on research, I worried about running into Maxwell Aaron Dane. With our high valuation, Milla, as CFO, only gave the top investment firms the opportunity to bid. But I never expected the highest offer to come from MDC, the conglomerate owned by Carmen and Max's family.

Rejecting any consideration of the proposition due to personal issues with MDC's CEO was not only selfish but also insane. In the end, Milla and I chose the most advantageous course for the future of the company, including the retention of all developmental controls for upcoming and current projects. Now, even if I wished to back out, it was too late. Moreover, I'd spent too much time rebuilding myself to fall again. One day, if Max and I happened to run into each other, I would wish him well and move on.

Great. Now I was lying to myself, too.

"Maybe you're right," Milla agreed. "Carmen is the head of all technology development for MDC. She's not going to let her big brother take over any aspect of the companies she oversees without a fight. Besides, she's aware of your history with Max. She's the one who hid you from him when you left South Africa. She won't let him interfere."

Why did Milla's words seem like a bad omen to me?

I stretched and glanced at the clock. Well, now that going back to bed was off the menu, better hit the treadmill. "Want to join me in the gym? It's too cold for a run outside." I pushed off the mattress and headed for my bathroom.

"No." Milla yawned. "I think I'll catch an hour or so of sleep before we have to meet at corporate. Lex wants us to arrive thirty minutes early in case there are a few surprises. He's always trying to protect his adopted baby sister."

I leaned my head out of the bathroom. "He loves me, but you, on the other hand…" I hummed aloud. "You could put us all out of our misery and jump him already. That way all the sexual tension between you two will end."

Lex and Milla had had an ongoing thing for each other since Milla was in high school, but neither possessed the balls to act upon their feelings. I loved teasing them about it.

"On that note, I'm out of here. Sleep is calling my name."

Milla jumped off the bed and left me to my morning routine before I headed to the gym.

* * *

I started my run around five a.m., giving me a few hours before my nine o'clock meeting at corporate. I gazed out toward the beautiful view of Boston's midtown, while Pink blared her "girl power" songs in the background.

I am one lucky lady.

My success seemed surreal at times. Not many twenty-eight-year-olds get to say they went for a run in the home gym of their penthouse on the fifty-fifth floor of Boston's Millennium Tower. I had gone from a physically and emotionally exhausted and financially strained PhD graduate to one of the wealthiest entrepreneurs in the world in less than five years.

"See world, women are tech wizards, too." I fist-pumped into the empty room and caught myself before I fell off the treadmill.

I gave all the credit to Lex and Milla. They supported me when I needed them the most and encouraged me to make my vision a reality. I guessed I owed Max, too. If he hadn't broken me, I wouldn't have achieved any of the things I had accomplished to date.

A few years ago, I would have given up my whole life to please him, putting aside my dreams to fit into his world. I handed him complete control only for him throw it back in my face.

Never again.

I had buried that side of myself. No man would gain that level of trust again.

I tapped the button to run faster. I wanted to sort through my thoughts before the meeting. If only exercise made life easier.

Milla insisted I needed to get laid. Maybe she was right, but I wasn't sure if my equipment worked without BOB, my battery-operated boyfriend. My dreams highlighted my nonexistent sex life, and almost orgasming didn't count.

Oh hell, there I went again, back to thinking about Max. Well, I couldn't help it, since he was the sole experience I'd ever had.

Over the years, I went out with a few guys, but none of them gave me what I wanted or needed.

Dominance.

My lack of interest wasn't their fault; I picked men I could dominate, not the other way around. They were the polar opposite of Max. Once or twice, I contemplated starting a sexual relationship, but I'd ended things before we reached first base. One kiss and I lost interest.

"Arya, get off the treadmill. I've been calling you for the past fifteen minutes," Milla shouted from the doorway of the gym.

How long had I been running? I glimpsed at the wall

clock. Seven fifteen a.m. Shit. I jumped off the machine and lowered the stereo. "My bad. I left my phone on the bench and with the music so loud I couldn't hear it."

"Don't worry about it. Get moving. There isn't much time."

Man, she was already dressed. Did she even go to sleep?

"What's going on? We aren't due in the office until later in the morning."

"Lex called. He had to reschedule the meeting to eight o'clock. The MDC teams know we're all leaving town tonight, and they want to meet earlier in case extra time is needed to discuss the final logistics."

"There is no way I'll reach the office by eight o'clock. I haven't even showered yet. With the weather and traffic, I won't make it until at least eight thirty. You head over there and let Lex know I'm running late."

"I don't think so. Remember, he likes to shoot the messenger. I'm not in the mood to deal with his Irish temper."

This thing with those two was now getting on my nerves.

"Fine. Tell him that I'm stuck on a call or something. I'll get there as soon as possible. If he gives you shit, remind him that not everyone has a corporate copter on standby to pick them up for work."

"So speaks the girl with a brand new Maybach and a private jet."

I shot Milla the bird, snagged a water from the cooler, and chugged.

"Mmm," I hummed, as the chilled water slid down my throat and cooled my overheated body from the inside.

"So sad, after making a billion-dollar deal, girl gets lazy and starts running late," Milla remarked with a smirk. "Wait, you're always running late."

I rolled my eyes, rushed past her, and charged straight for my shower. I hoped I'd be only a few minutes late.

About the Author

Sienna Snow's love of reading started at a very young age with *Beezus and Ramona*. By the time she entered high school, a girlfriend had introduced her to Bertrice Small and Jude Deveraux, and an avid romance reader was born.

She writes sexy romance, some with a lot of heat and spice, and others with a bit of fantasy. Her characters represent strong women of different cultures and backgrounds who seek love through unique circumstances.

When she is not writing, traveling, or reading, she spends her time with her husband and two children.

You can learn more at:
SiennaSnow.com
Twitter @sienna_snow
Facebook.com/authorsiennasnow

31901060816495

CPSIA information can be obtained
at www.ICGtesting.com
Printed in the USA
FSOW03n1946260817
37980FS